"Are you still in love with Jon?"

He leaned forward, his blue eyes vivid in the lamp-light, accusing.

"I don't think so," Dani said with scrupulous honesty. "But since you came here, I've felt confused...."

He stood up and started pacing. "All my life I've been confused with Jon. All my life I've struggled to be recognized as a separate person.... When you look at me you see Jon. That about sums it up, doesn't it?"

"Not always, not every time."

He bent down in front of her, his face only inches from hers. "What about the other way around, Danielle? When you saw Jon, did you ever think that he was me? When you were with Jon, did you ever wonder if he could be me?"

Something stirred in her mind, a memory that had been suppressed. "No, never," she said quickly....

Dear Reader:

Meet twelve daring, passionate women!

You've seen many exciting changes in Harlequin books over the past few months, but one thing hasn't changed—our commitment to providing you with the most up-to-the-minute stories in romance fiction today.

In Superromance, we're delighted to introduce you to a bold new series, WOMEN WHO DARE. Through 1993, one book per month will feature a heroine who faces challenges head-on, a woman who will dare anything... for love.

And you will recognize some of your favorite authors as contributors to this new concept. In January, you won't want to miss Margot Dalton's *Daniel and the Lion,* in which physiotherapist Jamie O'Rourke saves the hero from himself. In February, Carol Duncan Perry drops modern-day stunt pilot Elizabeth Carmichael into perilous Prohibition-era Chicago in *The Wings of Time.* Dr. Caroline Charles shakes up the medical establishment in Janice Kaiser's March WOMEN WHO DARE title, *Cradle of Dreams,* and photojournalist Kelly Cooper stakes her life on her intuition when she finds herself held hostage in Sandra Canfield's *Snap Judgement.*

Whether emotional, adventurous, suspenseful or humorous, Superromance novels continue to reflect the ways that modern women live and love in today's society. I hope you'll enjoy all the wonderful stories our talented authors are planning for 1993!

Marsha Zinberg,
Senior Editor

P.S. We love to hear from our readers! Letters to the editor or to your favorite author can be sent to:

> Harlequin Reader Service,
> P.O. Box 1397
> Buffalo, New York
> 14240 U.S.A.

Double Take

MARGARET CHITTENDEN

Harlequin Books

TORONTO • NEW YORK • LONDON
AMSTERDAM • PARIS • SYDNEY • HAMBURG
STOCKHOLM • ATHENS • TOKYO • MILAN
MADRID • WARSAW • BUDAPEST • AUCKLAND

For my friend Margaret Carney,
because she loves birds, canoes and trees
even more than I do

Published January 1993

ISBN 0-373-70531-X

DOUBLE TAKE

ABOUT THE AUTHOR

"I've always been intrigued by grown-up twins," writes Margaret Chittenden. "Do they have identity problems? Are they naturally close or more likely to be rivals? If you fell in love with a twin, would you be attracted to the other one? *Double Take* is my exploration of this theme." The talented author lives in Washington State with her husband.

Books by Margaret Chittenden

HARLEQUIN SUPERROMANCE

16–THIS DARK ENCHANTMENT
40–SONG OF DESIRE
91–SUCH SWEET MAGIC
123–LOVE ME TOMORROW
175–TO TOUCH THE MOON
214–CLOSE TO HOME
310–THE MOON GATE
366–UNTIL OCTOBER
444–THE SCENT OF MAGIC

HARLEQUIN TEMPTATION

40–LOVESPELL
156–THE MARRYING KIND

HARLEQUIN INTRIGUE

183–THE WAINWRIGHT SECRET

Don't miss any of our special offers. Write to us at the following address for information on our newest releases.

Harlequin Reader Service
P.O. Box 1397, Buffalo, NY 14240
Canadian address: P.O. Box 603,
Fort Erie, Ont. L2A 5X3

Author's Note

The town of Murre Bay is fictional as are the people and events depicted, but the scenery, weather, life-style and wildlife are those of the great place I live in—Ocean Shores, Washington.

PROLOGUE

STANDING UNNATURALLY still so she wouldn't wrinkle the train of her wedding gown, Danielle smiled through her veil at her father's distinguished-looking but glum reflection in the tall, triple mirrors of the church's changing room. "Lighten up, Pops. This is my wedding day, not my funeral."

Harris Kelsey sighed. "I hate sounding like a disgruntled father, but I have to admit I'm not exactly thrilled about you marrying Jonathan Falkirk. I'm not sure he's right for you."

Dani's stomach coiled in a familiar knot but she managed to speak lightly. "You haven't approved of any man I've ever gone out with."

He smiled wryly. "True. But I'm still going to stick my neck out and ask if you're quite sure Jon is the right man for you."

About to say "of course" she hesitated, wondering why his question had aroused a feeling of panic, a feeling that there was some memory wanting to come into her mind, a memory she couldn't possibly allow. Something to do with snow, and lights gleaming and intense feelings that... Shaking her head, she studied herself in the mirror again.

She looked like the ghost of weddings past in the embroidered and beaded *peau de soie* wedding gown her maid of honor had talked her into, she decided abruptly. Given her blond hair and fair complexion, she should probably have insisted on the plain ivory dress she'd been drawn to. She shouldn't have allowed her father to talk her into this huge wedding either, even if he had insisted on paying for it. He certainly wasn't wealthy, but he'd wanted to show the Falkirks he was as good as they were. A mistake, all of it.

All of it? Wedding nerves, nothing more. "I'm sure," she said firmly.

"I guess I'm just not ready to hand you over," her father said in a doleful voice.

Dani made a face at his reflection, determined not to be drawn into a fight on this day of all days. "That's a fiendishly chauvinistic remark if ever I heard one. You make me sound like a baton in a relay race."

"You know what I mean," Harris said, evidently determined to be gloomy. "You're all I have left."

Still trying to hang on to her patience, Dani raised her eyebrows. "I take it we're not counting the glamorous Widow Pennington, or the gorgeous divorcée from the bank, or the ubiquitous Miss Farrelli?"

"I'm talking about family."

"You're forgetting the old rhyme—'your son's your son till he gets him a wife, but your daughter's your daughter all her life.'" Her voice was developing an edge to it. She softened it deliberately. "I'm twenty-eight years old, Dad, teetering on old maid status where your generation's concerned. I'd have thought you'd be relieved to have me off your hands—all that money for my med school expenses!"

His brow was still furrowed. "I wish I could have paid all of it, so you wouldn't have had to work your way through." He raised his hands in a helpless gesture, then let them drop.

"It was good for my character," she said briskly. It should have been good for something—all those years of school, hitting the books night after night, then struggling through three years of residency, all the time working at Falkirk's in what was left of her free time, on her feet, selling dresses, smiling, smiling, smiling, when all she wanted to do was sleep. "Besides, if I hadn't worked at Falkirk's part-time, I wouldn't have met Roxanne and if I hadn't met Roxanne I wouldn't have met Jonathan." Happy-go-lucky Jon, full of fun, teasing her, making her laugh.

"And now you're taking out this business loan for your practice. When your husband-to-be is a *Falkirk!* You should have let Jon set you up the way he wanted to."

"No way. Becoming a doctor was *my* dream, my responsibility." She squeezed his arm, though she felt more like throttling him. Why did he have to bring up all the old arguments at a time when she was supposed to feel serenely happy? "Would you please quit worrying," she coaxed. "Everything's going to be fine. Happy-ever-after stuff." She smiled at their reflections again, trying to jolly him out of his querulous mood. "Look how handsome we are. Mom would have been proud of us."

"I wish she could see you today." His blue eyes, looking suspiciously moist, met hers in the mirror. "You are so beautiful, my darling."

Beautiful was not an adjective Dani would ever have applied to her tall, slender, verging on thin body, high-cheekboned face and boyishly styled hair. Occasionally she managed to look halfway elegant, but that was about it. A beauty should be colorful, exotic, exciting—a scarlet rose, heady to the senses, like Adrian Falkirk's wife.

"You aren't so shabby either," she said, determined not to let her father wax sentimental—it was going to be hard enough keeping her own emotions under control today without him falling apart. She had missed her mother dreadfully during all the wedding preparations, knowing how wholeheartedly Mom would have thrown herself into helping to choose the dress and flowers and set up the reception. Watching other mothers-of-the-bride during endless dress fittings, her pain at times had been as severe as the first agony of grief she'd felt when Louise Kelsey had died so prematurely in a two-car collision three years ago. "Mom would fall in love with you all over again if she could see you now," she said, blinking back some moisture of her own. "Pierre Cardin must have designed that tux with you in mind."

Harris preened a little, straightening his bow tie under his stiff wing collar. "I do look rather dashing for an auto mechanic, don't I?" he said with a smug smile.

"James Bond as played by Sean Connery."

Grateful that she'd finally managed to cheer her father up, Dani turned carefully to peer into the anteroom where her four attendants had withdrawn to give her a few minutes alone with Harris. They were still bustling around in there, adjusting each other's petticoats, checking their already perfect makeup, steaming invisible wrinkles out of their blue lace-trimmed dresses.

The organist in the church, which was on the other side of a narrow walkway, was playing an encore of the *Romeo and Juliet* theme, the fourth and last of the selections Dani had chosen to entertain the guests before the "Trumpet Voluntary," which would herald the entry of the bridesmaids. Why an encore? Dani wondered.

"What time is it?" she asked.

Her father looked at his wristwatch, squinting to see the numbers. "Seven minutes after two." He frowned, running a hand over his thinning gray hair. "Weren't we supposed to start at two?"

A tiny tremor of alarm shivered down Dani's spine. "What do you suppose is holding things up? The photographer must be through with the guys by now."

"I'll check."

He was back before Dani could start worrying seriously, but his facial expression didn't reassure her. "Jonathan and Adrian aren't here yet," he announced.

"But when we arrived their father said everything was okay on their side." Something cold was clutching at her stomach.

"Carter says he didn't want to worry you. He says he's been calling Jon's condo at regular intervals and there's no reply, so Jon and Adrian must have gone somewhere else before heading out this way."

"Why would they do that? All the Falkirks are compulsive about punctuality. Why choose today to change the habits of a lifetime?" She cast a worried glance at her father. "You don't suppose Jon's had an accident?"

"If he has you can patch him up after the ceremony. He doesn't have to worry now he's marrying a doctor." He frowned ferociously at her in the mirror. "If he hasn't had an accident, I'll punch him out and you'll still have to fix him up. How dare he keep my daughter waiting."

"Something's wrong," Dani said tightly.

"What's the holdup?" her maid of honor asked, poking her head around the archway that divided the two rooms. "Isn't somebody supposed to give us some kind of signal when it's time to assemble outside?"

"Jonathan's late," Dani said, trying and failing to sound unconcerned.

"Overdid it at the stag party?" Pam asked.

Dani shook her head. "The guys had their party on Wednesday, just as we did."

Pam shrugged, smiled encouragingly and withdrew. Dani could hear her whispering to the others.

"Jon went out to dinner last night with an old school friend who flew in for the wedding," Dani told her father. "He said he was planning on cutting the evening short so he'd be bright-eyed and bushy-tailed today." She forced a smile. "I wouldn't put it past him to stop in at the store to make sure they're all managing without him. The anniversary sale is in its third day." She wasn't sure if she was reassuring her father or herself.

In the church, the organist had started over on the preliminary music. The wedding guests must be feeling restive. Especially Jon's family—his father, mother, two sisters, Jacqueline and Roxanne, and their husbands, Jacqueline's three mischievous sons, Roxanne's giggly daughter. They were an energetic lot, not inclined to spend much time sitting still.

Where *was* Jonathan? He wouldn't really have gone to the store, would he? Jonathan was an executive vice president and cochairman of the family-owned Falkirk's Department Stores as well as general manager of the Seattle branch. The company had been started by his grandfather, Raymond, in San Francisco and had since spread up the West Coast. His twin brother, Adrian, held the same positions, but he was manager of the original flagship store. He had come up from the Bay area a few days ago to act as Jon's best man. Adrian's wife, a former Miss California, had come with him, of course. No doubt she was also sitting in the church, drawing all eyes. A bosom like hers ought to be banned from public display.

Could Adrian be the reason for Jon's tardiness? Maybe he was trying to talk his twin out of marrying Danielle Kelsey. He'd never seemed too delighted at the prospect of their marriage. Such an irritating man—he couldn't seem to say anything to her that didn't have sarcastic overtones. Since the first day she'd met him he'd let her know in countless ways that he didn't like her any more than she liked him. Which was too bad, considering that he and Jon were so close. Identical twins usually were, she supposed, and Adrian and Jon were certainly identical—elegant, strikingly good-looking, intelligent. With the difference that Jon was more open and never snide. Well, she'd just have to learn to put up with Adrian and his wife, Marta. The Falkirks held a monthly business meeting and family get-together that all members were required to attend.

"What time is it?" she asked again.

"Two-twenty." Her father sounded nervous.

Something was cockeyed here. Jon knew as well as she that another wedding was scheduled at three-thirty. They were supposed to have all their guests and belongings cleared out well ahead of that time. September was a popular time for weddings, but it had seemed the best time to choose. The designer was scheduled to start work on the interior of Dani's new offices next week. She'd be opening her clinic at the end of October. If they'd waited until after she started her own practice she wouldn't have been able to get away for the honeymoon in Bermuda that Jon wanted.

"What time is it?" she asked again.

Her father automatically lifted his wrist to look at his watch again, then his head turned as someone walked past the nearest window. "Here's Jon now," he said with an audible sigh of thanksgiving.

Smiling with relief, Dani turned to see the tall, powerfully built, dark-haired man hurry past the next group of windows. Almost at once she realized that something was definitely wrong.

"It's not Jonathan, it's Adrian." Her stomach was doing back flips.

"How on earth can you tell?" her father asked.

"It's not easy," she admitted. "But there is a difference in the way they walk—Adrian always goes hell-for-leather, Jon kind of lopes along. Plus whenever I see Adrian he has a smirk on his face."

"Well, whichever this one is, he's certainly not smirking," Harris murmured as the door opened and Adrian stood framed in the opening. The grim expression on Adrian's strong-featured face as his brilliant blue eyes met hers filled Dani with foreboding.

"I'm afraid we have a problem, Danielle," he said. He never had called her Dani—that would have been a friendly thing to do and in the eight and a half months she'd known Adrian he hadn't once made friendly overtures.

She took a deep breath that got stuck halfway to her lungs. "What have you done with Jon?" she asked in a choked voice.

He looked taken aback. "What have I...nothing's wrong with Jon. He's fine. He's just...Danielle, I'm sorry to have to tell you this...Jon's not coming."

The statement hit her like a blow to her solar plexus. Fumbling behind her, she found one of the dressing room's rickety little chairs and sat down on it hard.

"Don't sit down," Pam yelled, shooting into the room like a pint-size rocket. "You'll crease your dress."

"To hell with the dress," Dani said numbly.

Pam stared from her to Adrian, her normally rosy-cheeked face blanching. "What's happened?" she demanded.

Dani hadn't taken her eyes from Adrian's solemn face. Her mind was screaming, *It isn't possible, Jon wouldn't do this to me, Jon loves me.*

Dani's father took a step toward Adrian, his face as red as a boiled lobster, his hands clenched and raised. "Where is he?" he demanded in a choked voice. "Let me at him."

Adrian looked alarmed for a moment, then brushed past Harris to stand in front of Dani. "I'm sorry, Danielle, there's no easy way to tell you this. Jon can't go through with the wedding. He's in love with somebody else."

This wasn't happening. It was some kind of joke Jon had dreamed up. "Jon doesn't know anyone else," she said lamely. "I mean, there *isn't* anyone else..." She swallowed hard. "Who is it?"

Adrian took a breath. "He had dinner last night with..."

"An old school friend," Dani interrupted. "I know all about that. Jon told me he was going to. Claud somebody, they were in school together." Abruptly her mind flickered a reprise of Jon's sheepish expression when he told her about the dinner date. Her blood ran cold. "You're telling me Claud's a *woman?*"

Adrian nodded. "It's Claude with an *e*. Claude Les-
lie. She and Jon were very close years ago when we all
lived in San Francisco. Claude was our senator's
daughter. They hadn't seen each other since Claude
went back East to edit a fashion magazine. Jon thought
it would be fun to invite her to the wedding. But when
he saw her again..."

"Bye-bye Danielle," she said bitterly. "Just like
that." She lowered her head and her veil fluttered across
her face. Snatching it off, along with its elaborate orange blossom headband, she tossed it to one side,
wishing she had something heavier to throw. "It didn't
occur to him to tell me himself?" she demanded. "Like
this morning, maybe, before I went through this whole
dressing ritual? Before the guests were lined up in the
pews waiting for the 'Bridal Chorus' to announce my
glorious entry?"

Aware that her voice was rising hysterically and that
her attendants were now hovering worriedly behind her,
she closed her eyes and made a tremendous effort to
calm the staccato beating of her heart. A minute later
she looked directly at Adrian again, some part of her
mind noting how impressive he looked in his cutaway
black coat, every bit as striking as Jon would have
looked.

Her entire body felt cold now. She might never feel
warm again, she thought. "He spent the night with her,
I suppose?"

Adrian raked a hand through his thick dark hair in a
manner that was a duplicate of Jon's and left it, like
Jon's, attractively tousled over his forehead. She
couldn't bear this, couldn't bear to look at him....

"I knew nothing about this, Danielle," Adrian assured her. "I was getting ready to pick up Jon at his

condo when he showed up at the house. Marta and my parents had just left for the church. That's when Jon told me what had happened. He kept insisting he couldn't tell you, couldn't face you, didn't know what to do. He's in a terrible state. He didn't sleep all night, he said."

"I'll bet," she muttered.

"Maybe when he's had time to think about it..." He didn't sound as if he believed what he was saying any more than Dani believed what she was hearing.

Danielle stood up. For a second she was afraid she was going to swoon like some nineteenth-century maiden; all the blood seemed to have deserted her brain, she couldn't think, couldn't believe... "Somebody's going to have to tell all those people the wedding's off," she said carefully.

"Oh God," Pam exclaimed behind her. "This can't be happening. I don't believe Jon would do this."

"Obviously we have to believe it," Harris exclaimed. His face was still red. "I knew the Falkirks couldn't be trusted," he yelled at Dani. "I just knew instinctively. I told you Jonathan Falkirk wasn't right for you. Maybe next time you'll listen to me." He turned abruptly on Adrian, shaking a fist in his face. "Don't think you're going to get away with this...we're going to sue, breach of promise...do you have any idea how much money this wedding—"

"Dad!" Making a supreme effort, Dani took a deep breath and let it out slowly, willing herself to be calm. Putting her hands on Harris's shoulders, she gazed pleadingly into his angry face. "I need you to make an announcement," she said evenly. "Just a bare announcement that there isn't going to be a wedding, okay? Nothing vitriolic about Jon, just something dignified and direct. Can you manage it?"

"What about you?" he asked. "Are you going to be okay?"

How could she possibly be okay? She was never going to be okay again. "I'll be fine," she assured her father. "Please. Do this for me."

To her relief, his color was returning to normal. Now that his outburst was over, she was pretty sure she could rely on him to carry out her wishes with tact and good taste.

"Danielle." Adrian took a step forward as her father left the room. He had one hand extended as though he were going to touch her and there was an unusually sympathetic expression in his eyes. She didn't want his pity, couldn't bear it if he touched her. She couldn't bear to even have him in the room. How dare he stand there gazing at her with Jon's vivid blue eyes, looking like Jon's mirror image, emphasizing what she had lost? "Thank you for coming to tell me, Adrian," she said, sounding to her own ears like a hostess being polite to an unwelcome guest.

Then she noticed there was a large white handkerchief in his outstretched hand. He hadn't intended to touch her after all—she should have known that.

She hadn't even realized she was crying. But now she could feel the hot prickling of tears in her eyes.

Adrian didn't seem to want to meet her gaze now. Probably he was embarrassed by her weakness. Probably he thought she ought to keep a stiff upper lip, take it on the chin, present a bold front, face the music. The Falkirks didn't believe in excesses of emotion. Even Jon...

Jon. Oh God, Jon.

She was becoming hysterical, she recognized. Stereotypical female behavior. That's why it was called hysteria, from the Latin *hystericus*—of or suffering in the uterus. *Well done, Doctor Kelsey,* she congratulated herself—at least one of her brain cells was functioning.

"Goodbye Adrian," she said, still in that falsely polite voice. "Tell Jon, tell him..." She couldn't go on. Taking the handkerchief from him, she backed up until she found the chair again and sat down, mopping ineffectually at her eyes. She didn't want Jon's brother to see her fall apart. Drawing herself up, she took a deep breath. "Go away, Adrian," she said through clenched teeth. "You've delivered your message. You should be delighted by all this. You won't ever have to see me again."

His square jaw tightened and he looked for a second as if he were about to answer back, then he pressed his lips together and turned away.

As soon as the door closed behind him, Dani's bridesmaids gathered around her, squatting alongside her, their lovely faces distorted with sympathy, the warmth of their affection evident in the hands that touched her. "That bastard," Pam muttered and Dani found herself wondering quite objectively if she meant Adrian or Jon.

She was cracking up, no doubt about that. Spreading Adrian's handkerchief very carefully across her knees, she began folding it neatly, lining up the corners as precisely as possible. Pam knelt beside her and put her arms around her. "Don't hold it inside, honey," she murmured. "Let it go, just let it all go."

But there wasn't anything there to let go. She wasn't even crying anymore. There was nothing inside her but emptiness—cold, hard emptiness.

CHAPTER ONE

Two years later

"YOU HAVEN'T IMPROVED a bit," Dr. Reuben Green said flatly, scowling at the tall, dark-haired, elegantly suited man seated on the opposite side of his desk.

Adrian Falkirk grinned. "Thanks a lot, old buddy."

Why on earth had Reuben decorated his office in such a nauseating shade of green, he wondered. Did he want his patients to feel worse? He couldn't see why Reuben had to look so severe, either. He had come here expecting sympathy and medication—something to get him back in shape, preferably something that would act quickly.

"You haven't followed any of the advice I gave you four months ago," Reuben went on, frustration clearly etched on his saturnine face. "Your blood pressure's even higher than it was—not dangerously so...yet...but it's an indicator. Your cholesterol level's down a little, but it's still far too high. You're still smoking too much, probably drinking more than you should."

"Mine was not your basically friendly divorce, Reuben," Adrian reminded him. "Marta had set her heart on separating me from all my worldly goods. I'm lucky I still have clothes on my back. How can you expect my blood pressure to be normal?"

"The divorce was final two months ago," Reuben pointed out. "Your habits haven't noticeably improved," he added as Adrian pulled a pack of cigarettes from his shirt pocket and lit up.

"Pot calling the kettle," Adrian said.

"I smoke only four cigarettes a day and I don't inhale," Reuben said virtuously. "And I'm not at risk like you are. I'm a tranquil, happily married, easygoing—some say lazy—individual. You're a compulsive, hard-driving workaholic who buries his emotions six fathoms deep."

"I do not," Adrian protested.

"When was the last time you yelled at someone, threw something, admitted you were suffering? I've heard you make all kinds of joking references to your divorce, but you've never once confessed to bleeding inside." He leaned forward. "You have to change your ways, my friend. I've no ambition to be a pallbearer at your funeral."

"I'll make sure my father doesn't invite you."

Reuben glared at him. "With an attitude like yours, why did you bother to come back to see me?"

About to set his jaw stubbornly, Adrian realized Reuben's reaction was justified. He'd come here for help. Why the hell was it so hard for him to admit to weakness? Stupid question. He knew why. Family credo. Falkirks are strong. Falkirks are healthy. Falkirks don't whine.

Maybe they should.

"A couple of days ago," he said carefully, "I was reading a memo and quite suddenly I couldn't make out the words. The blurred vision only lasted a minute or so, but it scared hell out of me. Add to that a general rundown feeling, coffee jitters without the coffee, constant headaches and chronic insomnia and you begin to get the picture." He leaned forward, meeting Reuben's sympathetic gaze. "I'm ready to do anything you tell me. So give it your best shot, old buddy. What'll it be? Sleeping pills? Tranquilizers?"

"Would that it were so easy." Reuben shook his head decisively. "No pills. Nobody ever died of insomnia, people *have* died of sleeping pills. However, I *am* going to suggest something drastic. If you remember," he said with noticeable sarcasm, "I instructed you last time to cut down on the booze, cut down on the cigarettes, cut them out altogether preferably, follow some diet restrictions, take some time off work, go count cows somewhere pastoral. How much of that did you do?"

Adrian stubbed out his cigarette in the doctor's ashtray and grinned wryly. "I took a weekend off right after the divorce. A long weekend."

"And did what?"

"Played golf."

"Very good. Golf can be very relaxing. Fresh air, plenty of walking, good conversation, no competition, no hostility."

His eyes were holding Adrian's very levelly.

Adrian repressed a ridiculous pang of guilt. His golfing partners had included the CEO of an advertising company who wanted Falkirk's as a client and had pitched himself continuously, the company lawyer, who was even more competitive than Adrian, and Falkirk's chief financial officer, whom the lawyer suspected of some creative mathematics. By the time they had reached the eighteenth hole, Adrian's stomach had been tied in knots. The fact that he'd shot a sixty-eight had meant less than nothing.

"It's been a busy period," he said, hoping Reuben would appreciate the understatement. "We've still got that class action suit going with the union, the company's annual meeting is coming up, we've been having problems with increased shoplifting and vandalism..."

"No time to stand and stare."

"Exactly. But I have been eating more fruit and vegetables *and* I gave up pizza. That was a big breakthrough." He hesitated, then confessed, "I haven't quite managed to quit eating meat. I've always been a steak-and-potatoes man."

"I didn't say you had to give up meat altogether, you can eat lean cuts in moderate amounts."

"Four-ounce portions. Can't even see it on the plate. There isn't a restaurant in this country serves four-ounce portions."

"You're probably right. Most restaurateurs haven't caught on yet to what they're doing to our arteries. In the meantime, you'll just have to cut the servings in half—or even better, ask for an extra plate and share with a friend." He laughed. "I can just see you doing that at one of your power lunches." He raised his eyebrows. "Now, tell me what kind of exercise you've been getting. Jogging, I suppose? Chugging along like a machine, checking a stopwatch every once in a while to make sure you're beating yesterday's pace? Handball, played competitively? Killer tennis?"

He had him there, Adrian had to admit. "I like to win, sure," he allowed. "Doesn't everybody?"

Reuben sighed again.

"So what's the something drastic?" Adrian asked.

Reuben looked at him steadily. "I want you to take six months off work."

Adrian laughed. "You're out of your mind."

"No, *you* are. You want to sleep nights, get rid of your headaches and vision problems, feel good again,

you need a complete change of life-style. Evidently, the
only way to get you to break your bad habits is to get
you away from Falkirk's, away from responsibility and
deadlines and competition. I want you to go someplace
that's in the back of beyond. Someplace where you can
practice slowing down, mellowing out. If you don't...''

"If I don't, what?" Adrian wasn't really listening.
When Reuben had made that reference to somewhere
that was in the back of beyond, Danielle's name had
flashed into his mind. Fate was taking a hand, he'd
thought, which was ridiculous. Adrian Falkirk did not
believe in fate. Every man was responsible for his own
success or failure in life.

All the same, it was odd that he'd run into Pam
Hunter on his last trip to Seattle a few weeks ago. Pam
had told him that Danielle had left Seattle after Jon had
stood her up at the altar. Instead of opening her new
practice in Seattle, she'd buried herself alive in some
place called Murre Bay, a small beach community on
Washington's coast. She'd bought a practice there from
a GP who was retiring. Pam had said that she'd managed to get out of her lease, and she'd persuaded her
banker that an already established practice was a via-
ble alternative to her original intention.

Danielle.

He could still picture her as he'd last seen her—sitting there in her bouffant-skirted wedding gown, her
spine ruler straight, head held high, slate blue eyes filled
with hatred for the messenger who had brought the bad
news. The Snow Queen, tall and shining white, as illus-
trated in a book of Hans Christian Andersen fairy tales
he and Jon had owned in childhood. Only the tears
blurring the clean, strong bones of her face and the
slight tremor to her wide mouth had revealed her pain.

Another image. A July 4th gathering of the Falkirk clan in Seattle, the year Danielle was engaged to Jon. Rory, one of his sister Jacqueline's boisterous sons, had burned his arm on the barbecue while trying to catch a baseball. Danielle had taken charge, of course, with her usual quiet competence. It wasn't her skill that had impressed him so much—she was trained to respond to medical emergencies after all. But the calm and infinitely gentle assurance that had radiated from her face as she touched the boy and spoke to him had stayed with Adrian ever since, surfacing in his mind in times of trial, comforting him.

He was suddenly aware that Reuben had stopped talking and was looking questioningly at him. "Six months," he echoed sarcastically. "How the hell can I take off for six months?"

"Said you were ready to do anything I recommended," Reuben reminded him. "What's the problem? Can't afford it? Falkirk's not doing so well?"

"The company's doing great." He frowned. "We had a couple of poorer than expected quarters, but sales increases in July and August were the sharpest in more than a year, indicating profit growth is recovering and..." He broke off, aware that Reuben was gazing at him in an exasperated way.

"Okay, so I get carried away," he admitted. "I love my job. So sue me."

Actually, it wasn't quite true that he loved his work. Increasingly, of late, it had become something he *had* to do, something that sapped his energy. Somewhere along the way he'd lost the pride he used to feel walking through the huge store, sensing the satisfying hum of a well-run organization all around him, knowing he had a large share in making it all happen. Somewhere along the way he had become soul dead.

Reuben leaned back in his brown leather chair. "You are thirty-five years old, my friend. Exhibiting this self-destructive pattern at your age, you are three times more likely to get coronary heart disease in the next decade than the rest of us."

Shocked, Adrian stared at him. "In the next decade!"

"What I said." Reuben's bushy eyebrows slanted upwards. "Change your ways, however, and there's a good chance you'll be one of *my* pallbearers."

"Tempting proposition," Adrian said, straight-faced.

"Just look at yourself," Reuben said, gesturing.

Adrian realized he was sitting on the edge of his chair, his fingers drumming on the arms of it, his whole body tensed as if for flight. He made a conscious effort to relax, but couldn't quite manage it. He'd forgotten how. God, he felt wired. Yet weary to the bone. And that sudden loss of vision had terrified him. Maybe Reuben was right. Maybe he did need a vacation.

Danielle.

Something drastic, Reuben had said.

Yes.

DANI SMILED FONDLY at the woman sitting on the other side of her office desk. Steff Carmody was seventy-two-years old, slim as Dani herself and even taller. She was wearing a neon blue spandex jogging suit with a chartreuse sweatshirt over it. Steff didn't believe in dark clothing for wintry weather—drab days called forth all her brightest apparel. Her long white hair was tied back from her thin weathered face with a fuschia-colored ribbon. "There's no need for you to worry prematurely, Steff," Dani said. "According to the lab report, some questionable cells showed up in your pap smear. We need to find out what's going on, that's all. I'm going to refer you to a gynecologist in Baxter—Dr. Wellington. You'll like him."

"I never worry, Kelsey, you should know that by now." Steff's gravelly voice sounded as cheerful as ever. "I've taken care of myself all my life, done everything I was supposed to do to stay healthy. I intend living forever, nasty little cells notwithstanding."

Her brown eyes danced with humor. Dani could only hope her confidence wasn't unfounded—the pap smear *was* questionable.

Steff raised her eyebrows. "I do have one question."

"Name it."

"How tall is this gynecologist?"

"How tall?" Dani blinked. "About my height, I suppose—five-eight. What's his height got to do with anything?"

Steff grinned. "I prefer a really short GYN man, that way when I'm hanging out in the stirrups I can't see what he's doing."

Dani was still smiling when she opened up the next patient's chart on the small table outside the examining room. Her standard questionnaire form was on top, indicating a first-time patient. She stepped aside as her short, plump nurse came out of the room. "Got a real hunk in there for you today," Laurie whispered as she passed by.

Dani raised her eyebrows, then glanced down at the chart again and read the name printed boldly at the top of the form. Shock stopped her breath halfway to her lungs.

Adrian Falkirk.

Her brain stopped functioning. So did her heart. It was a full minute before she could breathe freely again. Then she buttoned her white coat as if she were donning armor, unbuttoned it again, retied the bow of her tan silk blouse, adjusted the waistband of her skirt and ran both hands over her hair to make sure it was neatly in place.

What the hell was she doing? She'd never been a fidgety person. This was ridiculous behavior for a thirty-year-old professional woman. Taking a deep, shaky breath, she clutched the chart to her chest, fixed a smile on her face and opened the door, determined not to let Adrian Falkirk suspect that she was in any way affected by his sudden reappearance in her life.

He was standing with his back to her, studying a height-weight chart on the wall, hands in the pockets of his snug-fitting blue jeans. A brown leather bomber jacket fitted just as snugly across his broad shoulders. From the back, he could be Jon. Then he turned. He was still a close copy, his features as strong as Jon's, his mouth just as firmly set, the vivid blue of his eyes and slightly curling black hair half as startling—and deadly—a combination.

He looked unwell, though. There were shadows under his eyes, his skin was pale, his forehead more furrowed than she remembered, lines of strain on either side of his well-shaped mouth. His face seemed thinner, which emphasized his square jawline. In spite of these changes, he still exuded enough Falkirk power and strength and masculinity to stop her dead in the doorway as if she'd walked into a wall.

Her heart seemed to have swollen to twice its size, filling her chest cavity so that it was almost impossible for her to breathe.

"How are you, Danielle?" he asked in a matter-of-fact way, as though two years had not elapsed since their last meeting. His left eyebrow still had that cocky tilt to it, she noted.

She was finally able to find enough breath to speak. "What the hell are you doing here?" she exclaimed, forgetting all her good intentions about remaining calm.

He blinked, obviously taken aback by her harsh tone. Hardly surprising. "You always were straightforward, Danielle," he commented with a faint smile.

She shook her head. "I'm sorry. That was inexcusable." She attempted a laugh that didn't come off. "You're about the last person I ever expected to find in one of my examining rooms." Closing the door behind her, she gestured at the examining table, desperately trying to recover her usual composure. "Take a seat and we'll start over, okay?"

She probably still sounded hostile. Well, what did he expect—that she'd welcome him with a parade and all flags flying?

"What *are* you doing here?" she asked.

He indicated the chart in her hand. "The reason's in there. I need a doctor. I understand you're the only doctor in town."

She flipped through the pages, hoping he wouldn't notice that her fingers were shaking. All the old pain was roaring through her—her heart contracting now as if a giant hand had reached inside her to squeeze it.

And she'd thought she was over all that. She'd truly believed she no longer cared about Jon, no longer grieved over losing him. Fat chance. The pain was as fresh and sharp as on the day it had been inflicted. It must have lain there inside her all this time, dormant, just waiting for something to trigger it into hurtful life.

With an enormous effort she managed to focus on the papers. Adrian had last been seen a month ago by a Dr. Reuben Green in San Mateo, California. Dr. Green had recommended a temporary change of life-style. Thumbing through the lab reports she could certainly see why.

Dr. Green's accompanying sealed letter would have amused her if she hadn't been so shaken up. Obviously he was Adrian's friend as well as his physician. "This patient requires constant monitoring," he had written. "He has the disposition of a mule, his impatience would try a saint, and he's adopted enough bad habits to lay low a half-dozen ordinary mortals. Apparently, he has no idea what the word vacation means and he's never heard of the forty-hour week. I haven't prescribed medication for his elevated blood pressure or cholesterol, because he's the type who would rely on the medication and do nothing to improve the underlying conditions."

She glanced up. "Dr. Green implies you never take vacations."

"Sure I do," he said with that familiar, sarcastic note in his voice. "Marta and I have always taken a month every year."

"To go where?"

"Marta's favorite watering hole, of course—Las Vegas."

"Gambling, drinking, nightclubs, shows."

He nodded.

"Dr. Green was right," she said. "Somebody forgot to tell you that vacation means rest, respite, intermission."

One corner of his mouth twitched. "Maybe somebody forgot to tell Marta husbands had any say about where vacations should be spent."

Dr. Green had added a postscript: "Adrian has recently gone through a traumatic divorce action which no doubt has a bearing on his medical condition."

So Adrian and the beauteous Marta were divorced. Dani wasn't sure if she was surprised or not.

Setting the chart down, she forced herself to meet Adrian's eyes. They were of such a vivid blue that in order to describe them she would have had to resort to innumerable clichés about cornflowers and hyacinths and summer skies, none of which would have done the color justice. "Let me get this straight," she said as evenly as possible. "This change of life-style your doctor recommended—you've decided to pursue it here?"

"Right here in Murre Bay."

"Why?" she demanded.

He shrugged. "Dr. Green advised me to take off for the back of beyond. I didn't know any place like that, but I'd bumped into Pam Hunter in Seattle Falkirk's a short while before and she told me you were practicing in Murre Bay and it was a very quiet sort of place—out of the mainstream."

"It's not that far out," she said briskly. "We may have an area of only nine or so square miles and around twenty-five hundred full-time residents, but often during the summer and always during clam-digging season, the population swells to fifty to sixty thousand. Gets pretty busy downtown, especially on weekends. Where are you staying?"

"I've rented a house on Scoter Lake." He hesitated. "Your nurse said you live on the oceanfront?"

"Scoter Lake's pretty quiet," she conceded, ignoring his question.

"I figured if I came here I'd save a lot of research time and I wouldn't have to break in a strange doctor," he said after a moment. "Seemed an efficient way to go about it."

Was he telling the truth about his reason for coming here? she wondered. Or did he have some ulterior motive in mind? That was ridiculous. What ulterior motive could there possibly be?

Probably he'd told the simple truth. It was more efficient to go to a place he'd heard was peaceful, rather than spend time trying to find a suitable alternative. It would never occur to him that he was turning someone else's life inside out. "Efficiency's important to you, is it?" she said stiffly.

"One of my problems," he admitted.

"How are you feeling now, this minute?" she asked.

"Tired and wired. Mild headache. Seems to hang around most of the time. Slight heartburn—that's a recent development, probably due to eating alfalfa sprouts." His sudden rueful grin was so like Jon's it stabbed her in every vital organ she possessed. To cover up her reaction, she put her head around the door and called Laurie in to assist, then picked up her stethoscope.

"Take your jacket and shirt off, will you please?" she asked, relieved that her voice came out even. "Does the indigestion come soon after you eat or at other times?"

"After I eat. Reuben assured me it *was* indigestion," he added, after he'd pulled off his jacket and peeled his polo shirt over his head.

His muscular chest was matted with as much dark hair as Jon's. It arrowed downward beyond the waistband of his jeans. An immediate sexual response jolted through Dani's body, leaving her winded. Keeping her face expressionless, she walked around behind him.

"Reuben Green already gave me the fifty-dollar lecture," he said over his shoulder. "I'm hoping you'll spare me. Lot of fuss about nothing, wouldn't you say? *I* think all I need is a few pills, some extra vitamins maybe."

Withholding comment, Dani settled the stethoscope ear tips in place, and placed the diaphragm against his back. His warm flesh shrank away minutely from the cold contact and she was immediately assailed by another sexual jolt.

She couldn't do this; couldn't possibly examine this virile, half-naked man who was the absolute double of the man she had once loved. Two years ago she had erected a wall behind herself, a wall that blocked out the past. She hadn't known it was necessary to build another barrier in front, one that would keep out unwelcome intruders.

"Dr. Kelsey?" Laurie said, and Dani realized the nurse was wondering what the hell she was listening to in there for so long. *Hang in there,* she scolded herself. Adrian Falkirk was not Jon Falkirk. He was a patient, she was a doctor. If she couldn't maintain a professional distance from an attractive male she had no business staying in practice.

Steeling herself to pretend the man was just an anonymous collection of muscles and bones and internal parts, she managed to complete the examination with her professionalism intact. Then she instructed Laurie to draw some blood and told Adrian she'd see him afterward in her office.

Briefly, while she waited for him, she stood at her office window, gazing out at Murre Bay's long, curving beach and the wide expanse of Pacific Ocean beyond it, gray today under a fitful sun. Breakers thundered in with the tide, foaming high. The sandy beach was deserted except for masses of gulls lined up facing into the wind, a huge flock of sandpipers wheeling and dipping in unison above the waves. A single tern flew by, wings beating deliberately, head turned down at a right angle. As Dani watched, it plummeted straight down into the swells to catch its prey.

Looking at the ocean was her favorite therapy. When she had first come to Murre Bay she had spent hours gazing at it, letting its rhythms enter her nervous system and calm her thoughts. It had never failed to give her strength. It gave her strength now.

By the time Adrian showed up, she was busily making notes in his chart in her usual neat handwriting. Theresa, her receptionist-secretary, would enter them into the computer later.

Adrian's tall muscular frame looked as sexy as Jon's in jeans, she noted—she'd mostly seen him in suits before. A designer suit *would* look a little out of place at the beach, she reminded herself sarcastically. Gesturing Adrian into a chair, she studied the EKG printout Dr. Green had sent along then closed the chart and looked up, schooling her face to show only objective interest. "How long are you planning to stay in Murre Bay?" she asked.

"A month or so. I want to get back to the store for the Thanksgiving sale. Reuben wanted me to commit to six months, but of course that's not possible. Falkirk's, San Francisco, would fall apart. So would I. I'm not used to idle living."

"You're resisting this whole program, aren't you?" she said flatly. "Are you so happy with your current life-style?"

To her surprise, he answered without hesitation. "Tell you the truth, I've been fairly miserable." He looked away from her, gazing through the window that overlooked the ocean. "I had this . . . episode," he told her. "A sudden loss of vision after a particularly stressful day. I imagine it's in Reuben's report. It made me realize . . ." His voice trailed off, then he continued. "Roxanne's daughter, Katie, has a gerbil. She has a transparent plastic ball she puts him in from time to time. He runs all around the house inside it, ricocheting off walls, rattling in and out of rooms. Roxanne says it's good exercise, but it always bothers me. Now I think it bothers me because I identify."

At that moment he seemed very vulnerable to her. Her heart went out to him, then she reminded herself to be objective. "In that case, why are you in such a hurry to return to the rat race?" she asked.

He shook his head. "Damned if I know."

He looked so genuinely puzzled that she almost laughed, but stopped herself in time. "How about keeping your options open," she suggested. "See how you like taking life easy. Maybe you can go on from here to Hawaii, find yourself some better weather and a palm tree to sit under."

"You don't want me hanging around Murre Bay for six months?"

She didn't want him hanging around six days. There were plenty of other places he could go to recuperate. She didn't need the aggravation.

"How do *you* like Murre Bay?" he asked. "Bit slower than Seattle."

"That's what I like about it."

"It must suit you, I guess. You look great."

"Thank you." Why should a casual compliment make heat flood her body? Was she really that insecure?

"I was surprised when Pam told me where you were. It was hard for me to imagine you out of the city. You and Jon always seemed to enjoy the urban scene—nightclubs, theater, concerts, parties."

"Maybe someone forgot to tell Jon a fiancée had any choice," she said with some dryness of her own. That wasn't fair. After all her years of hard work, plus the trauma of losing her mother, she had desperately wanted to be happy, to have a home of her own, someone to love. She'd been perfectly willing to go anywhere Jon wanted to go, even if it meant being someone she wasn't.

He raised his eyebrows. "Jon knew you'd canceled the lease on your office space, of course, but he didn't know where you'd gone."

"I didn't find it necessary to leave him a forwarding address." Her voice sounded tight.

He was studying her face as though he were trying to reach inside her mind and see what was hidden in its deeper recesses. She remembered that intense blue gaze; she'd caught him looking at her that way several times in the old days, though he'd always averted his eyes when their glances crossed. This time she was the one to shift her gaze—she couldn't quite meet his eyes no matter how she despised her own weakness. She wasn't yet over the shock of seeing him, she supposed.

"Jon really was sorry, you know," he said after a short silence.

"I know," she managed. "He wrote me. My father forwarded the letter."

"He was also sorry you'd felt it necessary to leave town. He was afraid the move might have caused you financial hardship."

"Finances weren't my major concern."

He studied her face for a moment, then nodded. "I guess it would have been tough seeing him and Claude around town. Your proposed clinic was up the hill, wasn't it? Clear view of Falkirk's."

She was surprised he'd even thought about how that would affect her. Perhaps he had more sensitivity than she'd given him credit for.

As long as they were being so personal, she might as well indulge her own curiosity. "Dr. Green says you and Marta are divorced now."

"Yes."

"I guess the Falkirk twins just naturally resist domestication." It was a nasty thing to say, but she was still rattled. He'd had no business coming here, threatening her hard-won equilibrium.

"I wouldn't say that," he said with a short laugh. "Jon's nicely settled in now."

She flinched. That was a typical Adrian Falkirk remark—jocular, but designed to hurt.

He leaned forward, his mouth tightening, and surprised her by apologizing. "That was a rotten thing to say, Danielle. I'm sorry. I had no intention of taking potshots at you, believe me. I was irritated because you took it for granted the divorce was all my fault."

"It wasn't?"

He sighed. "Well, she did leave me. For a movie star, no less. Jack Pelham. All those macho automobile racing films. He wasn't the first other man in her life, possibly not the last. Marta's side of the story is that I spent all my time at the store and she was lonely. My version is that I started spending too much time at the store after she began playing the field. Take your pick."

"I'm sorry," Dani said perfunctorily, annoyed as always by his flippant attitude. There was one more question she had to ask, not just out of curiosity. "Does the family know you're here?" she asked. One thing she didn't need was an invasion of Falkirks.

He shook his head. "I told them I had to have time off, of course, and why. Dad thought I should stay with him and Mom in Seattle, but being around Dad is never exactly stress-free. So I said I was planning on exploring the Oregon coast." He laughed shortly. "Which I did on the way here. My assistant manager and my secretary are the only people who know where to get in touch with me, and that's only in case of emergency. I'm taking Reuben's advice to heart, you see."

Did that mean Jon didn't know where he was? She sincerely hoped so. If she had this strong a reaction to seeing Adrian, how would she react to running into Jon in one of the local stores?

It was time to get back to business. Putting her hand flat on the closed records folder, she started talking again before he could relay any more personal information. "I won't be able to assess your complete medical condition until we get the lab results, of course, but right now I'm in full agreement with Dr. Green. Your problems are mostly due to stress. You are at risk and you need to mend your ways. However, you needn't worry that I'm going to lecture you. You're a big boy now. Neither Dr. Green nor I nor one of your old family retainers can do this for you. It's your life. You have to take steps to improve your health yourself.''

As he nervously took a pack of cigarettes from his inside jacket pocket, she pulled a prescription pad toward her. ''Don't even think of lighting that in here,'' she said evenly without looking up.

He replaced the pack in his pocket at once. ''Sorry, automatic reflex.''

''I'm writing you a prescription for some gum that contains a small amount of nicotine. It will help you quit if you really want to.'' She handed the slip to him, adding a low-fat diet guide for good measure.

''What do I do for a social life in Murre Bay?'' he asked as he folded the papers.

''You might try the Sandbox,'' she suggested. ''It's a new bar on Seaview Way.'' It was difficult to keep a straight face; the Sandbox was a no-alcohol bar with a strict taboo against smoking. ''It's just the sort of place you'd enjoy,'' she added with relish.

He smiled wryly, obviously analyzing that comment, but this time she had her defenses in place. Only a slight jerking of her heartbeat indicated that she was still responding to memories of Jon.

''I would also suggest that you walk every day,'' she went on.

He raised his eyebrows. ''Where to?''

Dani laughed shortly. ''You really are goal-oriented, aren't you? It doesn't matter where to, or how far, or how much time you should allot to it—just walk.''

''Aimless wandering makes me nervous.''

''You'll get used to it.''

He grimaced. "That's what Reuben said about fruit and vegetables, but I still can't face life without steak and eggs."

"Eat fish instead. You can buy it at Phil's Market, fresh off the boat. The lingcod is marvelous. As you're living on the lake you can go fishing for trout and bass. It's open season all year around here. And fishing's very good for you. The time you spend fishing is added on to your life, rather than being subtracted from it."

He crooked an eyebrow. "That doesn't sound very scientific."

She actually managed a smile—she was proud of herself, she was going to get through this interview even if her nerves *were* drawn as tightly as bowstrings and her stomach tied up in knots. "It's my dad's theory," she said.

He frowned. She wondered if he was remembering, as she was, the last time he had seen Harris Kelsey, when Adrian had brought her the crushing news that had changed her life. She wondered what he'd say if she were to tell him Harris still hadn't forgiven the Falkirks for what he called "this tremendous insult."

Had *she* forgiven Jon? She had thought so. She had also thought she'd stopped loving him. But judging by the emotion that was throbbing through her at this moment, she had been mistaken. She must force herself to remember that Adrian was not Jon. As far as she knew, Adrian was blameless. It was hardly his fault he was a carbon copy of his twin. She must treat him as if he were any other new patient asking her for advice.

But why the hell had he chosen to come here when he had a whole world to choose from?

"Anything else?" he asked after a moment.

She took a deep breath, calling upon all the composure she usually possessed. What would she advise that mythical other patient if he had overdosed on stress? "Watch a few sunsets. They get pretty spectacular here sometimes. So do the stars—no streetlights. Don't worry about sunrises, sleep late. Dig a few razor clams—the season started yesterday and it lasts a month or so, until November 17th, that's why there are more people than usual in town. Noon till midnight, odd dates only. Limit of fifteen—but you don't *have* to take fifteen, this is not a competitive sport. You can get a license at Phil's. If you need more excitement, you can drive into Baxter—it's half an hour inland, on the Prescott River. It's not the major port it once was, but it's been building up recently, renovating the waterfront, putting in a marina, an esplanade and a farmers' market, turning itself into quite a tourist spot. There's even a big new shopping mall. And some pretty good fishing." Why was she babbling on? "Come back and see me in a week or so," she concluded, adding dryly, "if you haven't expired from boredom by then."

She stood up, signifying that she was through, but he didn't follow suit. Nor did he comment on her hostile tone. Looking up at her, he asked, "Do you do all these things, Danielle? Fishing, clam digging, hiking, star gazing?"

"As often as I can," she said.

"Could we do them together?"

"I don't think that would be a good idea."

"Why not?"

Evidently, he'd conveniently forgotten that he'd treated her like dirt when she was engaged to Jon. Probably he thought if she would accompany him he wouldn't have to waste time "researching" the local females. All the same, she could hardly tell him she couldn't bear to look at him because her heart didn't recognize the difference between him and Jon.

Again, she knew she wasn't being very scientific—it was her *brain* that couldn't seem to work out the difference, but it felt more like her heart. The strong chemistry that had existed between her and Jon was evidently confused about the identity of the man sitting opposite her. It was affecting her with tremendous force, clamoring in her blood, making her want to touch him, go to him, *be* with him.

She became aware that Adrian was waiting for an answer to his question. "I have a boyfriend who might object," she blurted out.

"Oh, I see." His strong features were washed clean of expression now. "Somebody local?"

"Brian Milburn. He owns the Surf and Turf restaurant."

"I've seen it. Great-looking place."

Brian would be astonished to hear himself described as her boyfriend, Dani thought. He'd also be delighted. He'd been trying hard to move their friendship into what he referred to as phase two for the last six months. But she wasn't interested in getting seriously involved with any man.

"You realize," Adrian said, getting to his feet in one lithe movement, "my rehabilitation program will not be complete if I don't have any friends. I've always been a gregarious sort of individual."

"Then I'm sure you'll make friends in Murre Bay. It's a friendly town." How was she managing to keep her voice so steady when her body was aching with the strain of hiding her incredibly stupid reaction to him?

He smiled wistfully, startling her. She hadn't thought Adrian Falkirk had a wistful bone in his body. "Couldn't you even consider dinner?" he asked.

Why was he turning on the charm? His resemblance to Jon wouldn't be nearly as strong if he'd only stick to his old sarcastic hostility. "Sorry, I have a date," she lied.

"Tomorrow?"

"Tomorrow's Wednesday. Dr. Stanislaus and I have a free clinic in Baxter on Wednesday evenings. Stasny's the doctor I bought the practice from. He lives a few miles north of here."

"Thursday, then?"

She set her jaw, hoping determined body language would impart strength to her voice. "Give it up, Adrian. I'm not going to dinner with you."

"Why not?" He hesitated, looking at her with his old derisive expression. "Is it that you're still angry with Jon? And with me by extension? After all this time?"

Just what she'd really like—word getting back to Jon that she was still suffering. Why couldn't she tell him straight out that she was fully recovered, get him off her back. She *had* been fully recovered, until he came along, stirring up old memories, old responses.

Before she could guess his intention, he took both her hands in his and looked steadily into her eyes. His hands were large and competent. Her own seemed to be swallowed up by them. She hoped he couldn't feel the frantic beating of her pulse. "We're both walking wounded, Danielle," he murmured. "Can't we team up? Can't we possibly be friends?"

She shook her head, seemingly unable to snatch her hands free, desperately hoping he couldn't tell that his touch was causing her heart to ricochet against her ribs. Secondhand chemistry, she reminded herself.

"Come on, Danielle," he murmured, turning on the charm again, laugh lines crinkling at the corners of his eyes. "For old times' sake?"

What old times' sake? Adrian didn't belong to those old times. It was *Jon* she had loved. Only Jon. She had *disliked* Adrian. *Always.* At last she was able to draw her hands away from his. She looked at him coldly. "I've spent the last two years trying to forget old times," she said.

CHAPTER TWO

BECAUSE OF A MAN'S carelessness with a handsaw—when would do-it-yourselfers learn caution?—it was six o'clock before Dani got away from her clinic. As she drove home along Seaview Way, the sun was making its downward journey, trailing gauzy veils of purple and salmon pink, painting a wide path of eye-dazzling light across the now quiet ocean. As always, the sight reminded her of her childhood conviction that the sun sank into the sea every night. She never had figured out why it didn't sizzle.

It wasn't really possible to welcome an emergency, of course, but she had certainly welcomed the distraction. She had felt wrung out after Adrian left. She'd found herself remembering the fencing club she'd belonged to in college. The thrusts and parries and feints of their conversation had seemed almost as competitive, the combative energy racing through her bloodstream had left her just as exhausted. Her only comfort lay in knowing Adrian couldn't possibly have recognized the turmoil he had aroused.

What the hell was she going to do? He'd been right about one thing—she was the only doctor in town. She could hardly refuse to accept him as a patient. Especially without giving him a reason.

One month. She'd have to see him at least once a week. Three more visits. Surely she could manage to get through three visits. Dear God, was she really still in love with Jon?

She had to stop thinking about Jon...and Adrian. Somewhere in the mists of memory, she had read of an Englishwoman who had been advised by Queen Victoria to think of England while having sex, in order to keep her mind on a higher plane. Perhaps she needed a similar distraction. Determinedly, she put her mind to work on the clam chowder she would cook for her solitary dinner. Steff Carmody had brought in a dozen large razor clams, dug the previous afternoon, cleaned and ready to go. She'd throw in some carrots and potatoes and celery stalks, an onion, lots of spices and a few red pepper flakes, thicken it with flour, add hot skimmed milk and have enough food for a week. If her stove behaved.

Soon after moving to Murre Bay, she had bought a small two-bedroom house on the ocean, which she was now having enlarged. While work was in progress, she'd stored all her furniture and rented a trailer, which she'd had parked behind the house. The trailer wasn't very big, barely spacious enough for one person, and its propane-fueled kitchen facilities were unreliable.

The builder's pickup was still in her driveway when she pulled in. Chet Caswell's hours were as unpredictable as hers. Her spirits lifted. She was glad Chet was still around—she felt lonely this evening. Which wasn't all that unusual. Her forcible and abrupt separation from Jon had left a hole in the fabric of her life that she had yet to fill. As much as she liked Brian Milburn, his company did not always provide her with what she craved. Even after all the months that had passed since Jon's betrayal, there were still times when she felt... hollow.

She tracked Chet down in the almost completed living room. He stood looking out one of her new bay windows at the sunset. Almost everyone in Murre Bay stopped whatever they were doing to view a good sunset—one of the things she appreciated about the place. Chet didn't look as if he were truly enjoying the experience, though. His young shoulders had a definite slump to them.

"How's it going, Chet?" she asked, joining him by the window.

He gave her a sideways smile that looked forced. "Great," he said unconvincingly.

"Uh-huh." She studied his gloomy profile for a minute. "Subcontractors giving you fits?"

"Don't they always?" He sighed, and worried his light brown hair with the fingers of one hand. "The plumber finally showed up. He brought the fiberglass shower stall for the upstairs bathroom. Only problem was, he couldn't get it in through the doorway up there because it was bigger than the one we ordered. We waited a month for it, so I suppose it'll be another month before the right one shows up. One of the penalties of living so far out. We're going to have to redo the staircase too, a couple of steps are out of alignment." He shook his head. "I can't believe my dad *enjoyed* this work."

Chet's father had died of heart failure just before Dani came to Murre Bay. At that time, Chet had been studying for his real estate license in Seattle. He'd shot out of Murre Bay like a rocket the minute he'd graduated from high school, he'd told Dani. He hadn't ever intended coming back to live. Helping his dad during school vacations had made him determined to work with his head rather than his hands. He'd wanted to go on living in the bustling, exciting city and make a killing in Seattle's booming real estate market. But when his father died, his mother had needed him to carry on the family business. There were four younger Caswells to support. So here he was, twenty-two years old, saddled with unwanted responsibility, working at a job he hated, deeply resentful at having to fill his father's shoes and having a very tough time getting people in Murre Bay to accept him as a competent contractor.

All of which, of course, was why Dani had hired him.

"I'm going to make a pot of clam chowder," she offered. "You want to share it?"

Chet's face brightened perceptibly. "You're on," he said. "Time I get through a day like today, I don't have much patience left for dealing with the kids. You wouldn't believe how many problems they can come up with in a single day."

Her invitation had *not* been prompted by the fact she had lied to Adrian about having a date, Dani assured herself as she hunted down chowder ingredients. Certain lies were permissible. Everyone lied sometimes. Little lies—to save people's feelings, to make them feel better about themselves, to get out of doing something one just did not want to do—convenient lies. Lying to Adrian Falkirk had been necessary for her own protection.

They chatted companionably over a glass of wine while Dani prepared the chowder in the trailer's minuscule kitchen. His lanky body looking cramped in the small seating area, Chet chopped salad vegetables and reported on the work that had been done that day and the plans for the following day. Often, Dani felt impatient with the slow progress, but Chet was a perfectionist and she could see that she was going to be very satisfied with the final results, which was the important thing.

"If I could just keep Michael on the job, we might get along faster," Chet said moodily as they began to eat. "He's not much of a carpenter but he's strong as a horse. I could use his help putting up the last of the drywall in the new master bedroom."

Michael was Chet's younger brother and a constant source of conflict. Dani looked at him sympathetically. "He's taken off again?"

Chet sighed. "He went to a party in Baxter two nights ago and hasn't shown up since. I was mad at Mom for letting him go, but she says a boy has to have *some* fun."

Dani couldn't blame him for the bitter note in his voice. Michael was only eighteen, yes, but Chet was only four years older. "I thought you were going to tell him if he didn't shape up he'd have to leave and find work elsewhere."

His hazel eyes clouded. "Mom wouldn't back me up. Said Michael just hasn't found himself yet and I should be more patient with him."

Shaking his head, he straightened up in his seat. "Sorry, Doc. Didn't mean to dump on you." He grinned, abruptly looking as young as he really was. "This is the best clam chowder I've ever eaten. I'd have thought you'd eat out all the time, busy as you are." He glanced at her slyly. "At the Surf and Turf restaurant, maybe."

Nothing was hidden from the residents of Murre Bay—one of the major disadvantages of living in a small community.

"Cooking relaxes me," she said blandly, ignoring his innuendo.

"Uh-huh." He grinned again, obviously aware that she was deflecting his curiosity about her friendship with Brian Milburn. "And how was your day?" he asked carefully.

She grinned back, acknowledging his tact. "Busy. Interesting." No way was she going to tell Chet *how* interesting. Quite suddenly Adrian Falkirk's strong-featured face and startlingly blue eyes flashed into her mind, followed by a close-up of his powerfully made body, stripped to the waist, his chest matted with dark hair. Why did he have to look so much like Jonathan? Why had he chosen to come to Murre Bay, stirring up old memories that were better forgotten? She couldn't rid herself of the notion that he had some kind of ulterior motive. But neither could she imagine what that motive might be.

THE PHONE RANG soon after Chet left. It was Brian. "I was just wondering if you'd like to join me in the lounge for an Irish coffee," he said, his voice as tentative as usual.

Her immediate reaction was negative, and she kept him waiting for a response far too long while she tried to decide why. "I'm too tired," she finally offered lamely.

He didn't try to pressure her; he never did. Sometimes she thought she'd admire him more if he didn't always accept rejection so readily. Jonathan had always teased her into doing anything he wanted her to do.

That wasn't fair, comparing Brian to Jon, she thought as she washed the few dishes in the tiny sink, missing her dishwasher. Nice as he was, Brian would never come out of the comparison favorably. Maybe he was *too* nice. Or she was a fool.

The phone rang again. Her father this time. "Thought I might come down this weekend, heard the clamming was good," he said after his initial greetings.

Dani's heart plummeted. The last thing she wanted to face right now was the risk of her father running into Adrian Falkirk. "Sorry, Dad, I'm coming to Seattle," she improvised quickly, hoping she could get Stasny Stanislaus to cover for her. Sure she could—Stasny seized any opportunity to keep in touch with his former practise. "I need to do a little clothes shopping, there's a dance coming up at the Seaview Hotel."

"Who are you going to the dance with?" Harris asked at once, successfully distracted.

"Brian Milburn," she said, wincing over the lie. She'd already turned Brian down, afraid dancing might be too intimate an experience. The dance wasn't going to be held until December anyway.

"Seeing a lot of Milburn, aren't you?" Harris said shortly.

Determined not to get sidelined into a discussion of a love life that was in any case nonexistent, Dani quickly suggested they might see a movie while she was in the city.

"There's going to be a midnight showing of *The Rocky Horror Picture Show*," Harris said, brightening. Then a glum note entered his voice. "I suppose you'd rather see one of those weird French films of yours."

"I'd love to see *Rocky Horror* with you again, Pops," Dani said. "I'm not wearing a costume though, you're on your own there."

"Fair enough," Harris said happily. "I'll bring the noisemakers and the confetti and the other stuff."

Dani shuddered. Seeing *Rocky Horror* for the umpteenth time, pretending to enjoy the juvenile antics of the audience, would be her punishment for lying to her father, she decided as she got ready for bed.

"BUT WHY shouldn't I have given Mr. Falkirk an appointment?" Theresa asked. Sitting at her desk in the reception area, she gazed up at Dani, her brown, round-as-a-button eyes wide, a hurt expression on her pretty young face. "He called in just after we opened up this morning. Mrs. Callavero canceled out last night, so there was an opening. He said he needed to see you again. What was I supposed to do?"

"I'm sorry, Theresa," Dani said, knowing full well she'd overreacted to the sight of Adrian Falkirk sitting in the waiting room beyond the receptionist's cubicle. "I'm a little strung out this morning. Guess I didn't sleep too well last night."

Theresa's face showed immediate sympathy. "You need to drink herb tea. It would be far better for you than all that coffee." As usual, she was forgetting who was the doctor here. The next minute she was searching through the morning newspaper, looking for Dani's horoscope so she could diagnose the reason for her employer's unusual irritability. "Here it is," she said triumphantly. "Old friends may cause problems for you today. Try to disregard them."

"The friends or the problems?" Dani queried. Adrian Falkirk hardly qualified as an old friend, she thought. An enemy, maybe—at least an adversary.

Theresa made a face at her, then shook her dark curls. "Subconsciously, you must have known someone was going to give you a hard time. That's why you couldn't sleep.'' She looked suddenly concerned. ''I hope it isn't me,'' she said worriedly, then brightened. ''I'm not an *old* friend, am I? I've only been here six months.''

Dani's last receptionist, inherited from Stasny Stanislaus, had been close to sixty-five and immensely efficient. Dani had been sorry to see her retire. All the same, she was very fond of Theresa. The girl was a little scatterbrained, but warm and friendly. The patients adored her. She always read all of their horoscopes, too. And wrote the inspiring message on the waiting room's chalkboard every day. Today's was To do two things at once is to do neither.

''I can't imagine you creating any problems for me,'' Dani told her warmly and was rewarded by a beaming smile.

Dani had told the truth about her restless night. The trailer bed was not the softest. She'd spent most of the night lying tensely on top of the boardlike mattress, staring at the trailer's low ceiling, mulling over the undeniably sexual effect of Adrian's likeness to Jon, unable to let herself sink into the sound of the surf as she usually did. And now Adrian Falkirk was about to disturb her equilibrium again. Waiting for Theresa to show him into her office, she could feel her heartbeat revving up just at the thought of seeing him. Think of Queen Victoria, she instructed herself.

''I didn't quite understand the diet information you gave me,'' Adrian said as he sat himself down on the other side of her desk.

He had pulled the diet sheet out of his jeans pocket and was frowning earnestly down at it. He looked a little more rested this morning. Evidently he hadn't suffered from any disturbances in the night.

Just looking at him caused a definite constriction in her chest and groin, she noted. Those old familiar responses were sitting up and taking notice again. Some small area of her brain was obviously imprinted with physical memories of Jon. Maybe she should volunteer for neurosurgery, have the area cut out completely.

She hadn't been intimately involved with a man for a long time—maybe that was the problem. Perhaps sexual frustration had built up without her knowing it, to be projected onto the first truly attractive man to come along. Why hadn't it been projected onto Brian Milburn? Because, unfortunately, that kind of chemistry could not be summoned on demand.

"I'd have thought it was fairly straightforward," she said flatly.

"The one Reuben gave me was more specific," he insisted. "This one doesn't tell me how many ounces of anything I should have."

"Everything on it is low-fat—it doesn't matter how many ounces you eat, within reason anyway. You're not overweight."

"I guess that clears it up for me. Thank you." He eyed her guardedly. "Are you smiling or gritting your teeth?"

"Gritting."

"You're angry with me for being so dumb?"

"You've never been dumb, Adrian. I'm just feeling . . . irritable this morning, I guess."

His face lit with a smile so like Jon's it shocked her entire nervous system into overdrive. "Reuben Green told me hunger can make a person irritable," he said while she was still vibrating. "Something to do with low blood sugar. How about having dinner with me tonight? Protein's good for blood sugar, isn't it?''

Such hubris, she thought. Typical Falkirk behavior, of course. He was in town and he expected her to entertain him. As though their whole miserable history had never happened. Why? Why was he hounding her like this? What on earth could he hope to gain by it? ''I have a clinic,'' she reminded him stiffly.

''So you do. Lunch then. I hate eating alone.''

''Really?'' she said evenly. ''I rather enjoy it.''

He crooked an eyebrow. ''Is that a rejection?''

''Absolutely. I always have lunch sent in.'' Before he could volunteer to bring it to her, she said firmly, ''I catch up on my reading while I'm eating.''

''To do two things at once is to do neither,'' he quoted solemnly from Theresa's chalkboard.

How could she not laugh? How could she not soften toward him? If there was anything she appreciated in a man it was a sense of humor.

Nevertheless, she stuck to her refusal. She hadn't really lied. Sometimes she did read while she ate at her desk. But when the sun shone, as it was doing today, she took her lunch down into a sheltered spot in the dunes and relaxed over it, watching the birds, or the tourists.

ON THURSDAY, Adrian showed up in the middle of the afternoon with a cut on his left index finger that was hardly more than a scratch. He'd been cutting back salal around his house and had caught his finger on a piece of old wire. Theresa had fitted him into the schedule on an emergency basis. Judging by the starry-eyed expression on Theresa's round face when she announced his presence, she had already succumbed to the famed Falkirk charm.

"I wouldn't really call this a life-and-death situation," Dani said evenly as she cleaned up the cut.

Adrian gazed intently into her eyes. "I was afraid there was a danger of lockjaw."

He *knew* he was affecting her physically, Dani decided, forcing her hands to remain steady. "I'll have Laurie give you a tetanus booster to be on the safe side," she said gravely, and left the room before he could make any further propositions.

He was back on Friday, suffering from what he called the granddaddy of all headaches.

"Ran out of aspirin, did you?" she asked.

He hoisted himself onto the edge of the examining table and gave her a patently fake soulful look, accompanied by a sigh. "This is not the kind of headache that can be cured by medication, Doctor Kelsey. It needs more personal attention."

His eyes held hers. Against her will, she felt her body wanting to lean toward his. A woman could sink into all that blueness, she thought.

The Queen Victoria mantra wasn't working. Perhaps she should try hostility. "How much longer do you intend wasting my time?" she demanded.

"As long as it takes," he said promptly.

"To do what?"

He sighed again, very audibly, looking at her in exactly the same roguish way Jon had whenever he'd wanted to cajole her into doing something she didn't want to do. "Are you always so unkind to your patients?"

"My other patients don't..." She broke off, unable to think of a word that would fit the situation.

"Don't invite you to dinner?"

His strong face did not lend itself well to the ingenuous expression he was trying to adopt. Before she quite knew what was happening she had laughed.

"That's better," he said with great satisfaction, but before he could follow up on his advantage, she said, "As it happens, I do occasionally dine out with patients. Women patients. Or married couples. But I'm not going to dinner with you, Adrian."

"Why not?" he asked. "Look at it from my point of view. I'm stuck here in a strange place with nowhere to go, nothing to do and nobody to do it with. I know you. My brother treated you badly, but I am not my brother."

Dani had always prided herself on being fair-minded. He was obviously appealing to that trait. Had Jon advised him on how to break through her defenses? Why should he want to?

"Perhaps I'd like to make up for the way Jon treated you," he added reasonably.

"No one can do that, Adrian."

"Then perhaps I could improve your opinion of the Falkirks as a whole. It's only dinner, Danielle." He raised his hands, palms upwards. "I'm not going to give in, either. I'll just have to keep coming in here every day with some malady or other until you see the light."

She believed him. Falkirks had a lot in common with steamrollers.

"Theresa told me my horoscope today said I should go all out for everything I want," he added. "What was yours?"

"Don't allow yourself to be persuaded to do anything stupid."

"You're making that up."

"Absolutely." He was making her laugh again. And hostility could not survive laughter. Maybe she could use the laughter instead. Keep everything between them light and humorous. It was worth a try.

He was studying her face, possibly reading her thoughts. "Could you look upon dinner with me as a reward for my good behavior?"

"What good behavior?"

"I gave up smoking indoors," he said virtuously.

"And now spend all day out of doors, I suppose."

"I sat unmoving in my smokeless living room for a whole hour this morning. I can prove it too. Look at my teeth. They're worn down to the nubs."

She laughed again. It had been a long time since she'd enjoyed this kind of repartee. It was terribly hard to resist. Brian Milburn was pleasant company, but his sense of fun was sadly lacking.

She caught herself up. She was making comparisons again. "What about the rest of my suggestions?" she asked.

He smiled smugly. "I went fishing off my dock last night. Caught two beautiful trout." He sighed one more time. "I'm sure my headache would be completely cured if you'd just let me cook them for you."

"Adrian Falkirk cooks?" She was startled. Jon had always employed household help. So had his parents and sisters.

"You'd be surprised how many facets there are to my character."

"I'm surprised already," she muttered.

"Then why are you frowning?"

It was time to put her cards on the table, she decided. "I'm frowning because I don't trust this new-found friendliness of yours. You never liked me,

Adrian, don't even bother to deny that. And I certainly never liked you.''

He smiled. ''Ah, you're using the past tense. You see, I'm growing on you.''

''You are not.''

''But you're weakening, aren't you? The thought of me cooking for you intrigues you—you'd like to see if I can really do it.''

He hadn't denied that he'd never liked her, she noted. But he was quite right about her being intrigued. She could not for the life of her figure out why he was pursuing her so strenuously. As well, a domesticated Falkirk seemed tremendously exotic, up there with flying pigs. *And* she was getting a little tired of spending most of her evenings alone.

She could see Brian any time she liked, she reminded herself. But she knew even as she scolded herself that she was going to give in under pressure—not only Adrian's, but her own—and accept Adrian's invitation. Out of curiosity, she assured herself. Nothing more than curiosity. In the course of a whole evening he was bound to reveal his real purpose in coming to Murre Bay. Once she knew what he was after, she'd be able to deal with him.

THE HOUSE Adrian had rented was a large contemporary, featuring enormous windows. It was less than a mile from Dani's house, on Scoter Lake, facing south, thus offering a whole different aspect from Dani's. Though the surf could be heard from his deck, there was no other similarity. Instead of dune grass, his yard was covered with lawn partially invaded by wild strawberry vines and edged with gnarled and leafless pussy willows. The lake bank sloped down to dense thickets of cattails that were rapidly going to seed.

As Dani stood beside Adrian on the deck, sipping an excellent chardonnay, lights began coming on in houses all around the lake, sending shimmering paths out across the mirror surface of the water. The weather had turned warmer and the area was sheltered from the ever-present ocean breeze by Douglas firs, Sitka spruce, alders and high myrtle bushes, all of which were reflected blackly in the mirror calm of the lake. In the stillness, all her senses seemed honed to a degree that was seductive. The wine was crisp and dry and cold on her tongue, the salt-scrubbed air had never smelled so sweet. The sound of the surf seemed more rhythmic than usual, more hypnotic, the evening sky more intricately hued. In the distance a half dozen Canada geese flew by in perfect formation, outlined sharply against the sky. Seemingly affected by the same languor that was stealing over Dani, several pairs of mallard ducks were paddling lazily near the bank, occasionally tipping upside down in search of food.

A huge beaver appeared suddenly and swam in circles in front of the dock, then slapped his tail loudly on the water and dived for cover as a yellow canoe came into view. Quacking their displeasure, the ducks took off, landing some distance away. The canoeist laughed and called out, "Sorry, Kelsey!" and Dani realized it was Steff Carmody—no other white-haired woman in Murre Bay sported a purple-and-yellow parka. Steff's eyes glinted sideways at them as she paddled by.

The spurt of activity had broken the spell the silence had woven. "It's getting cold," Adrian said briskly. "Was the canoeist a friend of yours?" he asked Dani as she accompanied him inside.

"A good one, yes. Steff Carmody."

She had talked to Steff only that morning. The gynecologist had scheduled a cone biopsy and a D and C for the following week. Evidently he had found some cause for concern. Not Steff, Dani prayed under her breath. Not someone so full of life as Steff.

"Will your reputation be ruined now that she's seen you with me?"

She laughed. "Steff would love to see my reputation ruined. She thinks I'm too virtuous to be true." She shook her head. "Steff's a local character. She sees all, knows all and loves to gossip, but never maliciously."

"That's good to hear," Adrian said as he closed the sliding glass door. "I've been the victim of malicious gossip too many times."

"Did you deserve it?" Dani asked lightly.

His eyes met hers. "No," he said solemnly, surprising her. "I take relationships seriously." He set his wineglass on the kitchen island counter and lifted a pan down from the rack hanging above. "That's why my marriage lasted as long as it did."

Dani couldn't think of anything to say to that. After a while, feeling awkward, she murmured, "I can't believe I'm actually having dinner with Jon Falkirk's brother. If anyone had told me a month ago..."

Adrian shot her an enigmatic glance and she let her voice trail away, then offered briskly to help. He put her to work making coleslaw with a plastic gadget that shot bits of cabbage all over the counter until she learned how to control it.

Adrian had baked the trout, she was glad to see, though he'd used butter when a low-fat substitute would have been better. But all in all, the completed meal was fairly healthy and certainly delicious.

"Okay, I'll admit it, I'm surprised," Dani said as they sat over decaffeinated coffee in Adrian's living room. A fire was crackling in the fireplace. She had just watched him unwrap the foil from a square of the gum she had prescribed for him. He hadn't smoked since she'd arrived, she realized. And he'd limited himself to one glass of wine. "You really are trying to reform, aren't you?"

"I want to live," he said simply.

She nodded, feeling awkward again. "Was it very bad, the divorce?"

He grinned at her. "Your medical degree is showing, Dr. Kelsey. That was quite an assumption, blaming my self-destructive behavior on my unhappy marriage."

"Doesn't it belong there?"

"Not all of it. Mostly I was working too hard, putting in fifteen-hour days, forgetting to delegate, allowing myself to get stressed out all the time. My job wasn't fun anymore. The store got so damn *big*. Most of my time was spent in meetings, coordinating things, settling disputes, not actually *doing* anything myself. The divorce, which was pretty bad, yes, was just the final straw that broke this camel's back."

"I always wondered..." She broke off.

"What I saw in Marta?"

She nodded. "Apart from her looks, of course. She wasn't exactly..."

"Einstein?" He laughed shortly. "I noticed that pretty quickly." He shook his head. "I guess many very young men are flattered into temporary insanity when a truly breathtakingly beautiful woman takes an interest. I was just out of college, still young enough to mistake beauty for intelligence—or virtue. I don't know how such disasters can be avoided unless we pass a law prohibiting a man from getting married until he's thirty years old."

"Jon was thirty-three when we got engaged," she pointed out. "He still didn't know what he wanted."

"Jon was a fool," he said emphatically.

Startled, she set down her cup on the coffee table and looked at him. He held her gaze and a silence grew between them that shimmered with tension.

Neither of them had dressed up for the occasion. People in Murre Bay rarely did. Though Dani usually wore skirts and blouses at work, she inevitably changed into jeans and T-shirts in the evening, unless she was going out on the town. Tonight she'd put on French-cut jeans and a favorite V-neck sage green sweater that came almost to her knees, livening it up with a green-and-gold scarf at her throat. Adrian had on tan chinos and a loden green sweatshirt. He'd joked about them dressing in his and hers styles.

Why was she thinking about their clothing, she wondered. As an alternative to Queen Victoria, probably. She certainly didn't want to think about the implications of what Adrian had said.

"This is a nice house," she said lamely, looking vaguely around.

There was a gleam in his blue eyes that told her he knew she was avoiding the issue. "Furniture's rather thrift store eclectic, don't you think? That's the problem with rented houses—can't blame the owner—I wouldn't furnish a rental with priceless antiques myself."

He'd made an effort to make the place look more homelike with pots of yellow chrysanthemums bought from Phil's Market and a few botanical prints he'd picked up at the local, surprisingly fine, art gallery.

He'd debated setting the round table in the dining area by the kitchen window, but had decided in favor of the island counter and bar stools instead. He hadn't wanted to make too much fuss this first time. It had seemed ... politic ... to keep things simple.

Danielle was nervous, he realized. He'd jumped in too soon with that remark about Jon. Trouble was, he was still smarting over her comment about being with Jon Falkirk's brother. He wanted her to see him as himself. Yet given their past relationship, how else would she think of him?

Setting down her coffee cup, she suddenly turned to him with an air of determination. "I still don't know the real reason you came to Murre Bay. I was expecting some major announcement this evening, at least some explanation."

He'd always known she wasn't a game player. And normally, he liked a woman who was straightforward. How he wished he could be just as open. But he didn't dare tell her the truth. Not yet. "The real reason?" he echoed, stalling for time. "I didn't fake that blood work, Danielle."

She had a wonderfully firm jawline, especially when she was angry. "You could have gone anywhere, seen any doctor. I don't buy that stuff about it being more efficient to come here. Why *did* you come, Adrian?"

He hedged. "Curiosity, maybe?"

"About what?"

"You."

Her face tightened. "You wanted to see what happens to a woman after she's dumped by a Falkirk?" She inclined her head. "Okay, you've seen. Amazing what a woman can survive, isn't it?"

He shook his head. "I knew you didn't think too highly of me, Danielle, but I didn't know your opinion of me was that low."

"Can you deny that you never wanted Jon to marry me?"

He met her eyes levelly, admiring the angry fire in their smoky blue depths. "No, I can't," he said honestly.

"You must have been delighted when he didn't, then."

"Not delighted, no. I hated seeing how hurt you were. I've...worried about you ever since."

"So now you've seen there's nothing to worry about." Her voice was still crisp.

He'd had his strategy all mapped out, he'd thought, but in her presence he kept forgetting it and she certainly wasn't helping him out. The Snow Queen was in her ice palace and the drawbridge was up and locked in place. Take your time, he told himself—when you don't know what to do, do it slowly.

Getting up, he brought the coffee decanter from the kitchen and refilled her cup. "I went to the Sandbox last night," he told her.

"The Sandbox?" He could almost feel her relax. A second later she laughed, rather sheepishly. "The alternative bar I recommended. How was it?"

"You sent me there without seeing it yourself? How could you?"

She picked up her coffee cup and regarded him mischievously over the rim. "That bad, huh?"

He gave a shudder that wasn't altogether a pretense. "Average age of the citizenry about ninety-two. Perry Como on the jukebox, Thank-You-for-Not-Smoking signs the sole decor, the only libations mineral water or club soda or some revoltingly pink concoction called a virgin strawberry daiquiri.''

''You're exaggerating.''

''Not a whole lot. The ambience was definitely not what you'd call lively. I'm not even sure the rest of the clientele were awake. Everyone was just sort of sitting around. Once in a while someone would say something. Fifteen minutes later, someone would answer. That was about it.''

''I heard there was an electronic dart board.''

''You heard wrong, doctor.''

She laughed again, no doubt amused at the expression on his face. It really had been a dirty trick, sending him to the Sandbox, and she knew it, obviously.

There was a companionable silence that he didn't want to interrupt. The dancing flames of the fire painted shadows on her face, deepening the hollows under her fine cheekbones. Her boyishly styled hair gleamed with soft gold highlights. He loved the way it curved behind her small ears, wished he could trace the line with his fingers. In the V-neck of her sweater the soft swell of her firm breasts had a creamy appearance. Taken feature by feature she was not a conventional beauty. But beauty was there all right—in her glowing skin and the inner strength and intelligence that shone in her grave and lovely eyes. She was very still, but not tense. She never had been a fidgety woman. He remembered her stillness. She seemed able to wrap it around herself, effortlessly projecting an aura that was soothing yet challenging at the same time. Challenging because it tempted him to find out what would disturb it.

''I figure you owe me a night out on the town,'' he said abruptly.

At once wariness clouded her eyes and he could have kicked himself. She had retreated into the palace again. "I'd like to see how much enjoyment you could get out of a night at the Sandbox," he grumbled, making a joke out of the invitation so she'd relax again.

It worked partially, but then she glanced at her wristwatch and he realized he'd frightened her off again. What to do now? Tell her exactly why he was trying to get her to spend time with him? Or play it casual, so perhaps she'd want to repeat the experience?

He never had been a patient type, that was the trouble. This pussyfooting around was alien to him. He wanted to crash through the palace walls, tell her directly why he'd sought her out, what he hoped to gain. He wanted to grab her and shake her and tell her...

"Do you work on Saturday mornings?" he asked as he escorted her to the door and helped her into her jacket. Did he dare suggest breakfast or would that be pressing his luck?

"The clinic's normally open from ten until noon." She hesitated, then grinned faintly. "Stasny Stanislaus is covering for me tomorrow, though. I'm planning to drive into Seattle for the weekend. I hope you aren't thinking up symptoms, the schedule's already full."

He shook his head. "I've achieved my objective. You came to dinner."

"I did, didn't I? I guess persistence pays." She raised her gaze to his. "Does that mean you're going to stop tormenting me?"

"Tormenting's rather a strong word, isn't it?"

A faint flush of pink stained her cheekbones. "Teasing then," she amended.

"I expect I'll come up with another objective," he allowed.

"Such as?"

He shook his head. "I'll let you know."

She smiled wryly. "I guess strategy doesn't work if the opponent knows what it is."

God, she was quick. She'd seen right through his careful moves. He raised his eyebrows. "You think of yourself as my opponent?"

"I have to," she said quietly.

Did this mean he was making headway? he wondered. Did it mean she was attracted to him and fighting it, or did it mean she liked him no more than she ever had? Best not to ask. "A friendly opponent, I hope?" he suggested mildly, wishing he could think of a way to keep her here a little longer. Maybe he should just take her in his arms and hold her until . . .

A beeper sounded off. Out of long habit, Adrian's hand went immediately to his pants pocket, but it was, of course, Danielle's beeper.

"May I use your phone?" she asked.

He watched her as she checked with her service, then talked to someone who was evidently having a problem, admiring the crisp but kind efficiency in her voice, the alert expression in her eyes.

"A child with a possible sprained ankle," she told him as she headed back to the door. "I'll have to do X rays to be sure it's not a fracture. Her father's bringing her in to the clinic."

So much for persuading her to stay. And she'd be gone all weekend. He wondered if she stayed with her father when she visited Seattle. Probably. Why shouldn't she? Would she tell Harris Kelsey that Adrian was in Murre Bay? He sincerely hoped not. Harris had made it very clear at that traumatic last meeting that all Falkirks were persona non grata where he was concerned.

Preoccupied, Danielle smiled at him as he opened her car door for her. Obviously her mind was already on the clinic and the patient she was meeting there. But at least she was smiling. When he'd first arrived in Murre Bay she'd looked at him with all of the old animosity. A smile meant he was making progress, surely? Theresa's chalkboard that morning had declared that, according to *The Way of Lao-tzu,* a journey of a thousand miles must begin with a single step. This one step would have to suffice for now.

CHAPTER THREE

THE BEACH WAS CROWDED with clam diggers, in for the weekend. Head down against the wind that was cutting clear through his jeans and ski parka, clam shovel over one shoulder, Adrian plodded along, dutifully getting his prescribed exercise, watching the various methods of digging, hoping he'd come across one that looked simple.

A few intrepid men and women in chest-high waders stood out in the surf, facing the shore. They would stare at the water for a few minutes, then suddenly lunge downward with a clam shovel and flip up a clam encased in a long, olive green shell. On the beach, men and women of all ages first beat on the sand with upturned shovels, then crouched down and dug like crazed terriers, flinging wet sand in all directions.

Engrossed, Adrian didn't see the white-haired woman in the canary yellow slicker until he came within an inch of falling over her. She was squatting down with her right arm buried to the elbow in the sand.

Apologizing, he backed away, then realized she was staring fixedly up at him, her brown eyes bright as a bird's. "Don't I know you?" she asked.

Before he could respond, she yanked her arm upward. She was clutching an extralarge clam, which she deposited in a string bag tied to a cord around her waist. "Spirited little beast," she commented, then stood up and gave him a wet, sandy handshake that was surprisingly strong. She was tall and thin with an austerely beautiful face. "Name's Steff Carmody. Saw you in Doctor Kelsey's waiting room, never forget a face." She fluttered her eyelashes flirtatiously. "Especially a handsome face."

"Adrian Falkirk," he said. Her name seemed familiar. So did her white ponytail. The woman in the canoe, he remembered. Danielle had said she was something of a gossip. She had said it fondly, though.

Looking him up and down the woman grinned, her weathered face settling comfortably into its laugh lines. "Just getting started, are you? You don't have a grain of sand on you."

"This is my first time," Adrian admitted. "I've been getting up my courage all week. Tell you the truth, I'm not sure where to begin. Everybody seems to have a different method. I always thought clams just lay around waiting to be picked up, but it all looks fairly athletic."

"Razor clams are not like other clams," the woman said. She hauled one out of her string bag and showed it to him. "This protruding white part is its neck, at the other end, pulled into the shell, a foot—a digger. Soon as Mr. Clam feels a disturbance he starts digging downward at a rate of nine inches a minute. Come on and I'll show you how to catch up with him. You need to get started—tide's turning and it'll be getting dark soon."

"How can you be sure he's *Mr.* Clam?" Adrian queried.

"My sister's grandson names all creatures great and small Mister. Mr. Horse. Mr. Cow. Mr. Clam. Chauvinistic little munchkin but we're hoping he'll grow out of it." To Adrian's amazement, she suddenly began stomping around in some kind of primitive war dance at the water's edge, then pointed out a small round depression that had magically appeared in the wet sand. "That's called a show," she said. "Go in on the seaward side with your shovel, dig about three fast scoops, then get down on your knees and follow through with your hand."

A couple of minutes later, he was flat on his face, right arm buried up to the armpit in wet sand, right hand clutching a slippery, sharp-edged shell. Just then the woman yelled, "Watch it!" and he saw, over his shoulder, that an extralarge wave was rapidly approaching. He wasn't about to let go, however, so he had only himself to blame when the wave broke over his shoulders. Soaked to the skin, wet hair straggling over his forehead, he finally staggered to his feet, triumphantly waving his first clam.

"Stubborn, aren't you, Falkirk?" the woman said. "I like that in a man." Grinning, she vigorously stomped away in another circle.

It took him a couple of hours to get his limit. By then bobbing, weaving flashlights glowed all the way along the beach, looking like fireflies. Adrian's pride in his achievement was immense. As he soggily squelched away from the clam beds, chilled to the bone, parka pockets weighing him down, muscles burning just enough to make him feel virtuous, he realized that for the first time in weeks—months—he didn't have a headache. Looking up at the dark sky where a few stars were glimmering, he drew in several deep breaths of salt-loaded air, feeling as healthy as all get-out. And immediately craved a cigarette.

"Need a ride?" a familiar gravelly voice called from a small pickup camper as it lumbered alongside.

He shook his head and gestured at his own BMW. He'd parked it some distance down the access road—no way was he going to risk getting sand in the wheel wells.

The camper moved on, then braked to a stop. The woman stuck her head out of the cab as he drew level. "How about a bowl of homemade soup?" she said. "I live fairly near you, 309 Scoter Lake Drive. Weird looking white house facing east with a square, glassed-in tower that looks like an afterthought, which it was."

Adrian grinned. "I know the house. Soup sounds great—soon as I get myself dried off."

She nodded, her white ponytail bobbing. "Bring your clams. I'll show you how to clean them."

He lit a cigarette as soon as he was in the car, inhaling all the way down to his wet socks. Trouble was, now that he was smoking less, the cigarette smoke tasted better than it had in years, curling around his mouth in a way that was sweet and warm and comforting, immensely satisfying.

Set a limit, he told himself. Five a day. Absolutely no smoking in the house, or anybody else's house. No smoking in the car either, he decreed, stubbing the cigarette out in the ashtray. No smoking anywhere comfortable. Standing up only.

He laughed at his own fierceness. He'd enjoyed the clam digging immensely, he realized. The whole experience had been fun. How long had it been since he'd thought of something as fun?

"I'M SEVENTY-TWO," Steff told him after she'd shown him how to purge and clean his clams. "Lived in Murre Bay ten years. Best thing about Murre Bay is that even though it's a small town, during the winter, anyway, it's not ingrown. Everybody comes from somewhere else. Lots of variety.''

She dipped two steaming bowls of soup from an enormous pan that was simmering on the kitchen stove and set them on a tray. "Follow me," she instructed, and led the way to a sun porch that looked out on the darkly glimmering lake. Heat from a freestanding wood stove in the living room kept the porch cosy. Track lights illuminated it. A square antique oak table had been set for two. "Refrigerator soup," she informed him as they sat down. "Start with chicken stock, throw in everything that's in the fridge: squash, turnips, parsnip, leeks, onions, potatoes, carrots, zucchini, add a large dollop of pesto and a few dumplings and there it is.''

It was terrific soup, thick and rich and fragrant, scalding hot. It seemed possible his feet might eventually thaw if he ate enough of it. He smiled gratefully at her. "How do you like living in Murre Bay?" he asked.

She looked at him solemnly. "Being a city person, you may not know that most birds are very territorial. They stake out a spot—and from then on it's *their* spot. Bird song, when it's not an invitation to a female or a threat to a male, is often a proclamation of ownership. Many animals have the same instinct."

Her bony, weathered face split in a grin at his obvious bewilderment. "I have this theory that it's no different for humans. For everyone there is a special place that will give him or her optimum happiness—a sort of natural habitat. The trick is to find it. Murre Bay is my place. Have you read the police blotter in the local paper? Stray dogs, injured ducks, an occasional driver without a license, a few drunken juveniles at a beach party—that's about the extent of the crime scene. My sister and her family come visiting from New York— can't believe I leave the hoses and sprinklers and barbecue out all summer and nobody rips them off. Find it hard to believe myself sometimes.''

He frowned, suddenly remembering he'd heard her name before he came to Murre Bay. ''You said your sister's from New York. Are you too?''

''I am.''

''You're *that* Steff Carmody? Madison Avenue? The Model Agency?''

''The very same.'' She was obviously delighted he'd heard of her.

''What brought you way out here?''

''Came out years ago on a shoot, when I was modeling myself. Not much at Murre Bay then, no hotels, no big houses, just ocean and woods and a few cabins in amongst the dunes, but I thought it was the most beautiful place on earth. Always figured I'd come back some day, find Prince Charming and settle down.'' She laughed. ''Left it a little late for Prince Charming, I'm afraid. Time I got here I was a confirmed old maid. But the place is still beautiful.'' She waved a hand at the kitchen window. ''Look through there on a clear day and you'll see the Olympic Mountains.''

He had already noticed that the dramatically saw-toothed tops of the rugged Olympics could be seen above the tree line to the north from many vantage points in Murre Bay.

''How d'you know who I was?'' she asked as she refilled his bowl and buttered him another slice of crusty French bread.

''My wife—ex-wife—is Marta Renfrew.''

"The Sharon Rose perfume girl? She was your *wife?* Didn't even know she was married. Heard she was a bit of a nym..." She pressed her lips together.

"She was," he said dryly. "That's why we're no longer married."

He didn't really want to talk about Marta. He wanted to talk about Danielle.

As though she'd read his mind, Steff said, "Kelsey was visiting you a couple of nights ago, right?"

"Last night. She came to dinner." He looked at her curiously. "You call everyone by their last names?"

Steff grinned. "Always. I'm what is known hereabouts as a character. Have to maintain my image."

Setting her empty soup bowl aside she leaned her elbows on the table, resting her chin on cupped hands. Her brown eyes were bright chips of curiosity. She was obviously hoping for confidences. Maybe it wasn't such a good idea to talk about Danielle. He had no idea how much—or how little—she might have told this woman.

He shrugged casually. "Danielle and I met a few years back. Haven't seen each other for a long time." Changing the subject abruptly, he said, "Don't you miss the Big Apple?"

She shook her head, then laughed. "Tell you the truth, I get homesick once in a while, so then I hie me to the airport and climb aboard a jet. Two or three days in Manhattan and my battery's juiced up for another year. Only thing I miss is feeling useful, having a real purpose. But I don't exactly vegetate, and I go into Seattle every month or so. I may not look it but in my finer moments I'm something of a clotheshorse. Can't get by for long without Nordstrom's, Falkirk's and The Bon."

Adrian winced. "I'd like to have seen a slightly different order of importance there."

She frowned in a puzzled way, then sat back and stared at him with sudden hostility. "Falkirk. Of course. You're one of the twins. Are you the one who dumped Kelsey?"

He shook his head. "His brother."

The hostility was gone. "You're Seattle based?"

"San Francisco."

"So what brings you to Murre Bay?"

He filled her in briefly on his health situation. "Somehow I seem to have misplaced my joy in work, my joy in living," he concluded. "I thought I'd see if I could get it back."

She smiled wryly. "Had some of the same problems myself. Workaholism—late twentieth century version of the black plague." She smiled at him. "So you came to consult Kelsey?"

He nodded again.

"Well, you certainly chose the right person. Kelsey's the best. She cares. She even does house calls when necessary." A sly grin flashed across her face. "Guess you found that out."

Her eyes were solemn again. "When Kelsey first came to Murre Bay she was hurting. Took me two months to find out the reason. She talked about feeling crushed, rejected, unable to trust her instincts. Since then I've watched her recover. She's happy now, I think, or at least content. So I have to ask you, Falkirk—did you come here as friend or foe?"

"Friend, definitely."

"Good," she said. "Kelsey needs a friend."

"I understood she had several."

"That she does. But old friends are usually the best. Kelsey often seems . . . lonely."

"I thought she was seeing someone. . . ." He let the question hover in the air.

Steff frowned, then snorted. "You mean Brian Milburn? You don't have to worry about *him*. Brian's a nice enough guy, but a bit of a gloomy Gus. Kelsey needs someone who's fun, someone to play with. Everyone needs playtime."

"She told me she goes clam digging and hiking on the beach," he offered.

Eyes narrowed and glinting, she grinned saucily at him. "Wasn't talking about that kind of playtime."

He laughed and she joined him. "I think we understand each other," she said with great satisfaction. "Exactly how good an old friend were you?"

He decided to trust her. "Not as good as I wanted to be."

"I see." She met his gaze steadily and he had the weird impression she was gazing directly into his soul. "You love her," she said at last, making it a flat statement rather than a question.

"Yes." It was the first time he had admitted it aloud.

"Tell me about it."

"I've never talked to anyone about it."

"So maybe you should."

It was evident to Adrian that those steady brown eyes of Steff Carmody's had seen much that was good in over seventy years of living, much that was bad. They were still studying him intently, but with sympathy now, rather than curiously.

"My sister Roxanne was the first to meet her," he began. "Danielle was doing her residency at a local hospital, working part-time at Falkirks, Seattle. Roxanne is general merchandise manager there. They both headed up a committee for a theater benefit for abused children—and became friends. Roxanne invited Danielle to my father's house for our annual Christmas Eve party. I arrived alone—Marta had stopped off to visit a friend, probably male. I met Danielle.''

He hesitated, then plunged on, encouraged by the warmth of Steff's eyes. "There were sparks. Right from the start. We talked. There was a sing-along. Christmas carols. I liked her. More than liked her. Then Jon arrived.''

He laughed shortly. "Jon knows me as well as I know him. He saw right away that Danielle . . . interested me. He's always been intensely competitive. He set out to charm her. At first she didn't respond. Like everyone else, she was confused by the likeness between us, I suppose. But then Marta showed up and Danielle immediately became more interested in Jon.'' He shrugged. "I don't blame her, of course. I'd had no business letting myself be attracted to her. I was a married man.''

He sighed. "A month later, she and Jon were engaged.''

"Did he ever love her? Or was he just that competitive?''

"I don't know. My feelings for Danielle were such that I wasn't able to examine the situation too clearly. Falkirks have monthly get-togethers, you see—social as well as business. Naturally, Jon brought Danielle along on the social occasions. And I . . . every time I saw her, I . . .'' He shook his head. "All the time Jon and Danielle were engaged, I was busy fighting my own attraction to her.''

"You said Marta was your ex-wife. You're divorced now?"

"Yes."

"So. You got divorced. It occurred to you that Jon had already dumped Dani. So you thought you'd have a go at her yourself."

"I wouldn't put it quite so..."

"Crudely? But is it true?"

He nodded.

"Does Kelsey know you're in love with her?"

"No way. She has no idea what I'm doing here. And she definitely doesn't trust me." He hesitated. "I wasn't always pleasant to her after she and Jon became engaged. The only way I could...cover up...was to be rude to her, to act as if I disliked her. I guess I was a pretty good actor. She believed me."

"You're sure you aren't just being competitive yourself?"

He met her gaze. "Quite sure."

Once again, Steff was regarding him very directly. "What I should probably do is tell you to leave Murre Bay, leave Kelsey in peace."

"*Is* that what you're going to tell me?"

She shook her head. "I'm going to ask you a question."

He braced himself, squaring his shoulders. "Fire away."

Her brown eyes warmed. "What can I do to help?" she asked.

"THIS IS BRIAN," the voice on Dani's answering machine said tentatively. "I was wondering if you'd like to join me for a walk on the beach. If you get home in time. If it's still daylight and you're not too tired after driving from Seattle.''

Brian always sounded as if he were trying to talk her out of accepting his invitations. Often, he succeeded. This was probably one of those times. Three hours *was* a long drive.

"Adrian Falkirk," the next message announced. Nothing apologetic or tentative about that voice. "I'll call back later."

Dani immediately dialed Brian's number. A hike on the beach was just what she needed after her rowdy middle-of-the-night outing with her father. Of course she wasn't running away from Adrian.

When Brian drove up five minutes later, she suggested they drive farther south to where the Prescott River emptied into the ocean.

The wind had dropped during the day and the sun shone warmly on Dani's bare head as they strolled along. This beach was more gravelly than the ocean beach and the waves splashed musically over small rocks and seaweed clusters and empty crab shells. Right now the air was so wonderfully clear she could even see Mount Rainier's glacier-topped crown poking up, a rare sight from this distance. "I like it here," she said with a heartfelt sigh. It was a litany of hers, repeated every time she came back from the city.

"I'm glad," Brian said, taking her hand in his.

Usually she didn't permit even that small an intimacy, suspecting that Brian might try to advance further if she granted him even an inch, but what harm could there really be in a little hand-holding?

She smiled up at him. He was as tall as Adrian and Jon, but slender and wiry rather than muscular, quite handsome, but somehow not at all sexy, at least not to her. His sandy-colored curly hair was thinning slightly, though he was only thirty, but he didn't try to conceal the fact, which pleased her. An all around nice guy, no doubt about it. There was also no doubt that he liked Dani a lot—more than was comfortable, actually, though usually he was very comfortable to be with.

"Penny for them?" he asked.

"I was thinking about *The Rocky Horror Picture Show*," she lied hastily, and went on to describe the costumes some members of the audience had donned in an attempt to look like Dr. Frank-N-Furter, Magenta, Riff Raff and Columbia.

"I'd like to see that," Brian said wistfully.

One of the things that frustrated her about Brian was that he would say something like that without ever coming out and asking her to go with him. Not that she *would* go with him. She thought of Adrian's persistent pursuit of her during the previous week, then realized she wasn't being fair—first comparing Brian to Jon, now to Adrian.

"You'd hate it," she said firmly, then drew his attention to the line of seal heads bobbing along some distance out in the harbor. The seals were obviously watching their progress with interest. A lone murre waddled along at the water's edge, looking like a small penguin.

For a while they discussed the oil spill that had slicked the local beaches the previous year, coating and killing many of the birds and other sea life. Both she and Brian had helped in the rescue attempts—that was how they had first become acquainted. Engrossed in the conversation, Dani didn't pay any further attention to their surroundings until they were a couple of hundred yards from the tall, dark-haired man in a blue ski parka who was standing near the water's edge, gazing toward them, smoking a cigarette.

Adrian.

Even though she couldn't make out his features at that distance, she recognized him instantly. She also knew, by the motionless quality of his muscular body, that he had recognized her.

It was at that moment she admitted to herself she had suggested this beach because she had been afraid of running into him on the other one.

How had he known? He couldn't have.

"Let's go back," she said abruptly, interrupting Brian midsentence. "I'm cold."

Brian looked surprised, for which she couldn't blame him. For once there wasn't a breath of wind stirring and she was quite warm in her fleecy gray sweats. But typically, he swung around immediately, perfectly willing to head in any direction Dani wanted. This time she had to acknowledge she was running away, but she wasn't about to examine her reasons. She was also determined not to let go of Brian's hand, though every instinct within her was urging her to do so. All the way back, she imagined she could feel Adrian's gaze on the back of her head.

"How about dinner tonight?" she suggested as they reached Brian's station wagon.

Brian looked as delighted as she'd known he would. He was so...predictable. "It'll have to be at Surf and Turf," he pointed out.

"I like Surf and Turf." This simple statement made his gray eyes light up and caused his grip on her hand to tighten.

She felt like a fraud.

All the same, she enjoyed their meal together, even though Brian was constantly being consulted by his staff on some minor problem or other. There was something very comfortable about being with a man who didn't stir her senses in any way. Instead of verbal fencing she could enjoy a normal conversation about the changeable weather, the latest news from the Middle East, the encouraging increase in the Dow Jones average.

She had dressed for the occasion in one of her most feminine outfits, a peach-colored silk blouse and matching lamb's wool cardigan with a long slim navy blue linen skirt. She had also applied careful makeup. Brian's expression told her he appreciated her efforts and his occasional touch on her arm, far less tentative than usual, made her aware that by seeking to avoid Adrian, she'd encouraged Brian to think she was finally beginning to care for him.

"Why don't you stay until the restaurant closes?" he suggested over coffee. "We could have a quiet drink together. At my apartment perhaps?" He reached across the table to take her hand in his. There was a hopeful expression in his gray eyes and something possessive in his grip. He had been trying to get Dani to visit his penthouse apartment in one of the oceanfront condos for a long time. Was he thinking they might extend the evening beyond the drink?

She wanted to snatch her hand away, but forced herself to let it lie unresistingly in his. What on earth was wrong with her? She'd wanted him to be less tentative, but now that he was being just a little more aggressive she felt uneasy.

"I have a patient coming in early in the morning," she said hastily.

As usual, Brian accepted the rejection without question, and a moment later, while he was talking to his chef about some white sauce that had turned out unforgivably lumpy, Dani was able to excuse herself and leave.

Halfway across the parking lot, still shrugging into her coat, she hesitated. Three young men were standing in the shadows at the kitchen side of the restaurant. Something about the way they were lounging against the wall, talking in low voices, seemed . . . odd.

Two of the men were strangers to her—burly types dressed all in black. With them was a lanky youth with tow-colored hair, cut into spiky bangs across his forehead, straggling in long skinny strands at the back. It was Chet's brother, Michael, wearing bicycle shorts, a fleece-lined denim jacket and combat boots. "He's looking for attention," Chet had complained when she'd commented on Michael's haircut and his weird assortment of clothing.

Chet would be relieved that his brother was back in Murre Bay. No matter how he complained about Michael, he was obviously fond of him.

Dani stood watching the men for a minute as she fumbled through her purse for her keys. As she opened the car door, one of the men said something to Michael and he whipped his head around to look at her. She half waved, dropping her hand when he turned abruptly and strode away around the corner of the building. The other two kept staring at her and she hastily got into her car and drove out of the parking lot, feeling an unaccountable and unusual sense of menace.

Who on earth were those two young men? she wondered. They didn't look familiar to her at all. Usually by this time on a Sunday the weekenders had all gone home. And the younger members of the clam-digging set didn't go in for all-black clothing. The two had looked more like young hoods than tourists.

Shaking herself slightly, Dani tried to relax the tension that was cramping her shoulder muscles. She was being silly. The shadows and the fact that Michael had hurried off had combined to give the group an air of secrecy, that was all. Possibly Michael hadn't checked in at home yet and he'd wanted to avoid recognition in case Dani told Chet he was back in town. He'd told his companions she was the town doctor, probably, and they'd been curious about her.

All very logical. Yet her feeling of unease lasted until she was back in her trailer. Even then she didn't feel quite as secure as usual. She found herself closing the drapes on the windows that faced the ocean—something she did only when the sunlight was bright enough to be blinding. It was the very first time she'd felt unsafe since she came to Murre Bay. She didn't like the feeling one bit.

CHAPTER FOUR

"NOW THEN," Dani said briskly, sitting down at her desk and flipping open Adrian's chart. "I have the results of your blood work and I'm happy to say you seem to be on the right track."

This time Adrian had waited until his Tuesday appointment before coming into the clinic again. In the meantime, Dani had convinced herself that of course she could treat him like any ordinary patient.

Unfortunately, the decision made when he was out of sight did not hold together in his presence. Neither did she. There was the same jolting awareness when she looked at him, the same crackling of the air between them, the same constriction in her chest.

Be businesslike, she scolded herself. You are a professional, act like one.

"Since Dr. Green examined you," she continued, "your cholesterol level has gone down a few points and the high-density lipoprotein is up." She glanced at him. The same intent blue gaze that had always disturbed her was fixed on her face. Somehow managing not to skip a beat, she went on, "Did Dr. Green explain to you about high-density and low-density lipoprotein?"

He nodded solemnly. "High-density is the good guy in the white hat, low-density's the villain with the handlebar mustache."

She wasn't going to laugh. She'd already discovered that laughter weakened her defenses. "That's one way of putting it, I guess," she said evenly. "HDL hauls cholesterol away from your artery walls, LDL dumps excess cholesterol onto them. So the idea is to raise the HDL level while depressing LDL. Eating cholesterol-free foods and foods that are low in saturated fat and exercising regularly does the job in both cases."

She closed the chart and clasped her hands together over it. Whenever this man was around, she needed something to hang on to. "I guess all I can tell you is to keep up the good work. How's the nonsmoking and antidrinking campaign coming?"

"I'm down to five cigarettes a day. Outdoors only. And I've switched to regular gum. Lack of nicotine isn't my problem—it's the oral satisfaction that I miss."

Was that a suggestive smile hovering at the corner of his mouth? "The drinking was never a problem, Danielle," he went on. "I drank too much socially, yes, but only because I was usually buying drinks all around. Had to keep up the macho Falkirk image, I suppose. Whatever—I've no problem sticking to a single glass of wine with dinner."

"Good. Then I guess I'll see you in another week to check on progress. Not much point in having your blood work done again until the middle of next month. Dr. Green can do it for you when you get home."

"Are you dismissing me, Danielle?" he asked.

There was an amused note in his voice that unnerved her. "I have other patients," she pointed out. "As long as you don't have any particular problems . . ."

"But I do." He had raised that left eyebrow of his and was leaning forward. She had to force herself not to lean to meet him. Usually she didn't like people to invade her space, but somehow when Adrian did it acted on her like a magnet. If a magnet was cut in two, she remembered abruptly, each piece became a magnet in itself. Adrian was Jon's identical twin. In their mother's womb a single ovum had divided into two parts. Perhaps what she was feeling was the effect of Jon's magnetism, shared at conception with his brother.

Ridiculous theory. She pushed herself far back in her chair, trying to make her change of position look like a natural shifting rather than a fearful withdrawal.

A rueful smile played around the corners of his firm mouth, but he didn't comment. "I'm getting restless," he explained.

"Restless?" she asked warily.

"I have to keep stopping myself from calling San Francisco to see how things are faring at the store. I'm a floor person, you see, not an office person. I spend a lot of time walking the departments—that's a lot of walking in a 900,000 square foot store. Now I find myself walking it in imagination, worrying about the new electronics department, the restaurant remodeling, listening for my beeper. For years I've been married to that beeper. It doesn't seem to matter that I *know* my assistant manager will be working flat out. She's hoping for a store of her own, so she's anxious to prove herself capable of handling my duties. And she's certainly got competent help—I trained the division heads myself. But I worry just the same. And of course worrying creates tension. I think I need something to occupy my time."

A teasing sparkle had entered his blue eyes. "My nanny used to say the devil finds work for idle hands," he added.

She'd forgotten about the nanny. The twins' mother's social activities had left her little time for her children, according to Jon. Dani had often blamed Jon's charming but selfish expectation that she would fall in with his every wish on that nanny's doting affection. Obviously Adrian had been affected the same way.

"Beachcombing is palling already?" she asked dryly. She hadn't expected Murre Bay to satisfy a Falkirk for long. Probably he was about to tell her he was off to a more exciting locale.

She frowned, shifting her weight again—why on earth should that thought make her feel so irritated?

"I *love* beachcombing," he said, surprising her.

Reaching into his jacket pocket, he pulled out a small green soda bottle and put it on the desk between them. "I almost forgot. I brought a gift for you. Proof that I'm following orders—walking the beach. I guess it washed up with the tide. Looks as if it came from Japan."

The bottle was etched with characters that did indeed look Japanese, which wasn't surprising. Every once in a while the local newspapers reported the finding of a bottle with a message in it from a Japanese student. And sure enough, there was a rolled up spill of paper in this one.

Dani looked suspiciously at Adrian's innocent expression, then upended the bottle and tapped the paper out. Opening it up, she read aloud, *"Moshi, moshi,"* and looked at him again.

"That's what Japanese people say on the telephone instead of hello," he said solemnly.

She looked back at the note. The message was short. "Be kind to Adrian Falkirk." How could she not laugh?

He laughed with her. How blue his eyes were. "Amazing, don't you think?"

"Astonishing." She replaced the note in the bottle and ran her fingers over the bumpy surface. It had retained the warmth of his body. Hastily, she set it down. "Where did you find it?"

His eyes glinted. "On the beach where you went walking with your boyfriend."

"Boyfriend?" she echoed before she could stop herself.

"I believe his name is Brian?" he said helpfully. "It *was* your boyfriend you were with, wasn't it? On Sunday? You were holding his hand. Seemed to denote a certain intimacy."

She looked directly at him. "Why do you keep chipping away at me, Adrian?" she asked.

"Perhaps I'm curious to see the woman behind the marble facade."

She shook her head. "You must have some kind of purpose that goes beyond curiosity."

"I do, indeed," he said cheerfully.

At last. "What?" she demanded.

He didn't answer for a moment and for the life of her she couldn't look away from his steady blue gaze.

"I don't think I'm ready to tell you what my purpose is," he said very quietly, then moved his head slightly sideways. "Let me amend that, I'm not sure you're ready to be told."

While she was still trying to figure that out, he added, "What I was trying to say earlier in my very devious way is that I'm lonesome. I'd like to take you out tonight. For a glass of wine, maybe, if you can't manage dinner." He laughed. "I'd even settle for a virgin strawberry daiquiri."

Quite suddenly, a reason for his apparently single-minded pursuit occurred to her. Murre Bay's population was divided almost equally between retirees and young people with families. There were very few single people, especially in Adrian's age group. After a week of living here he'd probably discovered that. He was not the kind of man who would be content for long without the company of a woman.

Which meant that Adrian Falkirk wanted to use her because nobody else was available. It was as good a reason as any she could think of for his behavior. And of course she wasn't going to allow him to pressure her into keeping him company so he wouldn't be bored.

This decision gave her a feeling of great relief. "I'm sorry, Adrian, I don't think it's a good idea for me to see you socially. The doctor-patient relationship..."

"That's a cop-out," he interrupted.

Which was quite true, of course.

"You're blaming me for Jon's behavior," he said flatly. "I can understand you'd be resentful, but..."

She leaned forward, suddenly feeling very angry, and welcoming the anger. "Let me set you straight on something, Adrian. You seem to have the idea I've spent the last two years simmering with resentment because Jon left me standing at the altar. That isn't so. At the time I was angry yes, hurt yes, and perhaps even resentful. But once I got over my..." She hesitated. What was a good euphemism for broken heart? "... over my wounded feelings, I realized that if Jon really did fall in love with Claude—and as he married her, I guess he must have done—I certainly wouldn't have wanted him to go through with our wedding."

"He could have told you himself, though."

"True." She lowered her head. "It's history, Adrian. I've put it all behind me."

"If that's the case, why is it so impossible for us to be friends? What have you got against me?"

Could she have become his friend if he wasn't Jon's brother? Possibly. Especially if he wasn't Jon's double. But unfortunately, he was. He was standing now. Only her desk separated them. She could feel the ache in her body starting again, the ache that made her want to lean toward him.

"Why do you want to see me anyway?" she asked, taking the offensive. "You were downright nasty to me when I was engaged to Jon."

"I was, wasn't I?" His voice was subdued now, but he was still looking at her directly. "Do you remember the night we met, Danielle?"

A warning signal went off in her mind. What was he leading up to now? She shook her head. "No," she said emphatically.

He sighed as though that was the answer he'd expected. All the sparkle had gone out of him. He looked tired suddenly. And drawn. Nodding briefly, he turned away again.

She had hurt him, obviously. She wanted to go after him, apologize. For what? She shook her head. Of course she wasn't going to go after him. She'd wanted him to leave her alone. Possibly he would do that now. So she should be happy. Shouldn't she?

"How about an early dinner at my house tonight?" Steff asked.

Dani didn't hesitate. "I'd love to," she said into the telephone. Steff would be going into hospital on Friday—the next day. Probably she needed company, though she would never admit it.

That wasn't the only reason she'd accepted, she realized as she hung up the phone. She'd felt…off-center somehow, since seeing Adrian on Tuesday, as though she'd behaved badly where he was concerned. But how else could she have behaved? She'd *had* to discourage him. It wasn't his fault she kept confusing him with Jon, of course, but the fact was there and there wasn't much either one of them could do about it.

STEFF WAS A wonderful cook. The mingled smells of garlic and onion greeted Dani at the front door. "Coq au vin," Steff announced as she tossed Dani's jacket onto a chair. She never did stand on ceremony. "Remembered it was your favorite," she added with a smile, preceding Dani into the kitchen. She gestured vaguely at the kitchen door. "Falkirk went out to the garden to collect the last of the tomatoes for our salad. I've an idea he might be sneaking a smoke while he's at it."

Dani stopped dead in the hall archway. "Falkirk? Adrian Falkirk's here?"

"Sure is. We met on the beach last Saturday. Clamming. We've seen each other a couple of times since— becoming pretty good friends." Steff's voice was bland, her back turned as she tore salad greens into a wooden bowl. "Understand he's an old friend of yours."

"Is that what he told you?" Dani had to make a conscious effort to keep anger out of her voice.

Steff shot her a quizzical look over her shoulder. "You don't like him? What's not to like? Seems a fine man to me. Not to mention gorgeous. If I was thirty years younger I wouldn't let you near him." She laughed. "Twenty years younger, even."

"I was engaged to his twin brother Jonathan," Dani blurted out. "Jon dumped me the day of the wedding. I told you all about it ages ago."

"So you did. Seems a shame to blame Falkirk for his brother's transgressions, though."

Dani sighed. "I don't dislike Adrian because Jon dumped me, Steff. Right from the beginning he treated me like . . . he was mean to me—miserably mean. Now he's suddenly shown up in Murre Bay and acts nice as pie. I don't know why. But I do know I don't trust him. I've been doing my damnedest to avoid him, Steff. I wish you'd told me he was going to be here."

Steff squinted at her as she put the salad bowl aside. "Methinks you protest too much, Doctor dear. Gets to you, doesn't he?"

"Not in the least," Dani said firmly.

"Ha!" Steff exclaimed. Then she went to turn on the sun porch track lights. Dani pulled knives and forks out of the kitchen drawer and followed her, feeling very put out. "Did I ever tell you about my sister and me?" Steff asked her. "We were a classic case. She opted for marriage and kids. I insisted all I wanted was a career. Sometimes she thinks I got the best bargain. On the other hand, I know that *she* did. Living alone is okay in small doses, Kelsey, but not for a lifetime."

"What's this minilecture got to do with Adrian Falkirk?" Dani asked tightly.

"He's an eligible guy. Whatever happened between you in the past, he likes you a lot. Trust me on this. Why not give him a chance?" Steff's brown eyes could be mesmerizing sometimes.

She shook her head. "You're wrong this time, Steff. I don't know what Adrian's after, but I'm absolutely sure it has nothing to do with my best interests. He used to dislike me intensely."

"Not true," Adrian said behind her.

She hadn't heard him come in. Yet there he was, standing at the kitchen sink, rinsing tomatoes under the faucet. "Pass me some paper towels, will you, Danielle?" he asked.

She obliged, then couldn't stop herself from asking, "What do you mean, not true? The very first time we met you were rude to me."

He dried the tomatoes carefully before darting a sly sideways glance at her. "You told me you didn't remember the first time we met."

"I didn't," she said hastily. "It just came back to me. I certainly don't remember all the details, but I do remember you getting nasty at some time during the evening. And you sniped at me in that same sneery sarcastic way whenever you and Marta made one of your monthly pilgrimages up from the south."

Adrian nodded, his blue eyes studying her face. "There was a reason for that," he said ambiguously, then grinned, looking beyond her. "I'll save it for some time when our hostess isn't hanging on every word."

"Better than a soap opera," Steff said admiringly.

She and Adrian laughed, but Dani still felt indignant. How he could twist things around to suit his own purpose! she thought, then wondered, again, what that purpose was.

She also wondered, as they began eating, how he'd managed to coerce Steff into inviting her without telling her he would be among those present. That it was his idea she had no doubt, though again, she couldn't begin to guess at his purpose.

"What's happening at the Sandbox?" Steff asked Adrian abruptly, surprising Dani.

Adrian smiled. "Looks as if we might have a deal."

"What deal?" Dani asked. "Last I heard you didn't want anything to do with the place. Boring, you implied. Moribund."

He looked sheepish. "I went back on the weekend and got talking to the owner. Josh Andersen, you know him?"

"Kelsey knows everyone in Murre Bay," Steff said.

"Nice old guy," Adrian said. "Rotten businessman but a great personality. Recovering alcoholic. Used to go deep sea fishing off Alaska, has some tales to tell that would curl... well, that's another story too. I came up with a few ideas for him." He grinned at Steff. "Just as you thought, he was very interested."

"What kind of ideas?" Dani asked.

He leaned forward, enthusiasm making his eyes glow. "There are a couple of nonalcoholic bars in San Francisco, Seattle too. They do very well, not as much income as regular bars, but Josh says he's not out to make his fortune. I suggested he liven up the decor, put in a dance floor." His gaze was fixed on one of Steff's Boston ferns as if it were giving him inspiration. "A lot of people don't like going to a regular tavern," he went on. "People who are health conscious, single women who don't want to cope with drunks hassling them. But as I told Josh, that's no reason not to have any atmosphere at all. An espresso machine, more choice of soft drinks, freshly squeezed fruit juice, maybe hot hors d'oeuvres..."

"Can Josh afford to put in a dance floor and hire a band, not to mention an espresso machine?" Dani asked.

"Well no, but it wouldn't be a bad investment. . . ."

"You're thinking of investing in the Sandbox?"

"Josh and I are talking about it." He grinned at her. "I told you I needed something to occupy my time."

"You're supposed to be on vacation," Dani said irritably. "Recuperating. Relaxing. Taking life easy."

"Vegging out," Steff offered. "How come you're so uptight about this, Kelsey? It sounds like fun to me. I might even be interested myself." She grinned. "That is, if the news on Friday is as good as I expect it to be."

"It will be," Adrian said with complete conviction.

Obviously Steff had told him about her pending surgery. Steff, who never discussed her own private pains with anyone. The Falkirk magic was certainly working full-time. Steff was smiling confidently at Adrian, as though he could single-handedly arrange for her tests to be negative. Dani hoped they were both right; she didn't have a crystal ball herself. But there was nothing wrong with an optimistic attitude, she reminded herself.

Why *had* she reacted so irritably? she wondered as Adrian and Steff went on discussing the Sandbox. Because if Adrian got too involved with Josh Andersen, he might decide to stay on in Murre Bay after his month was up. And she just didn't want to cope with his effect on her any longer than she absolutely had to. It was far too exhausting.

It was obvious that Steff liked Adrian. And that the feeling was mutual. During the meal, Adrian was at his most charming, telling funny stories about himself and Jon when they were children, some of which Dani had heard previously from Jon. They had swapped identities from time to time to fool teachers, school friends, even their parents.

"Being a twin wasn't always funny," Adrian admitted. "There were times when I felt I was in danger of losing my identity entirely, times when I had to try to prove I was a separate and distinct person, occasions when I rebelled against the whole idea of being anybody's twin."

He looked at Dani somberly when he said that and she wondered guiltily if he knew somehow that she often saw Jon when she looked at him.

Jon would never have admitted to such vulnerability, she realized. Jon had always been quite sure of his own identity.

"Suppose you two take the canoe out for a spin?" Steff suggested, coming into the kitchen as they finished cleaning up the dishes. "I was just up in my tower. There's a splendid full moon coming up. Very romantic."

"Why don't we all take the canoe out?" Dani said.

Steff gave her a sly glance. "No way that canoe can hold three of us. Besides, I want to get my insurance papers together. I have to check into the hospital at the crack of dawn tomorrow."

"That reminds me," Adrian said. "How about I drive you into Baxter?"

Steff raised an eyebrow. "You think I might be too nervous to drive myself? What d'you take me for, a weakling?"

"I wouldn't dare suggest such a thing."

Steff snorted. "I'll drive myself, thank you very much. And just to show you how confident I am, I'm also planning on driving myself home the following day."

Unsmiling, Adrian looked at her, hands on his hips, long legs planted solidly. "One of the obligations of friendship is allowing friends to help you," he said. "I read that on the chalkboard in Danielle's clinic, so it must be true."

Steff gave him a long look, then softened visibly. "That's very kind of you, Falkirk. I'd be delighted to accept your help." Her eyes glinted mischievously. "There, how's that?"

He grinned. "Much better."

Steff made a shooing motion. "Okay. Now you two oblige me by giving my canoe an outing."

She'd enjoyed the evening in spite of herself, Dani had to admit as she pulled on her jacket and obediently followed Adrian out onto Steff's patio where the up-turned canoe was parked. It was a beautiful evening. A slight breeze was blowing off the ocean, carrying with it the roar of the restless surf. Just as Steff had promised, a huge yellow moon was rising gloriously in the eastern sky, etching mystery into the Douglas firs and spruce trees at the other side of the lake. Stars were just becoming visible.

"Ursa Major and Minor are my favorite constellations," Dani murmured as she picked them out.

"Why?" Adrian asked. She could *feel* him looking at her, feel the air between them, heavy with tension.

"Because of the ancient story," she said. "Jupiter fell in love with Callisto, a great beauty in her day. His wife, Juno, didn't take kindly to this, so she changed Callisto into a bear. There she is, see, the Great Bear—more often called the Big Dipper, which isn't nearly as romantic. And Little Bear is Callisto's son. Seems soon after Callisto became a bear, she saw her son and rushed toward him. He had no idea this big bear was his mom, and he was all set to run her through with his spear. So

Jupiter changed him into a bear also and lifted both of them up into the sky."

"Not too romantic to be stuck up there forever," Adrian commented, and she made a face at him. He smiled back at her, his eyes glinting.

A canoe ride on a quiet lake lit by that yellow moon was probably not a sensible idea if she was really intent on discouraging Adrian Falkirk, she thought.

"I like it here," Adrian said with great feeling as he looked around.

Astonished, she looked at him.

"Why so surprised?" he asked.

"I thought all Falkirks were urban animals." She hesitated. "It wasn't just that," she admitted. "Whenever I come back to Murre Bay, after a trip to the busy, artificial world of the city, I say the same thing. 'I like it here.' It's some sort of magic charm, I guess. Has Steff told you her theory about natural habitats?"

"She has." Again, he held her gaze, his eyes darkening. Then he shook his head slightly and bent to the canoe. "Heave ho," he ordered.

The canoe was heavier than it looked. It had always been waiting in the water when she visited Steff before. How on earth did Steff manage it alone? Even with Adrian on the other end, it took considerable effort to help turn it over and then to keep it level as they walked it to the boat ramp. When she was finally able to set her end down and straighten, she had to stretch to relieve a cramp in her lower back. Turning slightly to survey the sky again, she caught her breath and froze.

Directly north a plume of smoke billowed above the tree line, just visible against the band of light that glowed over Murre Bay's business section. For a moment she stared at the smoke, trying to figure out what could be causing it. It seemed too dense to be merely smoke from a wood stove or fireplace.

"That's downtown, isn't it?" Adrian said urgently.

A moment later, by unspoken agreement, they hurried toward the house. "I have to go, Adrian," Dani said. "Someone might be..."

"I'll go with you," he interrupted.

As Dani ran toward the street, Adrian paused to call through the door to Steff. He jumped into Dani's car as she started the engine, slamming the passenger door behind himself. "Steff's calling 911," he said.

As they turned onto Seaview Way they could see orange flames flickering at the center of the column of smoke. The smoke itself had darkened. "It's right downtown," Dani muttered, leaning forward to urge the car onward.

"Either the library or the Methodist church," Adrian suggested.

She shook her head. "It's farther on." Surf and Turf? she wondered.

It *was* Brian's restaurant. By the time Dani swung into the side parking lot, the fire department was already in action. Hoses snaked into the restaurant through the side door. Several groups of people were gathered at a safe distance, talking excitedly. Brian himself was standing in the parking lot, visibly shivering in a thin sweater and slacks, his head back as he watched a fireman climbing around on the restaurant's roof. He winced as the man raised an ax and started knocking out shakes.

Pulling her medical bag and a lap robe from the back of her car, Dani went to put the blanket around Brian's shoulders. "Is everyone out?" she asked.

He nodded, tugging the blanket close to his throat and smiling gratefully at her. "We had plenty of warning. The smoke alarms went off. Not too many people in here on a Thursday night anyway. The fire started in the walk-in pantry back of the kitchen. Before we could get the extinguishers going it spread to the crawl space above. So far it seems to be contained in this end." He winced again as the fireman on the roof started sawing through tar paper and plywood. "Going to be more damage from that guy's enthusiasm than the fire itself."

"Was anyone hurt?" Dani demanded.

He shook his head.

"How could it start in a pantry?"

"That's what I'd like to know." Bringing his head forward, he rubbed the back of his neck, then frowned. "What the hell is that stupid idiot doing?"

Following his gesture, Dani saw a tall, dark-haired, broad-shouldered man in a blue parka racing toward the restaurant's front door. *Adrian.* Ignoring the smoke that was billowing out, he plunged inside. Dani's heart stopped beating. Seemingly paralyzed, she stared at the doorway for a split second as if she could make that familiar muscular figure reappear by sheer strength of will. "Adrian?" she said incredulously, and felt rather than saw Brian's quick, startled glance. Then she was off and running herself, hurling herself in through the door without any further hesitation.

Somebody yelled—one of the firemen wielding a hose beyond the swinging doors that led to the kitchen—but Dani was already inside the dining area, unable to see more than vague shapes of chairs and tables through the smoke. Dropping to all fours she saw Adrian crawling toward her, a little boy who couldn't be more than five years old tucked under his arm. The child was struggling in Adrian's grasp. "The kitty," he yelled determinedly. "We have to save the kitty."

At that moment, a dark shape rubbed up against Dani's leg and she grabbed for it. "I've got the cat," she told the child and he immediately stopped struggling.

"You okay?" Adrian asked, coughing slightly.

"I'm fine," she managed to choke out, although the smoke was already beginning to dry out her lungs. To her amazement, the cat was purring loudly, obviously unperturbed.

"Let's get out of here," Adrian said urgently and she nodded, hanging on for dear life to the cat and scuttling as rapidly as she could behind Adrian and the boy.

The outside air smelled wonderful. She and Adrian stood up and took several lungfuls. Neither the child nor the cat seemed to need any. "That's one way to cure yourself of wanting to smoke," Adrian commented as he carefully set the boy down at a safe distance from the restaurant.

A plump young woman in a quilted red jacket ran toward them, screaming, "Timothy!" Grabbing the child, she alternately shook and hugged him. "What on earth did you think you were doing?" she yelled at him.

The boy, a freckled-face redhead, seemed surprised by his mother's emotional behavior. "I saw the kitty through the window," he said matter-of-factly. "I just went to get him so he wouldn't get all burned, but then I couldn't find him."

His mother hugged him again. "Timothy's okay," Adrian said gently, taking the cat from Dani. "He wasn't in there more than a few seconds and he's small enough he was under the smoke. Luckily I saw him run in."

"He was right beside me," his mother exclaimed as Dani extricated the little boy from her grasp and began checking him over. "I didn't even miss him until I saw you bring him out."

Adrian watched Dani as she examined the child. The caring, nurturing expression that appeared on her face as she touched the boy with gentle hands stirred something inside him, as though those delicate fingers were tugging at his heart.

Still distraught, the mother snatched the child up in her arms as soon as Danielle pronounced him okay, clutching him tightly. "Don't you ever do such a thing again," she said grimly to the boy.

"I won't, Mama." Timothy was still perfectly calm.

"I don't know how to thank you," his mother said shakily to Adrian. "I can't believe the pair of you ran right in and brought Timothy out. You're real heroes."

"Adrian's the hero," Dani said. "I wasn't in there more than ten seconds."

"She saved the kitty," the little boy told his mother. Then he patted her face as if to calm her. "I'd have come out anyway, Mama," he added. "It was all smoky in there."

"Everybody all right?" a paramedic asked Dani, an oxygen mask in one hand, portable tank in the other.

She nodded, then grinned up at Adrian as the young woman walked off, still haranguing her child. "The man of the hour," she said. She had spoken lightly to cover up the fact that she had been badly shaken when she saw Adrian disappearing into the smoke.

There was an expression she couldn't quite interpret in Adrian's blue eyes. "You came after me," he said softly.

"Well, of course I did. I'd have gone after anybody dumb enough to dash into a burning building."

"Would you?" His eyes still held hers. For just a moment the flashing lights, the moving bodies, the throbbing of the fire engine motors seemed to fade away, leaving the two of them alone in a small oasis of silence.

"Are you all right, Dani?" Brian exclaimed, putting his arms around her from behind. "What on earth possessed you? You scared me to death running in there like that."

She stiffened. "I'm fine, Brian. We're all fine," she added, pulling herself gently free and indicating Adrian and the cat.

Adrian held the cat toward Brian. "Yours, I believe?"

Brian backed off a step or two, clutching Dani's blanket close to his chest. "Keep that animal away from me. I've been chasing that damn cat out of the restaurant for the past three months. Someone in the kitchen keeps feeding it scraps. I can't find out who. Look how fat it is."

Adrian had pulled the cat protectively back into his arms when Brian refused him. It was a pretty cat, black and fluffy, with white feet and a white blaze on its face. Still totally unconcerned, he was purring like an outboard motor and nuzzling Adrian's chin. "Can't blame a cat for selecting a good place to eat," Adrian said mildly.

"You can when you're allergic to the damn things," Brian said stiffly, then sneezed to prove his point. "Too bad you didn't leave him behind," he said to Dani.

Dani looked at him narrowly, feeling very disappointed in him. She'd thought all along that eventually she might grow fonder of Brian, but she couldn't possibly care for someone who could even suggest leaving an animal in a smoke-filled building.

"This is Brian Milburn," she told Adrian without trying to hide her disapproval. "He owns Surf and Turf."

Still stroking the cat, Adrian looked thoughtfully at Brian, obviously remembering she'd told him he was her boyfriend. Brian was observing him rather sourly, she noticed. "This is Adrian Falkirk of Falkirk's department stores," she said.

Brian looked even more truculent. "What are you doing in Murre Bay?" he asked Adrian.

"Just staying here for a few weeks."

Brian made no attempt to hide his relief.

Childish jealousy, Dani thought, then immediately felt ashamed of herself. Brian had just gone through a very bad experience after all, even if the fire apparently wasn't as bad as it had looked.

Already the firemen were stowing their gear and wrapping a yellow warning tape around the outside of the restaurant. Someone had opened all the windows. Though the smell of smoke was still strong, there was little to be seen now. The fireman had descended from the roof. "You keep any gasoline in that big closet?" the burly fire chief asked Brian. "Oily rags, anything like that?"

"Why would I keep stuff like that in a pantry?"

"People do strange things. Someone had gas or kerosene in there, judging by the smell of that smoke. I have photos and someone's looking it over. I also have the kitchen blocked off. Don't let anybody in there. We'll clean up the debris after we've gone through it."

"Sure," Brian said disconsolately. He squared his shoulders. "How does it look?"

"Not too bad," the chief said. "Mostly the pantry and the crawl space above the kitchen—some damage to the ceilings and one kitchen wall."

Brian nodded, walked a few yards away with the chief and stood talking to him for a while. Then he came back. "Guess I'll go take a look," he said gloomily.

"You want me to come in with you?" Dani asked.

He looked gratefully at her. "Would you? I'd appreciate that." Putting a proprietary arm around her shoulders, he smiled tightly at Adrian. "Good of you to go in after that little boy," he conceded.

Adrian shrugged. "Just happened to see him." He smiled at Dani. "Pretty fast reflexes yourself, doctor."

Brian's arm tightened. Dani wanted to shrug it off, but knew such an action would hurt his feelings. All the same, this was no time for him to suddenly become possessive.

"I guess I'd better take care of my friend here," Adrian said brightly.

Brian watched sourly as Adrian went to put the cat in Dani's car then started walking back toward them. "He's a friend of yours?"

Moving out from under his arm as casually as possible, she avoided a direct answer. "We were having dinner at Steff Carmody's house. We saw the smoke from her front yard."

"Where'd he come from?"

"San Francisco." She certainly wasn't going to enter into any explanations as long as Brian was acting so surly.

"How come you haven't mentioned him before?"

"For heaven's sake, Brian, he just got here."

"He was on the beach on Sunday, wasn't he? You turned around when you saw him."

"I didn't particularly want to talk to him at that moment," she said with as much patience as she could muster.

"I'll take the cat home with me, if that's all right with you, Milburn," Adrian said cheerfully when he rejoined them. "I'm going to call him Boots," he informed Dani.

"What will you do with him when you leave Murre Bay?" Dani asked.

"I'll take him with me, of course." With a smiling glance at Brian, he added, "I like cats." That earned him another black look from Brian.

A few minutes later, the three of them gathered in the hallway between the dining room and kitchen, regarding the soggy, char-blackened, indescribably bad-smelling mess that had once been a well-organized food preparation area. The pantry behind it was totally destroyed, open to the sky. A fireman was sifting through the debris. The rest of Brian's staff were still huddled outside, talking in low voices about the fire, their faces worried.

"Guess I'll face this tomorrow," Brian said after a couple of minutes' silence. "I'll have to call the insurance company about getting in a cleanup crew. Probably have to redo the whole kitchen and part of the roof," he added gloomily. "Could be closed for a couple of months." Slinging Dani's blanket across a dining chair, he turned toward her, presenting his back to Adrian, patently excluding him. "How about a drink in the bar?" he asked her softly. "I doubt the smoke penetrated in there. I could use a drink after all this."

Compassion was clear in Dani's eyes. She was going to accept, obviously. How could she refuse a man whose pantry had just burned to a crisp? "We should maybe check back with Steff first," Adrian said evenly. "She'll be wondering... we did leave in rather a hurry—the canoe's just sitting there in the front yard. If it rains, it'll fill up with water."

"That's true," Dani said slowly.

"We could always come back and join Brian for that drink in a half hour or so," Adrian suggested straight-faced.

Dani giggled nervously. Evidently she'd noticed the black looks Brian was directing at him from time to time.

Abruptly, her face sobered. She seemed to be mulling something over and finally she put her hand on Brian's arm. The man immediately looked more cheerful. But Dani appeared very worried. "It just occurred to me," she began, then hesitated before going on. "Kurt Webber said something about oily rags or gasoline. Which would seem to indicate he suspects arson." She hesitated again. "I wouldn't want you to report this, Brian, because it could be purely coincidental, but I did see Michael Caswell and a couple of other young men hanging around outside here a few nights ago. They looked sort of... shifty, but that might have been my imagination." She glanced at Adrian. "Michael's the younger brother of Chet Caswell, the contractor who's working on my house," she explained. "Michael's something of a problem, I'm afraid."

"When did you see Michael?" Brian demanded.

She thought for a minute. "Sunday night, after we had dinner."

So that's where she'd been when he'd called her after seeing her on the beach. Adrian had guessed she was with the man who'd accompanied her, the man who'd held her hand. But he hadn't wanted his guess to be confirmed. Just how fond of Brian Milburn was she? he wondered.

"Sunday," Brian echoed. "Corky told me Michael was in here with a couple of bikers, while we were at the beach."

"I don't think they were bikers," Danielle said. "They were dressed in black, but..."

"Bikers wear black," Brian interrupted. "The point is, Corky had to ask them to leave. She said they were all being loud and obnoxious, making obscene remarks to her and the other waitresses, disturbing everyone. They refused to go until she threatened to call the police. Then they barged out, banging into chairs and cussing all the way. What time did you see them?"

"Around nine-thirty, I guess. But that doesn't sound like Michael, Brian. He's a bit of a pain, but he's usually fairly well mannered."

Brian ignored her. "They were in here at five-thirty. Why would they be hanging around unless they were up to something?" He nodded. "I knew that kid was no good. He worked here for a couple of weeks last summer, bussing. Late every day. Always sneaking outside for a smoke. I had to fire him."

"That doesn't prove..."

Brian wasn't listening. Nodding rapidly, he was obviously putting two and two together and coming up with half a dozen. "I'll call Webber right away." He turned away. "If those guys didn't cut the phone lines with all their haphazard chopping."

A hard guy to like, Adrian decided. What had he expected the firemen to do, stand by and watch the fire consume the entire restaurant?

Dani's face was showing disapproval too, he noticed. And felt uncharitable because the fact pleased him. "I asked you not to report this," she reminded Milburn, following him out of the dining room. "Let me talk to Michael first. He's never been in any serious trouble as far as I know. And Chet doesn't need any more problems."

"Nor do I," Brian said, picking up the phone at the reception desk.

"Wait, Brian, please," Danielle said urgently. "Let me at least call Chet and find out if Michael was at home this evening."

But Brian was already talking to the fire department, passing on what Dani had told him.

Obviously furious, Dani turned on her heel and charged back into the dining room where she retrieved her blanket. Then she headed straight for the restaurant's front door, with Adrian right behind her. He had an idea they wouldn't be having that drink with Brian Milburn after all. Somehow he wasn't at all disappointed.

CHAPTER FIVE

"DAMMIT MICHAEL, sit down," Chet exclaimed. "You're not going anywhere until we have this out."

"I promised to help the Lions Club janitor clean up the hall from the teen dance," Michael objected.

Michael always had a good excuse, a noble excuse, for avoiding chores or arguments. His expression right now held just the right amount of offended innocence.

"Well, if you promised . . ." Mary Caswell began.

Chet rounded on her. "Leave this to me, Mom. You want me to take care of this family, then let me do my job."

She looked hurt, of course. But then she always did lately. Wounded. Still pretty, but there was gray in her curly brown hair that hadn't been there when Chet's father was alive, and lines across her forehead that were fairly recent. But the biggest change in her was what Chet thought of as her flutteriness. She had never been a strong-minded woman, but she had been capable of firmness in the handling of her children. Now she was easily swayed by any argument. And all the kids took advantage of her. Paul and Chrissy and Linda were still in the den watching television and she'd told them to go to bed an hour ago.

Striding to the doorway, Chet raised his voice. "School day tomorrow. You know the rules. All of you get to bed and sleep right away. No arguments."

Obviously recognizing the exasperated note in his voice, they got up obediently and Paul turned off the television set, but they all looked at him as if he were something from under a rock, for God's sake. He remembered when they used to see him as some kind of hero. Big brother who lived in the big city and only came home on special holidays, bringing presents for all. As they filed out, their mother followed them, promising to bring them cookies and milk, to read to them, undermining his authority again.

Cursing under his breath, Chet returned to Michael in the living room. Mike was finally sitting down, but he'd turned on the radio and was rapping along with Hammer, head bobbing, fingers snapping. Sighing, Chet switched the radio off. He used to enjoy listening to the radio himself—he could remember Dad yelling at him to turn down the volume. Now he couldn't stand noise in the evenings. Sometimes he felt like a sour old man, some wizened old codger who disapproved of everything and everybody. Sometimes it was a shock to look in a mirror and see his own smooth, youthful face.

"Okay, Mike," he said evenly, determined to keep his temper this time. "What do you know about this fire at Surf and Turf?"

"Who, me?" Mike's hazel eyes were as wide and innocent as little Chrissy's. Which didn't mean he was innocent.

Stupid to ask, Chet knew. Ask Michael a question and he avoided direct answers on principle. Better to make an accusation and make it stick. "You were hanging around the place Sunday night with those punk friends of yours from Baxter."

"Who, me?" Mike said again.

Chet looked at him levelly. "You."

"So?"

That was almost a confession. They were finally getting somewhere. "You were kicked out of the restaurant earlier for creating a disturbance."

Mike's grin was designed to melt the coldest heart. "No sense of humor, those chicks in there."

"Women, Mike. Those are women. Working for a living. Just like Mom. You want some punk kid hassling Mom when she's cleaning hotel rooms? Those women are working to make ends meet, just like Mom and me, God help us. They're entitled to respect."

"You used to call women chicks."

"And Dad slapped me alongside the head every time I did it. You want me to do that?"

"You could try it." Still grinning, Mike playfully balled his fists and adopted a boxing stance.

Chet raked a hand through his hair and gripped the top of his scalp as though that would help him to control himself. "Okay, Mike, let's take it from the top again. You and your friends created a disturbance in the restaurant. You were asked to leave. You hung around outside. Four nights later someone set fire to the restaurant's pantry. Does all that seem like a coincidence to you?"

"I didn't set fire to nobody's panties," Mike said, eyes twinkling.

Chet hung on to his temper by a thread. "Pantry, Mike. P-a-n-t-r-y. It's a closet for storing cooking ingredients and dishes and stuff."

"Who told you about me being at the Surf and Turf?" Mike asked.

"It seems to be general knowledge. The waitresses told the restaurant owner, he called the fire chief."

"And Doc Kelsey saw me outside the restaurant," Mike finished cheerfully.

Chet wasn't about to tell him it was Doctor Kelsey who had called him fifteen minutes ago to let him know what was going on. She'd tried to stop Brian Milburn from calling the authorities until she'd had a chance to talk to Chet, but hadn't managed to prevail. Any minute now, someone was going to come looking for Michael Caswell. Before that happened, he wanted the truth.

"Doc Kelsey isn't involved in any of this, Mike," Chet said. He sure didn't want those friends of Mike's hassling Doctor Kelsey. He didn't trust them as far as he could throw them, which wouldn't be very far, judging by the size of them.

"Good looking chick, Doc Kelsey," Mike said appreciatively.

"Woman. She's been very good to our family," Chet reminded him. "She didn't even charge for the kids' school physicals this year."

He sat down in the armchair opposite Michael, feeling as frustrated as he always did when he tried to deal seriously with his brother. Talking to Mike, arguing with Mike, was like trying to walk on quicksand. You didn't make any forward progress, you just sunk in deeper.

"Do you think I like hassling you all the time?" he asked.

"You sure give a good imitation of it."

"I didn't ask for this job," Chet reminded him. "It wasn't my idea to come back here and try to hold this family together. For two bits, I'd take off and let you all drown in your own juices."

"Let's both go," Mike suggested eagerly. "I know a couple of dudes in Seattle would let us bunk with them till we could put a stake together. You and me, Chet, what do you say?" His eyes were shining. For one split second, Chet felt a yearning that . . .

It never took him long to come down to earth. "What do you suppose would happen to Mom and the kids?"

Mike shrugged. "Food stamps?"

Chet gritted his teeth. "I don't have a job lined up after Doc Kelsey's house," he said flatly. "Most people aren't willing to take a chance on someone my age. Sometimes I lie awake nights worrying about what's going to happen to us all. It doesn't help to have you to worry about on top of everything else. Give me a break, Mike," he added more softly. "All I want to know is if you had anything to do with that fire tonight or not. I have to tell you, it looks bad, especially as you don't have any way of proving where you were tonight."

"I was on the beach. I told you that."

Such a picture of injured innocence. Could Chet believe him? Mike had always loved the beach, ever since he was a little kid. He could sit on a log for hours, staring at the seabirds, drawing them in his sketchbook. Sometimes he hiked the beach for miles, lugging home chunks of driftwood that looked interesting. Chet had a sudden memory of him at four, jumping up and down over the waves in his little red swim shorts, laughing, tow-colored hair shining in the sun. Short tow-colored hair. Now it straggled over his shoulders. And he was wearing those damned combat boots again. He'd nagged his mother into buying them; now he wore them everywhere.

"I gotta go." Mike stood up abruptly, holding up a hand as Chet started to protest. "I didn't set that fire.

Didn't know anything about the stupid fire until you told me. That's it, Chet, take it or leave it.''

"Then you'd better stop in and tell that to Kurt Webber before he comes looking for you. It would look a whole lot better if you volunteered information instead of waiting for him to get around to trying to drag it out of you.''

"Okay.'' Mike was all smiles now that he was leaving.

"You do it, Mike,'' Chet said, standing up. "You do it, or don't bother coming home.''

Mike waved cheerily and was gone.

Was he really going to help the Lions Club janitor, Chet wondered. Probably not. Mike could make up the damnedest stories. It seemed to Chet that the only dance he'd heard about had been held on the weekend anyway. Surely the hall had been cleaned up before now. Maybe he should check with the janitor. Hell no, he didn't want to know if Mike was lying again. Sitting down again, leaning back in the chair, he closed his eyes. If only he wasn't so damned tired.

DANI HESITATED on the threshold of the hospital recovery room. Sitting next to Steff's bed, solicitously holding a glass with a bent straw to her lips, was Adrian Falkirk. She was beginning to feel almost fatalistic about the man. Everywhere she looked, everywhere she went, every time she turned around, there he was.

His eyes looked strained around the edges, red-rimmed, giving him a slightly scruffy appearance. How the hell had he spent the night? Had he really given up drinking? He'd supposedly intended going home directly from Steff's after they'd checked in with her to report on the fire.

Suppressing her irritation, Dani approached the bed, and smiled down at Steff. "How's it going?" she asked.

Steff managed a groggy smile as Adrian moved the glass away and set it down. "I must have drunk a gallon of apple juice. Never realized how soothing it is. That damn tube they stuck down my throat made it feel like raw hamburger." She smiled at Adrian. "Falkirk here has been keeping me company."

"Some company," Adrian complained with a grin of his own. "You keep nodding off on me."

"Shows I like you. Trust you. Feel comfortable with you. Something." Her voice was slurring now, her eyelids sliding closed. She fluttered them open and grinned lopsidedly at Dani. "Heard you and Falkirk are some kind of heroes. Good show, both of you."

"Dr. Wellington tell you everything's okay?" Dani asked her.

No answer. Her eyes had closed again.

"Those cells were precancerous, so you'll need to come in every three months for a Pap smear for a while to be on the safe side, but there's no sign of cancer in your uterus."

The lopsided smile hovered a moment then slid off Steff's mouth as it dropped open. A gentle snore was her only comment.

"I guess she wasn't lying here worrying," Dani said fondly.

"Dr. Wellington gave us the good word an hour or so ago," Adrian said.

"You've been here all day?"

He nodded. "She was the color of cottage cheese when they wheeled her in here. But then she came out of it and the nurse gave her a couple of shots of oxygen and she talked a blue streak for a while. Wore herself out. She looks pretty good now though, don't you think?''

"Better than you," Dani retorted.

She was trying—and failing—to imagine Jon sitting all day at the bedside of a seventy-two-year-old woman who wasn't related to him. Even if she had been related—Jon wasn't comfortable around sick people. He'd informed her of that as soon as he knew she was a doctor.

"Did you talk to Chet Caswell about the fire?" Adrian asked.

"Last night. And again this morning." She sighed. "Poor Chet. He's only twenty-two himself, but when his father died a couple of years ago he had to take charge of the family—his mother, Michael, three younger kids. He was living in Seattle, trying to get into real estate sales. Last thing he wanted was to come back to Murre Bay. But someone had to take over the business—it was the only way the family could survive. He's having a tough time of it already, without having to contend with Michael's problems."

She shook her head. "Michael denies knowing anything about the fire, but Chet says he's not sure he's telling the truth. I don't know what to think. Whenever I'm around Michael I feel I'm in the presence of an alien being. But he seems—gentle somehow. I really can't imagine him deliberately setting a fire. On the other hand, this morning Chet told me Michael didn't come home all night, and he didn't go to see the fire chief as he'd promised to." She shook her head. "I guess we'll just have to wait and see." She glanced at Adrian. He really did look awful. "Are you feeling okay?" she asked.

He smiled tiredly. "Didn't get a whole lot of sleep."

"What's the problem?"

"That's classified information."

"You look as if you were out on the tiles all night."
She was becoming irritated again. Why was he so determined to make a mystery out of everything?

"Apt choice of words," he said.

She frowned. "What's that supposed to mean?"

He laughed, his blue eyes glinting. "I'll make a deal with you. Come to my place when we leave here and I'll show you."

"Show me what?"

"Why it was an apt choice of words."

Dani sighed. "I have another patient here to look in on. And a house call to make after."

"That'll give me time to fix dinner for you."

"No, not dinner." If he kept feeding her, she was going to start feeling obligated to him. "I might manage coffee," she added, relenting. She felt responsible for him. She was his doctor after all. If he *was* drinking . . .

IT WAS SEVEN O'CLOCK when she parked in Adrian's driveway. He came to the door before she could ring the bell, his finger to his lips. "Didn't want you disturbing my babies," he murmured as he closed the door behind her.

She stared at him blankly and he laughed and held his hand out for her jacket. Then he took her arm and escorted her into the kitchen. There was a large cardboard box on the floor, lined with a colorful beach towel. In it was the cat Dani had rescued from the restaurant the previous evening. It was a moment before Dani noticed the four tiny, squirming kittens. They were almost hairless, blindly nuzzling into their mother's side. Sensing that she was being watched, Boots raised her head and roughly licked a couple of round fuzzy heads, then lay back contentedly.

"This is what I meant about an apt choice of words," Adrian said, kneeling down beside the box. "*I* wasn't out on the tiles, but obviously Boots was at some time in the fairly recent past. Good thing I gave her a unisex name, don't you think?"

Crouching down, Dani touched a finger to each of the tiny warm bodies, then lightly rubbed one of the mother's ears. Boots purred proudly. Dani glanced at Adrian and laughed softly. "This is what kept you from sleeping?"

He gave her a sheepish smile. "I thought he—sorry, *she*—was just feeling restless in her new home. She kept prowling around, meowing in this demanding way as if she were telling me to do something and do it now. I got up and brought this box out, thinking it might make an acceptable bed, but she acted offended. Then while I was getting myself a cup of coffee, she disappeared. About the time I gave up looking for her and went back to bed, I heard her meowing again and found her in my sock drawer. I guess she'd climbed in from the back of the dresser. Then I realized what was going on. Once she got started, she seemed to be managing just fine by herself, but I was so..."

He paused, looking down at the cat, an odd expression on his face. "I was so damned awed by the whole process, I stayed up the rest of the night watching. Did you know the mother cat severs the umbilical cords with her teeth? Amazing! Then she cleans off the kitten with her tongue and eats the afterbirth." He laughed. "I don't know how I imagined it would all get taken care of, but actually seeing it was...exciting. This morning she carried the whole litter into the box, one at a time.

So I could wash my socks, I guess." He rubbed the cat's head gently. "Thoughtful of her, wouldn't you say?"

Dani couldn't picture Jon sitting up all night with a pregnant cat anymore than she had been able to imagine him sitting by Steff's bedside. Watching Adrian's large competent-looking hands touching the cat with such delicacy was causing a meltingly tender response inside her that must have shown on her face. Looking up, Adrian caught his breath audibly. He stood up, holding out his hand. Thinking he meant to help her to her feet, she gave her hand to him and he pulled her up.

But then he didn't let go. For a second he stared at her, his face shuttered, eyes darkening. She could not look away, or ignore the sudden clamoring in her blood.

"Let's just try an experiment," Adrian muttered. Then he tugged on her hand, pulling her toward him. The next moment she was held tightly in a grip of iron.

His mouth was not at all gentle. It moved on hers insistently, hungrily, drawing breath from her, giving it back hotly. She felt his hands moving over her hips, pulling her body hard against his, felt his body's stirring and the bone-melting, churning response of her own. She was trembling as though with a chill, yet her body felt feverishly hot. And still his mouth moved on hers. When her lips parted involuntarily, he took the movement as an invitation, his tongue darting at once inside her mouth. The pounding in her ears was as loud as the surf in a winter storm. The storm was inside her, beating urgently against her heart, her groin, her mouth, racketing through every nerve to her brain, lifting her tighter against him. Her fingers wound in his hair and she held on to it tightly and wouldn't, couldn't let the kiss go.

Then one of them murmured something that was almost a moan and she came back to her senses and realized that she was doing something she had never intended, never expected to do.

When their bodies parted they were both breathing hard. The storm he'd called up was still raging inside her. For a full minute, she fought between identifying the emotion as desire or anger. Anger won. "You and your brother still have some kind of juvenile rivalry, is that it?" she demanded. "You have to follow in his tracks, find out what his women are like? Is Claude next?"

His gaze was inscrutable, giving away nothing of his feelings. She felt ashamed of her outburst. "I'm sorry," she said abruptly.

Turning away, she walked over to the small dining area and stood looking out the large picture window, her hands gripping the back of a wooden chair. Yard lights were on and she could see a great blue heron stalking rhythmically along on his sticklike legs among the reeds at the edge of the lake, his long narrow bill darting occasionally into the shallows. As she watched, the bird caught a small fish and tipped its head back to swallow, then went back to stalking. Birds had an enviably simple life, she thought, only survival to consider. Food and safety. No emotions to worry about.

She hadn't even recovered her breath yet, but it already seemed impossible, unimaginable, that she should have responded to Adrian as she had. What on earth could she say to him . . . how excuse herself for leading him to believe . . . She needed to be alone, needed time to adjust to what had just happened.

"It's for me to apologize, Danielle," Adrian said behind her. "I made a mistake, I guess. I thought you were beginning to feel..." He sighed and didn't finish the sentence.

What had she been thinking of? She hadn't been thinking at all, that was the problem. She had simply reacted. Had she imagined for those few wild lost moments that those were Jon's arms holding her?

As he stood there, Adrian lightly touched her shoulder and a tremor went through her. She hated the concrete evidence of her weakness. And hated even more the desire of her body to turn toward him, to lean against him. If she was still being reminded of her love for Jon, there was something sick about her response, surely—doubly disturbing when long-dormant emotions were being projected onto Jon's twin brother. Already she'd encouraged him to think she was attracted to him, when she'd intended all along to discourage him. And still she wanted to turn under the weight of his hand, to experience again those turbulent feelings she had experienced in his arms.

She had to get out of here. Now.

"Nothing has changed, Adrian," she said as firmly as she could.

"How can you say that, Danielle?" he protested.

But Dani was not going to stay and argue. She didn't dare. Pulling away from his restraining hand, she grabbed her coat from the closet where he'd hung it and headed blindly for the door, willing him not to follow her.

CHAPTER SIX

A STORM HIT THE COAST around midnight, roaring in out of the west, winds gusting to sixty miles an hour, lashing trees and bushes into a frenzy. One sure thing about Washington coast's weather was that any season could occur at any time of the year: sunshine and balmy breezes in November, hailstorms in May, stormy weather in August—or October. Since moving to Murre Bay, Dani had enjoyed standing at her living room window watching storm fronts as they came in over the ocean, dumped their rain and moved on, often trailing clear skies and sunshine behind them.

Living temporarily in the trailer, she didn't feel quite so secure. She tossed and turned in bed while the trailer shuddered with every gust and rain drummed on the metal roof. She felt as if she were trapped in a tin can that was being swept down into Niagara Falls. She could only hope that the roof would hold up under the onslaught.

Lying there, almost deafened by the noise of the elements, she was unable to close her mind to thoughts of Adrian Falkirk and the kiss they had shared. No matter that she couldn't understand his motives, she had been terribly unfair to him. She couldn't let anything like that happen again.

It would be best if she avoided him from now on, she decided. She'd write him a note, maybe, suggesting that he consult a physician in Baxter. She'd recommend Dr. Platt. He'd referred a couple of patients to her. It was time she returned the favor.

She had to get some sleep, she scolded herself, turning over one more time. Usually she only worked two hours on Saturday, but tomorrow she was giving flu shots all afternoon.

Another gust of wind rocked the trailer, making the windows rattle. Tomorrow, she would ask Chet to take time out from working on her new bedroom suite. If he were to finish the living room she could bring her Hide-A-Bed sofa out of storage and sleep on that. The thought comforted her and finally she slept.

In the morning, she tried not to remember the dreams she'd had in which Jon and Adrian had blended together into a single person, then split apart.

Shortly after dawn, she put on her sweats and a down parka and walked across the dunes. The storm tide had brought in enough logs and seaweed to make walking higher up on the beach difficult, but the area closest to the water was clear. The rain had stopped, but the wind was still gusting and the ocean was turbulent, the rollers breaking far out and crashing in to shore. Huge inky clouds hovered on the horizon, pregnant with the promise of more rain. The seabirds were grounded, huddling together in large groups.

She would take a chance and walk to the jetty as usual, she decided. With any luck she'd be back in the trailer, changing for her day's work, before the rain started in again. Pulling her knitted hat down over her ears, she set her sights on the signposts that warned of the dangerous undercurrents in that area and incidentally marked the end of her mile walk. Then she stepped out briskly, keeping a wary eye on the squall line. She didn't hear the jogger's footfalls until he ran up along-side her.

Adrian Falkirk, of course.

"Good morning, Danielle," he said, slowing to a walk.

She nodded, but kept her face turned forward as though she were concentrating on getting her correct exercise. Typical, she thought, even after yesterday's moment of passion, he was still too formal to call her Dani.

"Couldn't sleep?" she asked when the silence between them became uncomfortable.

He laughed. "I was too busy counting the shakes as they blew off the roof. And thinking."

If he expected her to ask what he was thinking about he was crazy. It was unnecessary in any case. The memory of that passionate embrace was alive between them, as if it were writhing in glowing colors on the turbulent air.

"I *have* been sleeping well since I came to Murre Bay though," he added. "Better than I've slept in years."

"Good."

Silence again. He'd adapted his stride to hers so that they were perfectly in step. She was so *aware* of him.

"Quite a coincidence we'd hit the beach at the same time," she said.

She could feel him smile at her, as if the air between them were electrified. "Steff happened to mention that you always walk at this time of the morning."

"Steff is altogether too talkative. I'll have to speak to her."

"Don't blame Steff, please. I wormed it out of her in a devious manner."

"That I believe." She stopped and looked at him, exasperated by her own awkwardness. His dark hair was blowing in the wind, flattening against his forehead. In his gray sweats and quilted navy blue vest, he looked rugged and much more clear-eyed than he had yesterday. Macho. Virile.

Feeling awkward, she cast around for something to say. "How are the kittens?" she asked finally.

His mouth curved in the wry smile that always made something twist inside her. "Fine," he said. "Feel free to visit them any time."

"I want you to stop in at the clinic," she informed him. "I'll be there all day today."

"There was a time I would have decided that invitation meant my immense charm was finally wearing you down," he said. "But from the tone of your voice and the look in your eyes I get the idea this suggestion is not meant to give me pleasure."

"I'm going to refer you to Dr. Platt in Baxter. You can pick up your records and take them to him."

When she would have walked on, he took hold of her arm and stopped her. Then he turned her to face him, holding her shoulders now. A tremor shivered through her, but it was not from cold. Amazingly, she could feel the warmth of his hands even through her down parka. Imagination, she decided.

"We need to talk, Danielle," he said.

She shook her head. "There's nothing to discuss," she answered firmly. "I made a mistake yesterday, allowing myself to be..." She broke off. "Let's just say I had a weak moment."

"And because of that you're going to cast me out of your life? You're going to let a man with a nervous breakdown wander around Baxter looking for some strange doctor with the unwelcoming name of Platt? Because *you* had a weak moment?''

"You've hardly had a nervous breakdown," she protested.

"Ha!" he exclaimed. "I'm going to. Any minute. Just watch me."

The Falkirk magic was working on her again, making her want to laugh, making her want to lean in to him, making her want to repeat last night's kiss. She bit her lower lip, fighting the almost irresistible impulses. Maybe she needed to resurrect the Queen Victoria mantra, or recite the multiplication tables. Something was obviously needed if she couldn't resist the Falkirk magnetism on an open beach with the wind howling around them and a new storm about to break over their heads.

The pressure of his hands increased on her shoulders. "Don't do this to me, Danielle," he said solemnly.

She seized on the irritation that flicked across her nerves. "Why is it so impossible for you to call me Dani like everyone else?" she demanded.

His eyes looked deeply into hers. "Because I don't want to be like everyone else where you're concerned. I want to be Adrian Falkirk and I want to call you Danielle because it's a lovely name and it echoes in my mind that way. Danielle." His voice softened dramatically, caressing every syllable.

"Adrian, I can't..." She didn't know what she'd started out to say. His hand was touching her cheek, his thumb brushing over her lips.

"Danielle," he said again, looking at her mouth.

He was going to kiss her. She wanted him to kiss her. No, she didn't. Panicking, shrugging his hands away, she continued walking, head down into the wind. At once he fell into step alongside her. "Adrian," she began again. "I'm a doctor. It isn't ethical for me to treat a patient who keeps . . ."

"Kissing you?"

"Exactly."

He gave an exaggerated sigh. "Then I guess I'll have to transfer to this Dr. Pratt."

"Dr. Platt."

"Whatever."

She had walked several steps before she realized he was laughing softly. Two more steps and she knew why. She'd given him a choice and he'd taken the one that suited him best. He'd give her up as a doctor, but not as a kissing partner.

Once again, she stopped walking and turned to face him. "Why, Adrian?" she asked. "Why are you pursuing me?"

He studied her face, a gentle smile illuminating his eyes, making them glow, laugh lines radiating from the corners. Devastating. "Have you looked in a mirror lately?"

"You're saying you're attracted to me?"

"You hadn't guessed?"

"After all that time of disliking me?"

"Circumstances change," he said ambiguously. "Besides, I told you at Steff's, I've never disliked you."

"But you also refused to tell me why you gave such a good impression of doing so."

"I'd rather you worked it out for yourself." He hesitated. "Until you do, I can't take the risk of you holing up in your ice palace forever."

"My ice palace? What on earth are you talking about?"

Another slow smile. "When you know me better, maybe I can explain. But believe me, whatever happened between us in the past, I'm..." He hesitated once more, and she thought he was going to take refuge in mystery again, but then he completed the sentence. "I'm very attracted to you now. You're a lovely woman, Danielle. Surely many men have wanted you. Why does it surprise you that *I* want you?"

"Adrian, I can't...I'm sorry, but I just don't feel anything like that for you."

"I don't believe you. The way you kissed me..."

"I think you'd better forget that kiss," she said. "I already have." A necessary lie, she assured herself.

He studied her face intently for a full minute, and she forced herself to meet his gaze, though she kept wanting to look away. Dammit, it was happening again; her body wanted to move toward his, her mouth wanted to part for his kisses, her hands wanted to reach for him, touch him. He smiled and her heart jerked. "You do like me, don't you Danielle?" he asked gently.

About to say no, she hesitated. She couldn't deny she'd come to enjoy his company when he wasn't actively pursuing her. Watching him with Steff, with the little boy he'd pulled out of the restaurant, noticing his gentleness with the cat, she'd come to see him in a different light, had begun to admit to herself that he wasn't the sarcastic, cocky, shifty-eyed, irritating man she'd believed him to be, but rather a kind, compassionate, amiable person.

She sighed. "I don't *dis*like you anymore, Adrian. I'd really like to be your friend. But..." How could she say it wasn't possible for her to be his friend as long as she saw Jon when she looked at him? She couldn't.

"I've decided you were right all along," Adrian said. "It isn't possible for us to be friends."

She gaped at him.

He grinned. "My feelings for you are too friendly for friendship," he explained. "I can't promise to stop wanting to kiss you. I can't seem to stop. Perhaps it's a sexual dysfunction on my part. Perhaps I need some kind of medication for it." Smiling, linking his arm with hers, he started them off walking again. "What shall we call it, an anti-Danielle pill? What ingredients would it require, do you suppose?"

Before she could even respond to his nonsense, he went on conversationally, "I'm going to pick up Steff around noon. I'll collect my records on the way. I certainly don't want to offend your sense of proper ethics."

Was he taking it for granted that if he was no longer a patient, he could continue his pursuit of her? Maybe she'd better start over. "I'm not sure you understand," she began, but then he suddenly stopped walking and looked toward the dunes, his hand above his eyes.

"I thought I saw someone in that old station wagon," he said.

The rusty old wreck had been stranded on the upper part of the beach for several weeks, obviously abandoned. Someone at the police department had told Dani they were trying to trace the owner before towing it out.

Standing beside Adrian, she squinted at the vehicle herself. And saw what he had seen—someone moving around inside it. Someone with straggly tow-colored hair. "It's Michael Caswell," she exclaimed, immediately heading in that direction. "The boy I talked to Brian about."

MICHAEL SHOWED THEM a sleeping bag he'd borrowed from a friend. He had two pairs of blue jeans, his bicycle shorts, combat boots and sneakers, a couple of sweatshirts and his lined denim jacket, a bag filled with apples and bananas, crackers, French bread and cheese he'd lifted from his mother's kitchen during the night. "I can probably hole up in this old wagon for a week or more," he proclaimed with a proud smile.

Dani had to bite her lip to stop herself from making motherly exclamations—*You slept in a car the last two nights? During that awful storm? Don't you have any sense at all? What if there had been an extrahigh tide, did you even check the tide tables? Don't you know Chet is worried about you? Not to mention your mother?*

Instead, she managed to limit herself to, "Very cozy."

Michael grinned at her through the open car window. "I might just become a—what d'you call it—one of those dudes who lives all alone and gets spooked when people come too close."

"A hermit," Adrian supplied.

"This is Adrian Falkirk," Dani said.

Michael stuck a hand through the window and shook hands. "The store guy." His smile was friendly. "I heard you were in town. Miss Carmody told my mom. My dad used to take me to Falkirk's in Seattle at Christmas. Electric trains in the window. We liked trains, Dad and me."

"Sergeant Banks told me a couple of days ago he's going to have this old wagon towed away," Dani said.

Michael made a face, then gathered up his bag of food and his backpack, and opened the car door. Getting out, he put the bags on the top of the wagon, reached into the back and dragged out the sleeping bag and began rolling it up. "So much for comfort," he said. "Guess I'll have to sleep on the beach tonight."

"You couldn't consider going home?" Adrian asked. He was trying to talk casually also, Dani noted.

"Chet told me not to bother coming back." Mike folded his lips together for a second, then shrugged. "Time I was on my own anyway," he added.

"You left something behind," Adrian pointed out, peering into the wagon's innards.

"Sketchbook," Mike exclaimed, reaching through the window for it. "Can't get along without my sketchbook. Gotta have something to do until I get hooked up with a TV again."

"May I see?" Adrian asked, still casual.

Shrugging, Michael handed it over.

Holding the book out of the wind at the side of the wagon, Adrian opened it up and showed it to Dani. All the pencil drawings were of birds. Seagulls captured in a few quick strokes. A flock of whimbrels on the golf course. One brown pelican, flapping upward from the ocean, his bill pouch ballooned to an enormous size.

"A man named Dixon Lanier Merritt wrote a poem that fits this sketch," Adrian commented. "A wonderful bird is the pelican, His bill will hold more than his belican. He can take in his beak Food enough for a week, But I'm damned if I see how the helican."

Michael threw back his head and burst into laughter, looking about twelve years old. That was part of the problem, Dani thought. Michael consistently acted like a twelve-year-old. But he had a man's body, albeit a lanky one. Not that he was mentally deficient in any way—he just didn't seem to want to grow up.

Something had to be done about Michael, she knew, but what? It couldn't be done by her, she realized, suddenly remembering to look at her watch. She had exactly fifteen minutes to get back to the trailer, shower, dress, and take off for Baxter to check on Steff. But nothing was settled between her and Adrian. She wanted him to realize...she shook her head. Later, she'd work it out later. If she didn't hustle, she wouldn't make it back home in time to open the clinic at ten.

"I have to go," she said hurriedly. "Michael..."

"I'll stay and visit with Michael," Adrian said easily.

"He should probably..."

"We'll work something out," Adrian assured her. He had flipped to the front of the sketchbook and was studying what looked like drawings of bird skeletons. "These are great," he exclaimed.

"I got to thinking if I knew what birds looked like inside, I'd be able to draw them better," Mike said shyly, looking over his arm. "I got books out of the library. I still don't have them right, though." Reaching past Adrian, he turned a few pages. "See here, this wing, the way it joins the bird's body, it's not right. That's a glaucous-winged gull—*Larus glaucescens,*" he added matter-of-factly.

"Well, I guess I'll just push off then," Dani said awkwardly.

Adrian nodded casually and gave a half smile. Michael didn't even turn around. "This murre, see," he was saying as Dani turned away. "*Uria aalge.* The way his head is turned. It took about six birds before I got that anything like the way it should be."

"You know the Latin names of all the birds?" Adrian asked.

"Nah. Quite a few, though. They just seem to stick in my mind."

"It's going to rain any minute," Dani said, but they paid no attention. Shaking her head, she gave up on them and started jogging, hoping to beat the rain to her door.

Adrian turned his head and watched her go, admiring the grace of her, the long strong legs pumping across the packed sand. With that knitted pink hat pulled down to her eyebrows she looked about fifteen years old. She'd sounded quite put out by his apparent inattention, he thought. A very good sign.

He became aware that Michael was watching him watching Dani. "How long have you been doing this?" he asked, turning back to the sketchbook.

"Long as I can remember," Michael said. "Used to get in trouble at school for drawing birds and animals, not paying attention."

"There are art schools . . ." Adrian began.

Mike laughed. "No way, man. Nobody happier than I was when I finally got out of school. 'Cept maybe my teachers. Celebration time in the faculty lounge." He shuddered. "No more school for this dude. No money for it, anyway."

A drop of rain splattered on the open sketchbook and Mike grabbed the book away and shoved it under his denim jacket for protection. "You want to sit out the rain in my pad?" he asked Adrian, throwing all his stuff back into the wagon and following it in.

"My pleasure," Adrian agreed, ducking in with him.

They talked companionably for a long time while rain pounded on the wagon and streamed down the windows—discussing birds and how they were put together, animals and their habitats, some rabbits Adrian had raised, a weasel that used to play hide-and-seek around the woodpile back of Michael's house.

At one point Mike pulled a half-smoked cigarette butt out of his jacket pocket and lit up, triggering an automatic yearning response in Adrian. "Sorry I don't have any to offer," the boy said.

"That's okay," Adrian replied, knowing he couldn't smoke in front of Mike anyway. Adults were supposed to set good examples, weren't they? Impulsively, he took a step he was pretty sure he'd regret later. "I gave it up," he said.

"Yeah?" Mike was interested. "Was it tough?"

Adrian nodded. It was tough right now, with the tempting smell of tobacco permeating the car. He clenched his teeth. It would get better; he'd read that somewhere.

After sharing a banana with Adrian and chewing his way through a small box of raisins, Mike picked up his sketchbook again and flipped through it. "The birds let me get pretty close," he said, then added wistfully, "I can't get 'em to stand still while I sketch them, though."

"An old college friend of mine and his wife run a wildlife refuge north of Seattle," Adrian told him. "Jorge and Consuelo Rodriguez. Maybe sometime I could take you to visit. Might even ask if they need a helper. They live in a rural area, have trouble keeping people."

"They have birds?"

"All kinds of birds. Also deer, raccoons, squirrels, whatever needs a home at any given time. People bring hurt or sick birds and animals from miles around."

"They'd let me touch the birds?"

"Not at first, probably. But after the birds got used to you, maybe."

"I'm real good with animals, too," Mike assured him. He had a faraway look in his eyes. "I'd sure like to live around birds and animals all the time. Like that dude, Tarzan.''

"I'm not making any promises or guarantees,'' Adrian warned him. ''I'll have to get to know you first, see how that works out. Then we'll see.''

"Fair enough.'' Mike's eyes were eager. "Man, I'd love a place like that.''

Was it safe now to try a question or two? "Heard you got in a little trouble couple of nights ago.''

Mike's grin faded. "The fire you mean? I didn't start that fire, Mr. Falkirk.''

"How about your friends?'' Adrian asked, remembering the conversation between Dani and Brian Milburn.

Mike shrugged. "Not while I was around.''

"They're good friends?''

"The best. Anybody in Baxter starts hassling me, they lean on him. Nobody hassles me anymore.''

"They live in Baxter?''

"Tacoma. They come out this way when things get too...'' He broke off and began whistling tunelessly, looking at the rain-drenched windshield with great attention as though it were possible to see through it.

When things get too hot in the city, Adrian interpreted. "They gang members?'' he asked.

Mike looked thoughtful, as if he hadn't ever considered such a thing. "Could be,'' he said at last. "I did hear Ox—everybody calls him Ox, I think his first name is Oscar—say something about wilding once.''

"You ever go wilding yourself?'' Adrian asked in the most casual voice he could muster.

"Nah.'' There was an almost wistful note in Mike's voice. Adrian wasn't sure how much more he could say without alienating the boy completely, but he knew he had to try. Mike was eighteen, not exactly an adolescent, and he was clearly flirting with danger. There had been an outbreak of wilding in Seattle lately. Gangs roaming the streets, beating up on anybody they took a dislike to, anybody who got in their way or otherwise displeased them. Gang association was creeping into the best of homes nowadays. The gang life-style could be tremendously appealing, especially to a kid who was bored and already partly alienated from society. The gangs could make any kid feel important, wanted, accepted. Today's world was a tough one; joining up with a gang was one way to ensure protection. Adrian remembered reading somewhere that the one thing gang members had in common was low self-esteem. But how could anyone help Mike build belief in himself? Self-esteem had to come from inside.

"A man is often judged by the company he keeps, unfortunately," he said mildly at last. Then when Mike didn't respond, he asked as casually as possible, "You tell your brother you didn't start that fire?" The larger questions would have to wait for a while, he decided. In the meantime, there was the question of how to get Michael Caswell to go home.

"Yeah, I told him."

Adrian could feel him withdraw, close himself off. But Adrian had to persist, he couldn't just ignore the problem.

"Heard he was a building contractor," he said.

"He took over my dad's business." Mike paused. "My dad's dead." He'd striven for a matter-of-fact tone, but to anyone who was really listening the pain was audible.

"How's the business doing?"

"Okay." Another pause. "For now. When Chet gets through with Doc Kelsey's place, it won't be so good. He doesn't have anything else lined up yet."

"Tough."

"Yeah."

Mike sounded relaxed again. "You tell Kurt Webber you didn't have anything to do with the fire?" Adrian asked.

"I didn't even go to see him." He hunched his shoulders. "I've got a record," he blurted out.

Don't show shock, Adrian told himself, remembering his own frustration when he tried to talk to his father. Keep him talking, and *listen.* "For what?" he asked.

"Shoplifting."

"When?"

"When I was six."

Don't laugh, either. The boy's face was totally solemn. "What'd you take?"

"Little things. Fishing lures mostly. At the hardware store. They were shiny, you know?"

"Uh-huh."

"I put them in my jacket pocket. It was easy. But then my dad found them."

"What did he do?"

"Made me take them back to the store and tell the manager what I'd done."

"Did the manager call the police?"

"Nah. But he sure was mad. Talked to me real cold, you know. I'd have felt better if he'd yelled at me. Told me if I ever did it again he'd have me put in jail and throw away the key." He shuddered slightly. "Man, I had nightmares for weeks. Dad said the nightmares were because I knew I'd done wrong, but he knew I'd never do it again, so I didn't need to worry."

"And did you do it again?"

"Nope."

"Then I think your dad was right. You don't need to worry. And if the manager didn't call the police you don't have a record." He hesitated. "Chief seems like a reasonable man," he offered.

"Maybe to you," Mike said with a snort. "You're a big, rich, important dude. Me—in his opinion I'm just a punk kid."

"Tough, isn't it?" Adrian sympathized. "I remember when I was your age . . ."

The boy stiffened as if expecting a lecture, but Adrian went on easily. "I had this little sports car, beat up, muffler tied on with rope, bought it with money I'd earned working for my dad. He wouldn't buy me or my brother or sisters a car. Said we had to learn the value of a dollar. You know how dads talk."

Mike grinned knowledgeably.

"That old car rattled like a string of cans going down the street," Adrian continued. "If I tried to get it up over forty, it would buck like a bronco. But it was red. If there's anything a police officer hates, it's a red car."

"'Specially with a punk kid at the wheel," Mike added.

"You know it. San Francisco's finest used to hassle me all the time, even when I wasn't doing anything wrong." He pulled a face. "Well, maybe thirty-eight in a twenty-mile-per-hour zone." What was he doing here, trying to arouse the kid's admiration for his own stupid actions? How else could he get Mike to trust him?

Mike laughed. "Cops here get on my tail every time I show up driving Chet's truck. I can imagine—a red sports car..."

A fellow feeling had been established in the station wagon now. And the rain was letting up. "The way I got out of it was," Adrian went on casually, "I got my dad to go to the police station with me, talk to the cops. They didn't leave me alone after that, but things got noticeably better."

"I don't have a dad, remember." There was a lost look in Mike's eyes that called forth Adrian's compassion.

"Must have been tough when he died."

"Scary. He was a strong dude, my dad. Big. Tough."

"So then Chet took over."

Mike made a face. "Sure did."

"You don't like your brother?"

There was a pause. Then Mike said, "We used to be real thick. Buddies. But when dad died it was like I lost Chet, too, like he turned into a stranger. Bossy."

What the hell else could he do but be bossy, Mike, Adrian thought. *All of a sudden he had to be a boss, had to give up his own life and come home and take care of all of you.*

"Suppose some responsible adult went with you to see Kurt Webber," he suggested. "Some big, rich important dude, for example."

"You'd come with me?"

Adrian nodded.

"Why? What's in it for you?"

Adrian shrugged. "Favor for a fellow bird-watcher." He groaned inwardly. Now he'd have to buy a bird book and do some studying. He barely knew the difference between a sparrow and a flamingo.

He let the boy think about his offer while he wiped off the inside of the windshield with the back of his hand and made a great show of checking out the sky. "Looks like it's letting up," he remarked into the silence.

"I guess I wouldn't mind so much if you'd go with me," Mike said at last.

BRIAN MILBURN was sitting at a table in his bar, gloomily gazing into a cup of coffee. In the restaurant, a cleaning crew was enthusiastically scrubbing walls and woodwork and ceilings. Beyond the swinging doors to the kitchen it sounded as though a demolition team were at work.

"How's it going?" Adrian asked, swinging a straight chair around and straddling it.

"It's going. That's about all I . . ." Brian had noticed Michael. "What the hell's that juvenile delinquent doing here?"

"We're on our way to see the fire chief," Adrian said easily. "Thought we'd stop in here and find out exactly what the complaint is."

"Arson." Brian's voice was flat. "Webber found traces of gasoline-soaked rags and newspaper tucked in a trash can under what used to be the bottom shelf of the pantry. Not my trash can. He also found a flammable liquid container. We figure someone snuck in and torched it while the chef's back was turned. The pantry's right next to the side door, not too difficult to get in and out without being seen. Didn't think it was necessary to keep the door locked as long as the restaurant was open. Not in Murre Bay."

"You have proof that Michael was involved?" Adrian asked.

"It's clear as day..."

"Suppose we start over." Adrian was trying to keep his voice patient. "Mike admits he was in here on the Sunday preceding the fire."

"Big of him," Brian snapped.

Adrian took a breath. Not only was Milburn irritating hell out of him, Mike had wandered over to look at a painting of a lighthouse that hung on the wall, as if this whole discussion had nothing to do with him. "I could do you a better picture than this with one hand tied behind my back," he told Brian genially, turning around to look at him. "Perspective's all off, and the color..."

"Yo, Michael," a woman said, coming into the bar from a back room. She was a young woman, slightly plump, with a mane of frizzy red hair caught up in a ponytail at one side. She was carrying a tray of clean wineglasses, which she began placing in a rack above the bar. Short as she was, the job wasn't easy for her and Mike began helping. "What you doing in here?" she asked. "You get to be 21 when I wasn't looking?" She looked over at Adrian and smiled. "Hi there."

"Corky Bunn, Andrew Falkirk," Milburn said.

Adrian corrected him and he shrugged, evidently determined to be unfriendly.

"Hey, neat," Corky exclaimed, leaning on the bar. "I heard you were in town."

Had everybody? Adrian wondered.

"I shop in Falkirk's whenever I get to Seattle," the young woman went on. "I love that Glad Rags department."

Glad Rags was a section Adrian had introduced in the San Francisco store to merchandise slightly defective clothing at bargain prices rather than return it to the manufacturer or sell it to jobbers. The department had proved immensely popular and was now featured in all branches.

The young woman went back to sorting glasses. "Wasn't it Corky who complained about Michael and his friends?" Adrian asked Milburn.

Brian nodded. "Bunch of young punks coming in here creating a disturbance..."

"She seems awfully friendly to Mike for someone who was insulted."

"Corky doesn't hold a grudge," Brian said, but Adrian wasn't convinced that was the whole story.

Getting up, he went over to the bar. "We're trying to get to the bottom of this incident in the restaurant with Mike and his friends last Sunday," he explained to the woman.

She made a face, then looked chidingly at Michael. "Nasty pair. You shouldn't be hanging around with characters like that, Michael, get you in trouble."

Adrian frowned. "Milburn told me you were mad at *Michael* for yelling and causing problems."

Corky had very round eyes, which grew rounder when she widened them. "Michael?" She looked over at Milburn. "Mike wasn't doing the talking, Bri, I told you that. He was trying to get his buddies to shut up. He kept telling them I was a friend of his and they shouldn't hassle me. Between us, we got them out of here. Mike wasn't hassling, he was helping." She aimed a punch at Mike's arm. "You better not bring those guys in here again, y'hear?"

"I hear you," Mike said, laughing and rubbing his arm.

Adrian counted halfway to ten, then let out the breath he'd tried to hold. "For God's sake, Mike, why didn't you *say* you weren't involved in hassling the waitresses."

"Never said I was. Mr. Milburn told Chet and the chief I was hassling. Doc Kelsey said I was hanging around. Nobody asked *me* anything, except did I start the fire. Which I didn't."

"You *were* hanging around the restaurant, weren't you?"

"No law against, far as I ever heard. I wasn't blocking the sidewalk. There isn't one." He seemed to think that was very funny.

"*Why* were you hanging around?"

Mike sighed. Nodding his head with each point as he made it, he finally gave out some information. "I got Ox and Scooter out of here, I went home. Chet started nagging. I came back. Ox and Scooter had been drinking at Peaches—the bar next door. I was trying to get them to camp out on the beach instead of driving all the way home to Tacoma and maybe having an accident. That's it."

"Were they in town on Thursday?"

Mike shrugged elaborately. "They don't sign in and out with me."

Obviously he was avoiding a truthful answer without actually telling a lie. Shooting a glance at him, Adrian let it pass for now and turned to Brian. "You heard what Corky said. And Mike. You going to be pressing charges?"

"You his lawyer?" Brian asked, his voice stiff.

"Just an interested bystander."

"We still don't know he's innocent as far as the fire was concerned," Brian pointed out.

"But you don't know he's guilty, either. Suppose we just let the authorities investigate and see what they come up with." He glanced at Mike. "Tell Mr. Milburn where you were Thursday evening."

"What's it to him?" Mike asked cheerfully.

Adrian gritted his teeth. "Trust me. Tell him."

Mike shrugged. "Okay. I was on the beach, way down by the harbor. Had me a little fire going, couple cans of beer."

"Your friends were with you?"

"Nope."

"You didn't see them at all that evening?"

"Might have seen them earlier, at the bowling alley."

Another one of Mike's throwaway confessions.

"But not later?" Brian persisted.

Mike's eyes glazed over. "Like I said . . ."

"Will you call Webber and tell him Mike wasn't involved in the hassling incident?" Adrian asked Milburn.

The man shot a hostile glance at Mike, then looked over at the bar where Corky was standing arms akimbo, her gaze fixed on him. He sighed. "I'll call him."

Mike brightened immediately. "All right," he exclaimed. "Guess I'm off the hook, huh?"

"We still have to talk to the chief. And Chet," Adrian told him.

"Busy day," Mike said cheerfully.

Adrian also had to fit in a trip to Baxter to pick up Steff and he'd hoped to get a chance to talk to Dani, too. He sighed. "Let's go," he said to Mike.

"I'm not sure I understand what your interest is here," Milburn said as Adrian turned away.

Truth, justice and the American way, Adrian felt like answering, but shrugged instead. He didn't like Brian Milburn, he decided.

KURT WEBBER wasn't too friendly, but he did allow that Brian Milburn had called him and it seemed there weren't any grounds for turning Mike over to the police department. "Yet," he added with a stern glance at Michael.

Michael told his story in a fairly straightforward way once he got over some initial blustering, but he insisted he didn't have street addresses or even last names for Ox and Scooter. Adrian wasn't sure that was true, but decided he'd work on Mike some more later.

By the time the interview was over, Adrian was anxious to be on his way to Baxter. But he wasn't at all sure he could trust Mike to report to Chet alone. There seemed nothing for him to do but to take the boy along.

TWO MEN WERE hanging wallpaper in Dani's living room when Adrian and Michael arrived in the middle of the afternoon. Michael elected to wait outside while Adrian checked on Chet's mood. "Old Chet might have a hammer handy," he pointed out.

It was immediately obvious to Adrian which of the men was Michael's brother. He had the same lanky frame and similar features, though his hair was shorter and slightly darker and his expression much more worried.

Adrian introduced himself, then waited while Chet carefully trimmed excess paper from the top of the strip of paper he'd just hung. Chet had done a terrific job on the drywall, he noted. His joints were excellent, the compound feathered out to a smooth finish. All cutouts were in precisely the right places. It was a big room, with a large multipaned bay window on either side of French doors, looking directly out across the dunes to the ocean. The sun was struggling through a thin layer of clouds, glinting off the foamy edges of the waves.

"Doc Kelsey wants me to finish off this room so she can camp out in it," Chet said as he wiped his hands on a towel. "Can't move the furniture back in until we're all through and get the carpeting down, but she says she's getting claustrophobic in that trailer."

Adrian nodded, aware that Chet was looking him over with great curiosity. Quite possibly all of Murre Bay knew of his interest in Dani by now. "I have Mike with me," he said as the two men shook hands.

He felt Chet's hand stiffen as he withdrew it. "He okay?" He asked tersely.

"He's fine."

Chet's face relaxed just enough for Adrian to realize he'd been genuinely worried about his brother, then tightened up again. "Where is he?"

"Outside." A little humor might help lighten the atmosphere. "He seemed to think it might be safer if I checked to see what you had in your hands before calling him in."

"Guess he's not as dumb as he looks," Chet said. His voice was grim, but there was a note of affection in it all the same.

Briefly, Adrian explained their visit to Surf and Turf and the agreement they'd struck with Brian Milburn, going on to repeat the conversation they'd had with the fire chief.

"Why the hell didn't Mike tell me all that?" Chet demanded, then glanced at the other man who was still hanging wallpaper, but obviously listening fairly avidly. Inclining his head at Adrian, he gestured toward the door and led the way into Dani's kitchen, a bright, efficient room that also overlooked the ocean.

"House looks good," Adrian said, admiring the neat blue-and-cream paint job.

Chet smiled, dropping ten years in the process. "It's coming along, I guess," he said modestly. "If we ever get the plumber organized we'll be pretty close to finished." A sudden grin lightened his face even more. "Had a guy and his wife stop by this morning. Said they'd been watching the remodeling and like what I've done. They want me to make a bid on enlarging their house. They own a small weekend place, but the guy's retiring in a few months and they want to move down here permanently." He shook his head. "Probably won't want me to start until the weather improves, but at least I know I've one more job in my future."

"Great," Michael said from the doorway. "Make sure you bid 'em up high enough, Chet. Can't go giving it away."

Chet looked at his brother, frustration and affection warring for domination in his expression. "Why the hell didn't you come home?" he demanded. "Mom's been worried sick about you." He raked a hand through his hair. "Don't say it," he said, holding up his hand in a traffic-stopping position. "I know I told you if you didn't see the chief you shouldn't bother coming home. That was a figure of speech, Mike. No way I'd ever kick you out. I'd think you'd know that by now."

"Could have fooled me," Mike said aggressively.

He was going to provoke a fight with his brother if he kept on in that tone of voice, Adrian felt sure. Time to intervene. "I'm here primarily as Mike's friend," he said to Chet. "I was thinking of offering him a temporary job."

Mike looked first astonished, then pleased. Chet looked as if he thought Adrian had lost his mind. "Doing what?" he asked.

"I need quite a few shakes replaced on my roof. Some brush cleared out around the yard. Fence needs repairing."

"Understood you were renting," Chet said.

"I am." He held Chet's puzzled gaze. *You're quite right,* he tried to communicate. *I don't need to do this work—it's to give Mike an alternative. Being employed by you isn't working out, is it?* "I'll check with my landlord first, of course," he said.

Chet glanced at Mike then back to Adrian. "We've tried Mike working for other people," he said flatly. "He didn't prove too reliable."

"I like Mr. Falkirk," Mike protested. "Besides, he knows some people who have a wildlife refuge. He's promised to take me to see them. Maybe get me a job there. You know how I like being around birds and animals and stuff."

Chet nodded, his face softening. "Guess one of us should be doing something he likes," he muttered, then shook his head, looking at Adrian. "You know something funny? That guy who came to see me this morning—Mr. Delman—when he said he liked my work, it made me feel...well, sort of proud." He shifted his gaze to Mike. "You remember when we were kids, Mike, Dad used to drive us around Murre Bay saying, 'I built that house, I put those gables on that one. See that deck, sure was a gut-wrencher working that one out.' He used to sound so proud."

Mike nodded solemnly. "I remember."

"Listening to Mr. Delman rave about this place made me think I might do that some day." Chet had gone a little pink around the ears. "Guess I'm saying construction might not be so bad after all," he said to Adrian. Leaning back against the kitchen counter, arms folded, he gazed thoughtfully at the tiled kitchen floor for a few seconds, then brought his head up and looked directly at Adrian. He and Mike had the same hazel eyes, Adrian noticed, but Chet's gaze was steadier, more mature. "If Mike'd rather work for you, it's okay with me, Mr. Falkirk. I know a carpenter's looking for work. If I'm not paying Mike I can afford to take him on." He shot a glance at his brother and grinned. "Be sure you pay him by the hour, though, not the job. Could take him six months to fix your roof, the pace he goes."

"Fix a roof fast as you can," Mike grumbled.

If he could foster that competitive spirit, this project just might work out, Adrian thought. He liked both Caswells and would like to see them succeed, each in his own way. He'd meant it when he'd said he was Michael's friend. He and Michael had gone together into Baxter, done a little shopping, looked around the mall Dani had told him about, which had provoked some interesting ideas he was going to explore later. Then they'd brought Steff home. "That's one tough old lady," Mike had said admiringly, after she'd harangued him about giving his brother more support. They'd even lunched together and Adrian had enjoyed the teenager's company. It was beginning to seem possible that Mike just might turn out okay. "You ever been in the Sandbox?" Adrian asked Chet on a sudden impulse.

Chet shook his head. "I'm not a big drinker, but I like a beer when I go out."

Adrian nodded. "I was thinking of work rather than recreation. Josh Andersen's going to be making some interior changes. Nothing big, but it would be a good showcase for your work. Could this carpenter of yours handle wainscoting, maybe a dance floor?"

"No problem."

"You might go see Josh, then. Tell him I sent you."

"I'll do that." Chet looked at him thoughtfully and Adrian could almost see him wanting to ask what he had to do with Josh Andersen.

A second later Chet fairly obviously reached the conclusion he shouldn't look a gift horse in the mouth. Offering his right hand to Adrian, he gave him a warm and very sincere smile. "I'm indebted to you, Mr. Falkirk, in more ways than one. Thank you." As Adrian turned to leave, he glared at his brother. "You go on home and tell Mom what you've been up to," he ordered. "She was on the early shift this morning, she'll be home now."

"Yes sir," Mike said, sketching a cheerful salute.

"You mean that stuff about being my friend, Mr. Falkirk?" he asked as they walked over to Adrian's BMW.

Adrian nodded.

"Can I drive the Beamer then?"

"You're not *that* good a friend," Adrian said flatly.

Mike laughed. "You're one cool dude, Mr. Falkirk. Now on, we're a team, you and me. You just tell me what to do, I'll do it."

Adrian managed to smother a groan. All he'd originally wanted to do was concentrate on his campaign to break down Danielle's defenses. Now it looked as if he'd acquired a son.

CHAPTER SEVEN

ADRIAN KNOCKED ON Dani's trailer door at seven
o'clock, feeling pleasantly weary. It had been a re-
warding, if busy, day. Though he could hear Dani
moving around inside, it took her a couple of minutes
to answer. He gazed out across the dunes to the turbulent ocean. No sunset tonight; the sky was still overcast
though the rain had stopped and the wind had dropped
to a breeze.

The door opened. "Adrian." Her voice sounded re-
signed. He was getting to her, no doubt about it. She
was wearing a short, blue silk robe over black stirrup
pants and ankle boots. A fetching but slightly strange
outfit. He raised his eyebrows.

"I was just getting ready to go visit Steff," she said.

She was blocking the trailer doorway, obviously not
intending to invite him in. He smiled up at her. "I'll
drive you," he offered. "I'm on my way there, too. I
dropped Steff off several hours ago, she was going to
take a nap."

"I checked on her early this morning. She was doing
fine." She laughed. "She was totally obnoxious. Kept
saying she'd told me she was going to be okay. Which
she had, of course. How was she when you saw her?"

"Tired but otherwise okay. Told her I'd fix dinner
and bring you along to share it. She's looking forward
to it."

He could see her mind scurrying, trying to find an excuse not to join them. No way she could do that without risking Steff getting hurt. Emotional blackmail, he reflected cheerfully. Worked every time.

"I came by to report on Michael," he added.

Again he could read her mind. She didn't want to invite him in. On the other hand, she could hardly keep him standing down there much longer—the breeze off the ocean was crisp and he was wearing only jeans and a lightweight sweater over a cotton shirt. *And* she was curious about Michael. "Come in," she finally said with a sigh, stepping backward.

The trailer's interior was cozily warm and as neat as he would have expected it to be. "I was here earlier," he told her. "At the house, not the trailer. Mike and I came by to talk to Chet after we took Steff home. We wanted to tell him what happened when we talked to Brian Milburn and then visited the fire station."

She stared at him, then laughed. "You've been busy, haven't you?"

When she laughed, the guarded expression left her face and her eyes lit up wonderfully. The silk robe's brilliant color reflected in them, too. Sometimes she could look so beautiful she took his breath away. As well, the robe had parted slightly as she backed up, giving him a quick view of the valley between her creamy breasts.

He forced himself to look away, and caught her glance just as she realized what had happened. At once, her hand came up to clutch the silken fabric.

Flattening herself against the stove, she gestured him into a small dinette area, then excused herself and disappeared into the back reaches of the trailer. When she reappeared she was wearing a black sweater that covered her up to the throat. Evidently she'd decided to try to avoid inflaming him any further. It wasn't going to work. With her short blond hair shining like honey in the light from an overhead lamp, shadows beneath her cheekbones, her body slim and lithe in the all black clothing, she looked just as sexy as ever.

Years ago, he'd dabbled with sculpture, mainly because his father and Jon had declaimed it a wimpy thing to do. He'd had no ambition to go on with the hobby, once Jon gave up tormenting him about it, but right now his fingers itched for clay to duplicate that perfect bone structure. God, he wanted to touch her.

"How on earth did you get Michael to go to the fire chief?" she asked as she slid into the seat opposite him and propped her elbows on the narrow table, cupping her face in her hands.

How easy it would be to lean forward and touch his lips to hers. He could almost taste the honey sweetness of her mouth on his tongue.

"Adrian," she said nervously.

He forced himself to lean back into an unthreatening position and saw her relax.

"Michael?" she reminded him.

He shrugged. "No problem. I offered to go with him." He frowned. "So often, when a kid seems rebellious he's really only scared. And I have to admit, if I was a kid, Kurt Webber would scare hell out of me." He shook his head. "Michael wasn't letting on he was scared of course, not him. Eminently casual, shrugging and grinning when Webber questioned him. Never actually coming out and saying he was innocent, just acting as if the whole thing were some kind of joke. But when I put my hand on his shoulder—as an alternative to wringing his neck—I could feel him quivering like jelly on a plate.''

"You like him."

He nodded.

"Did Kurt believe him?"

"I don't think so. But in the absence of proof, he let him go."

"Just like that?"

"Not exactly. First I had to explain to him that Michael had not been involved in the hassling at the restaurant on Sunday. Corky set that straight. Seems Mike was more hero than villain of that little incident. He even helped Corky eject his friends. Milburn passed that on to the chief." He debated adding that Milburn had done so reluctantly, but decided he wasn't that small-minded. "Anyway," he concluded, "Webber unofficially released Mike into my custody."

"*Your* custody! You're taking responsibility for him?"

"Looks that way."

"But Chet . . ."

"I'm afraid our friend Kurt didn't have a lot of faith in Chet's ability to keep his brother in line."

"But . . ."

"Mike and I talked it over with Chet," he assured her. "He okayed the arrangement. Mike will stay at home at night and weekends, but he'll be at my house weekdays, working on the yard, repairing the roof. . . . I wasn't kidding about the shakes blowing off."

"Why would you repair the roof? Isn't that up to the owner?"

"I checked with him. He's perfectly willing to pay for Mike's labor and the necessary materials. I explained it was partly social work, my theory being that Mike needs to get into the habit of work, just as I've had to try to get out of the habit.''

He leaned forward, unable to resist brushing into place a small section of her hair that had feathered out over her face, just above her ear, marring the clean line of the boyish cut.

She stiffened as his fingers touched her, but he removed them at once and she didn't comment. ''What makes you think he'll stick to the job?'' she asked after a few seconds' silence.

He grinned. ''That's what Chet wanted to know. I've a couple of aces up my sleeve, you see. Number one is a friend north of Seattle who owns a wildlife refuge. If Mike behaves, I take him there—maybe even get him a job there. He likes the idea, so maybe he'll work toward it. It's the old carrot on a stick method. The other ace is that Michael likes me. He looks upon me as a big, rich, important and also cool dude. So maybe he'll work better with me than his brother.''

Dani leaned back, staring at him, then she laughed and raked a hand through her hair, disturbing his careful smoothing. ''You really are something, Adrian Falkirk,'' she said. ''Have you always gone around solving people's problems, or is this a new you?''

''Same old me, Danielle.''

She had stopped smiling when he said her name. Probably she was remembering his reasons for using her full name. Yes, there was a certain look in her eyes—a look he'd seen there a long time ago and had seen on only rare occasions since.

''Danielle,'' he said again, looking at her directly. Her gaze locked with his, her eyes darkening. In that moment, he knew he was eventually going to win. She wanted him as much as he wanted her. He was sure of it. She was still fighting it as hard as ever, but it was there, no doubt about it. All he had to do was persuade her to stop denying it.

She stood up, tugging her sweater into place. He could almost hear the drawbridge clanging up. "Steff will be wondering what's keeping us," she said.

His pal Steff was much more likely to be keeping her fingers crossed for him, he thought, but wasn't about to say.

STEFF WAS UP and setting the table on her sun porch when they arrived, wearing an orange kimono with a wild-looking green dragon embroidered all the way down the back of it. She'd arranged her long white hair in a bun on top of her head, and jabbed two lacquered chopsticks through it. "Theme night," she announced. She looked sideways at Adrian. "I know you offered to cook dinner, but I decided you'd done enough for me, so I phoned Lieu's Chinese restaurant and ordered in all my favorites—almond chicken, mandarin beef, stir-fried vegetables, sweet-and-sour pork, egg rolls." She rolled her eyes at Dani. "Got my appetite back."

She grinned when Adrian scolded her for doing too much. "Thought you might get delayed," she murmured under cover of running water into a tea kettle.

"No such luck," he murmured back, then turned to see Dani watching the two of them suspiciously. "Problems with the drain," he invented, then wiggled the sink basket several times. "Okay now."

Giggling, Steff dug him in the ribs with a bony elbow. "How'd it go with Chet Caswell?" she asked, leading the way out to the sun porch.

He and Mike had filled her in when he drove her home from the hospital, but at that time he hadn't yet talked to Chet. "Good," he told her. "As long as Mike's employed, Chet can afford to hire another man, who'll most likely be a lot more reliable than Mike. With any luck it will all work out very well."

"It's great that you've taken an interest," Steff said, and Adrian began telling her about Michael's drawings of seabirds.

Jon would not have gone to so much trouble to help Michael, Dani realized as she struggled with her chopsticks.

Jon had always believed the only way to help anybody was to stand back and let them help themselves. "Help someone out this year," he'd often said, "and he'll be back next year looking for more."

Looking at that theory more clinically than she'd been able to when she was in love with Jonathan, Dani realized that in subscribing to it he had successfully avoided involving himself in anyone's problems.

When she *was* in love with Jonathan?

Hadn't she decided she was still in love with Jon? Why else would she have all these turbulent feelings when she looked at Adrian, when he touched her, when he kissed her? Her fingers clenched on her chopsticks as she remembered how small her trailer had seemed with him in it. And lacking in oxygen. There had been moments when she hadn't seemed able to breathe.

Steff had seated Adrian at the head of the table, with herself and Dani on either side—so they were quite close together. He looked extremely attractive this evening in a teal blue cashmere sweater over a grey-and-white striped shirt. He looked much better than he had when he came to Murre Bay, she thought. His face had filled out a little and he'd acquired a slight tan from spending more time outdoors. The pallid appearance had disappeared from around his eyes and mouth. Murre Bay was healing him, as it had once healed her. Unfortunately, now that he was so much healthier, he also looked even more like his twin. There—the way he'd just glanced at her—in that particular sidelong, humorous way that was accompanied by the quirky grin that lifted one corner of his expressive mouth. Jon all over again.

She averted her eyes, glancing at Steff, who seemed rather fatigued, she thought. She and Adrian should leave as soon as dinner was over. Besides, she needed to catch up on some reading material she'd brought home from the clinic. She sighed, thinking about going home to that empty, claustrophobic trailer.

Adrian was serving second helpings all around now. "Dig in," he said, as he repositioned his chopsticks in his right hand. He was able to wield them expertly, of course. Dani had the idea he would do most things expertly. "Having trouble?" he asked, glancing at her. "Hold them against your second and third fingers, like this. Thumb across the top. Use your second finger to manipulate them." Putting down his chopsticks again, he guided her fingers into place, his hands warm and competent on hers.

That quickly, it became easy to use the formerly impossible utensils. "Why *did* you take such an interest in Michael?" she asked hastily, afraid he'd noticed the tremor in her fingers when he touched her.

He shrugged. "Guess it goes back to when I was a kid. I recognize something of myself in Mike. I went through a period of rebellion in my own teens. Seemed as though Dad's plans for me were too cut-and-dried and not necessarily something I wanted to do. It was always Jon and Adrian will do this, Jon and Adrian will do that. What I really objected to, of course, was not being recognized as a separate unit.''

She barely managed to stop herself from flinching. *Guilty as charged,* she thought, wondering at the wave of sympathy that came over her.

''I gave Dad a pretty tough time for a while, staying out late, hanging out with a bunch of wild kids,'' Adrian went on. ''Fortunately I outgrew my problems without getting into serious trouble, but Dad wasn't too sympathetic. I never could get him to see me as a separate person.'' He frowned. ''I guess what I'm trying to say is that I empathize with Michael. Adults so rarely realize that when a kid is at his most unlovable, he's usually most in need of love.'' He laughed shortly, smiling at Dani. ''Sorry, didn't mean to pontificate.''

''That's okay,'' Dani said.

He looked startled. Her voice had come out softer than she'd intended. His story and his sensitivity to Michael's needs had moved her. That and the way his big hands were resting on the table. While he'd talked he'd finished eating and pushed his plate aside. His hands looked . . . empty, vulnerable. She wanted to put her hands on top of them. She wanted . . . him.

Did she really have to keep fighting the attraction that was between them? Did it really matter if her feelings were secondhand, left over from Jon? The facts were inescapable—she felt intensely alive in this man's presence. Since Adrian came to town her body had been making urgent demands. Why should she keep on fighting her own body? Adrian wasn't going to be here much longer. Two weeks, tops. If she went into it with her eyes wide open, knowing it was temporary, why shouldn't she have an affair with Adrian Falkirk?

Hardly ethical. But he wanted her. He'd said so. He wasn't worried about the ethics of making love to his brother's ex-fiancée.

Professional ethics were no longer involved. Theresa had told her when she left the clinic at noon, her expressive face showing both disappointment and curiosity, that he'd picked up his medical records. So he was no longer a patient. She was no longer his doctor.

He'd already kissed her. Which meant she knew passion could flare between them. It had been so long and sometimes she felt such a need....

We can always find excuses for doing things we want to do, she thought. She should pass that on to Theresa for her chalkboard.

Adrian's gaze was still holding hers and tension was arcing between them. Had he read her mind? He'd seemed to from time to time. Had her wanton thoughts communicated themselves to him? Whether they had or not, there was hunger in him, too. It showed not just in the intensity of his gaze, but in his hands, which had now clenched into fists on the tablecloth. As clearly as if he were saying the words again, she heard him repeat what he'd said to her on the beach that morning: "Why does it surprise you that I want you?"

"The passage from childhood to adulthood is not easy," Steff said.

Adrian was obviously startled by the sound of her voice. Had he, like Dani, felt that they were alone in the room while they gazed at one another?

Recovering, he grinned at Steff a little sheepishly, probably because she was looking very alertly from him to Dani. "You're a very wise lady," he said softly.

Steff assumed an all-knowing expression. "One of the few benefits of getting older," she said. Glancing at Dani again, she added. "I just wish I could get you two to wise up."

"What's that supposed to mean?" Dani demanded, then groaned as a wicked little glint appeared in Steff's brown eyes.

"Means the two of you have the hots for each other but won't admit it."

Dani felt herself flush to the roots of her hair, but Adrian was quite unfazed. "I had no idea you were so romantic," he said to Steff.

She made a face at him, then stood up. "I'm going to toddle off to bed," she announced. "You two will please clean up the kitchen for me before you leave." Putting her hands on Adrian's shoulders she looked directly at Dani. "The time is now," she said. "Talk to him." Then she turned around and left the room, leaving the two of them stranded in an awkward silence.

"Interfering old busybody," Dani said.

"But a loving one."

"True."

Their eyes met. And held.

"We're supposed to clean up the kitchen," Adrian said.

She smiled faintly. "It shouldn't take long. No pans."

"True."

He put his right hand on the table, palm uppermost. After only a moment's hesitation, she laid hers in it and felt a charge go through her. Her heart quickened in immediate response. "You're supposed to talk to me," he said.

She shook her head. "I have nothing to say."

"Me neither." He looked at her very directly, his eyes full of light. "Something's changed, hasn't it?"

She nodded.

Standing up, he tugged lightly on her hand to bring her to her feet, then touched her cheek gently with his free hand. There was only a step between them.

For a moment, she hesitated, then she took the step and felt his arms go around her.

"Danielle," he murmured into her hair. "There's something *I've* wanted to talk to *you* about."

Leaning her head back, she put her fingers to his mouth, trying not to flinch when he delicately closed his teeth over them. "Let's not talk about the past," she whispered. "Let's just forget we have that whole shared history. Let's call today day one, okay?"

His eyes looked deeply into hers. "That's what you want?"

She nodded.

CHAPTER EIGHT

EMBERS WERE STILL smoldering in the fireplace. Symbolic, Adrian decided. After checking on Boots and her brood, he placed kindling carefully over the ashes, stirred the glow into a blaze with a poker and added a couple of alder logs.

Dani had removed her coat and was standing awkwardly in the middle of the living room, looking around vaguely, probably having second thoughts, which he had to put a stop to immediately.

Throwing a smile her way, he crossed to the windows and closed the stiff linen drapes. No one overlooked the house, and it wasn't likely that Steff would be cruising by in her canoe, but he still wanted to create a feeling of intimacy. Taking Dani's coat he hung it carefully in the hall closet, then returned to take her hands in his. They were cold.

"Something to drink?" he asked. "I make a mean Irish coffee."

Her smile was tentative. No doubt about it, she was getting worried. "Sounds wonderful," she said.

Purposely, he hadn't turned on any lights. In the leaping shadows created by the fire, her eyes were luminous. Lifting her hands, he kissed them gently, holding her gaze. And felt a tremor go through her.

Her lips looked so soft. He remembered them as soft. Gently he brushed her mouth with his own and felt her immediate response. It was going to be all right then. He let out the breath he'd been holding.

"I'm not sure..." she murmured.

He had no idea what she wanted to say, but he did know this was not a time for talking. Nor was it a time for Irish coffee. It was a time for love.

Letting go of her hands, he cupped her face and kissed her again, deliberately restraining himself, gentling himself, so he wouldn't appear threatening. He had waited so long for this. He must not rush her now.

Her mouth moved under his tentatively, as if she were testing her own response. Letting her set the pace, he touched his lips delicately against hers, withdrawing as she withdrew, renewing the contact when she seemed to desire it, teasing himself unbearably by practicing such patience when he wanted to crush her to him and kiss her breathless.

And then he felt her arms go around him, her hands slowly moving up his back over his sweater until her cool fingers touched gently at the back of his neck.

Then and only then, he put his own arms around her and eased her close, sighing as he felt her body press against his. He thought that he could stand like this forever, with Dani in his arms, his lips on hers. But then the tip of her tongue touched lightly against his mouth and the patience he had leashed ran out. "Too much clothing," he muttered against her mouth.

As answer, she stepped away from him and lifted her sweater cleanly over her head, dropping it on the floor. A moment later her bra followed it.

She was so lovely. In the firelight he could see the curving lines that defined her waist, the firmness of her small but perfectly formed breasts. And, as she removed her pants and hose and boots in a couple of lithe movements, he saw the flat plane of her abdomen bisected by thin white briefs.

His hands reached for her buttocks and cupped them, learning the shape of her. Then he kissed her breasts, lightly, reverently.

Her own hands lifted to his shoulders, rubbing lightly over his sweater. "Too many clothes," she echoed and there was a sensual note of laughter in her voice that drove him mad.

Somehow he managed to strip without tangling himself in his clothing and when he straightened up from pushing the pile aside with his foot, she'd taken off her briefs and stood naked, waiting for him, firelight turning her flawless skin to pure enticing gold, her gaze running over him without embarrassment.

His body was excitingly male, sculpted in lines of athletic strength, shadowed on chest and abdomen and groin by night-dark hair. Shivering in anticipation of his touch, she heard her own voice moan softly as his hands stroked slowly and gently from her shoulders to her buttocks, then pressured her into moving forward into his arms.

She fitted against him marvelously well, she thought, and pushed away the thought of that other body she had loved. This body was warm and hard and aroused and being held against it felt wonderful. It had been such a long time.

Warmth filled her as he eased her down to the soft rug in front of the fireplace. She had never made love in front of a fire. Yet now it seemed the most wonderful place in the world to make love. The shadows dancing on the face above her lent mystery to his blue eyes and outlined his mouth, making it seem fuller, even more sensual than usual.

When his head bent to her breast, she touched his hair, gently at first, then more urgently as his lips tugged lightly at her nipple and a thrill of electricity jolted from it to her groin. His fingers were moving over her skin, heightening its sensitivity, stirring excitement in their wake, bringing her hips rising up against his.

"Slowly," she murmured to him, suddenly fearful that the glorious feelings he was arousing would climax too soon. She felt his lips soften in response and then he was rolling with her so that they lay on their sides, facing each other.

She wrapped her arms around him, marveling at his lean strength, the male hardness of his body.

He touched her with exquisite care, pulling away from her encircling arms so that he could have access to her breasts, her abdomen, her thighs, his lips following his hands over her, the shadows moving with him, so that they both seemed dappled in alternating bands of light and shade.

She touched him tentatively at first, then more boldly as she saw his pleasure. And as she moved and the firelight washed over them in changing patterns, she gave herself up to the joy of his lovemaking, quieting her mind when it wanted to question, to murmur warnings against opening herself up to heartbreak again.

When he abruptly rolled away from her, she was suddenly afraid—but only for the space of a few seconds. Then she saw he'd retrieved a familiar-looking package from a drawer in the coffee table. He'd been that sure of her, had he? She smiled at him gratefully, a little sheepishly. As a doctor, she'd lectured dozens of young women, and men, about the wisdom of using contraception, yet she'd come close to forgetting it herself. She was older but no wiser, she thought.

And then she stopped thinking as he knelt over her. He was such a big man, such an assertive man, that when he behaved with tenderness, the effect was devastating. She had always thought of herself as a strong woman, one not given to tremulousness, but now, looking at his stern face in the firelight, she felt herself trembling and didn't mind at all.

When he moved inside her, the trembling stopped and she became in that instant a woman driven by a need so great it was all-encompassing. Clasping him tightly, she urged him to a deeper connection, her mouth first accepting then demanding his kisses, her senses noting the clean, slightly salty taste of his lips, the clear intensity of his luminous blue gaze, the warm scent of his breath as it mingled with her own. A rhythm had established itself effortlessly between them, as though they had practiced it many times before.

All concept of time had ceased. But she had a sudden awareness of the night-dark world outside their small, firelit cocoon. Beyond the curtained windows, the wind had risen again, buffeting against the house from time to time, moaning softly around the sliding glass doors. On the beach waves would be foaming at their crests, thundering against the sand, then retreating, gathering strength for the next onslaught. Here on the firelit floor, wave after wave of blissful sensation was washing over her, building to a peak that was unbearable, yet which, conversely, she didn't want to end. When her climax came, it was more explosive than anything she had ever experienced in her life. It seemed to her then that she was out there in the wind-tossed night, and for just a second she could hear the triumphant roar of the surf.

Adrian lay still for a full minute, allowing her time to enjoy the sensations coursing through her body, then he began moving again and there was nothing gentle about him now. His kisses demanded entrance, the contours of his body were hard and unyielding against her own. And the pressure was building inside her again, her hips arching in rhythm with his. Once again, the pressure grew intolerable, and found its release, just as Adrian's voice said "Danielle" on an urgent note and the shadows around them lifted and shattered and then lay still.

A RED-WINGED BLACKBIRD was trilling outside his bedroom window. The distinctive four-note call was one of the few Adrian could put a name to, as Michael had pointed it out in the bird book Adrian had acquired the previous day.

Lifting his head, he glanced at the uncurtained window. The wind had dropped again and the sky looked fairly clear. He checked the bedside clock. Seven-thirty of a Sunday morning, arguably the happiest morning of his life. Turning his head, he gazed at Dani, almost unable to believe she was actually there, in his bed, where he'd imagined her so many times before.

She was still asleep, the curve of her mascara-darkened lashes feathering against her clear peaches-and-cream skin, her lips slightly parted, her breathing even and relaxed. Her hair was sleep-tousled and he stroked it gently into place, admiring once again the neat way it curved behind her ear. He was careful not to disturb her. They had slept very little, their hunger for each other seemingly increasing minutes after they satisfied it. He couldn't even remember when he'd half led, half carried her upstairs to his bedroom. He only remembered that she'd laughed softly when she found out his landlord's choice of a resting place was a water bed. "I've got to meet this man," she'd murmured. "I heard he was a ladies' man, this confirms it."

All the same, she'd enjoyed the novel experience, appreciating the subtle rhythms the swaying mattress added to their lovemaking. He kissed her lightly and she murmured in her sleep.

He wanted a cigarette. Badly. But he'd thrown out all he had on hand the previous afternoon, while his resolve was still strong. Fumbling in the nightstand for a stick of gum, he heard the distinctive hoot of a pheasant followed by a sudden clattering that made him leap from the bed in alarm, only to see from the window that Michael had arrived on a bicycle, which he'd just dropped on the lawn. He groaned. Monday, he'd told the teenager. Monday morning, maybe around nine. What the hell was he doing here now? And how could he most quickly get rid of him? He couldn't take a chance on Mike seeing Dani. This was a small town, and in spite of its veneer of sophistication, he couldn't risk tongues wagging about the town's only doctor.

Mike was wandering down to the lake, sketchbook in hand. Good. Maybe he'd find a duck to draw. Or if he had colors with him, he might try his hand at the sunrise, which was flushing the eastern sky with a bright wash of scarlet.

Turning, Adrian looked at Dani again, lying so relaxed among the vigorously tumbled sheets and blankets. He'd have to wake her, alert her to Michael's presence, then maybe the two of them could work out how to get rid of the boy.

After dressing hurriedly in sweats and sneakers, he knelt on the bed, hanging on to a rail of the brass headboard so he wouldn't lose his balance on the water-filled mattress. Touching her face lightly, he murmured, "Danielle."

Her mouth twitched slightly and her eyelids fluttered but didn't open. God, he hated to wake her. Maybe he should just go down and eject Mike then come back and climb into bed with her and . . .

Too late. Her eyelashes were fluttering slightly now. "Good morning," he said softly as her eyes opened.

She still wasn't completely awake. The slate blue irises were cloudy, sleep-dazed, and she couldn't seem to raise her eyelids all the way. "Hi," he whispered, touching her lips with a gentle finger.

Her mouth curved into a smile but her eyes closed instead of opening and she burrowed her head into the pillow as if she were fighting the very idea of awakening. "Come on, sleepyhead," he coaxed.

And then she turned on to her back and smiled sleepily up at him, her eyes finally fluttering open. "Jon," she murmured.

ADRIAN CONCENTRATED on the sound of his own sneaker-clad feet pounding on the damp, hard-packed sand. He was counting every other step, he realized. He had reached one thousand thirty-four as his brain fought to impose order on the chaos of his thoughts. He could hear Michael's footfalls echoing his own as the teenager ran beside him. One thousand eighty-one.

"We going to run all the way downtown?" Michael asked, sounding short of breath.

"And back," Adrian said shortly.

He could still see Dani's face blanching as she realized what she had done—the shock in her widening eyes followed rapidly and unmistakably by guilt.

How many times had people called him Jon by mistake? Hundreds. Thousands. But never in such circumstances, never when it meant the difference between joy and grief.

He couldn't even remember if he'd said anything. He only remembered backing slowly away from the bed, feeling as though he'd been doused by a deluge of icy water. She'd sat up in the bed, heedless of the covers falling away from her naked body, her beautiful naked body. And she'd held out one hand to him in wordless supplication.

Somewhere in there he must have turned away, run down the stairs, gathered up Michael and ushered into the BMW. He remembered the car's right front wheel bouncing over the potholes on the corner of Scoter Lake Drive and Dune Street. He remembered Michael chatting away about wanting to check out Adrian's yard to see what needed to be done, not meaning to disturb him. How he'd followed a huge cock-pheasant that was strutting and pecking across Adrian's front yard.

But Adrian's mind had been filled with the image of Dani's white face and ivory body and he had felt nothing but the continuing clutch of the nausea that had exploded inside him when he'd heard her sleepy voice murmur, "Jon."

Had he managed to tell her Michael was there? He thought so. And she'd have heard the car. She'd have got out of his bed, dressed and gone home, wouldn't she? He hoped so; he certainly hoped so. There was no way he could look at her again today.

"I've had it," Mike said, stumbling to a halt.

Adrian turned his head without slowing his pace. "Sit on a log until I come back," he said over his shoulder, then started counting again. One and two and three and . . .

"YOU GOT ANY of those good pizzas with the croissant crust?" Harris Kelsey asked the manager of the deli in Phil's Market.

"Make you some up?" the man offered.

Harris nodded, considering. "Make two." They weren't that big and he'd eaten only a bowl of oatmeal before leaving Seattle. Knowing Dani, she'd eat less than a half, but he could manage the rest easy.

Accepting the long skinny packages, he turned away from the counter and froze. Either Adrian or Jon Falkirk stood only a few feet away, dressed in a gray sweatsuit and sneakers, turned sideways to Harris. He was examining a couple of wedges of cheese, one in each hand. Setting one back down on the display counter, he put the other on top of a collection of items in a hand basket and strode toward the front of the store. With him was a tall, skinny, awkward-looking kid with a weird haircut. Not a Falkirk, that was for sure.

It was a full minute before Harris moved. Then he went in the opposite direction, not wanting whichever of the twins that had been to see him. What the hell was a Falkirk doing in Murre Bay? And did Dani know he was here?

He read the dietary information on the sides of several cereal boxes to kill some time, then, juggling the pizzas, he picked up a bag of cut greens and a bottle of salad dressing and headed for the nearest cash register, glancing around furtively to make sure the man had left.

By the time he reached Dani's trailer, he'd decided to say nothing, give his daughter a chance to tell him anything she had to say. But then the minute she opened the door to him, he found himself blurting out, "I saw one of the Falkirk twins in town. In Phil's. What the hell's he doing here?"

For a second he thought his usually strong daughter was going to burst into tears, but after she'd turned away to let him pass, she seemed to be in control again. "It's Adrian Falkirk, Daddy. What are *you* doing here?"

He set the grocery bag on her small kitchen counter and regarded her thoughtfully. She hadn't called him Daddy in twelve, maybe fifteen years. "Seems to me you keep putting me off whenever I call ahead, so I thought I'd surprise you. Brought lunch with me, too. Don't I get a hug?"

She managed a smile that didn't look too enthusiastic, but her hug was as loving as always, perhaps more so. He was even more alert. Dani had never been a clinging type. Something was going on here and he meant to find out what it was. Setting her away from him, he looked at her carefully. She was as pretty as ever, wearing narrow-legged jeans and the pale blue cable knit cashmere sweater he'd given her on her last birthday. Her honey-colored hair was newly washed, still a little damp, smelling fragrantly of shampoo, her face was innocent of makeup. She looked tired, he decided. There were delicate shadows under her eyes, small lines of strain at the corners of her mouth.

"How long has Adrian been here?" he demanded as she turned away and began digging coffee beans out of a porcelain container.

"For goodness' sake, Dad, take your coat off and sit down before you start the interrogation," she muttered.

He swore, which he rarely did in front of her. She didn't hear him anyway, she was grinding the coffee beans. Muttering to himself, he pulled off his jacket and went into her tiny bedroom to lay it on her bed. Then he slid into one of the padded benches that bracketed the small dining table. Restraining impatience, he watched her measure the grounds into the coffeemaker and add water. Then she turned on the oven and began unwrapping the pizzas he'd brought. It wasn't his imagination that she was delaying turning around.

Dani reached for a wooden salad bowl, scoured it with a garlic clove and emptied the greens into it, wondering how much she should tell her father. As little as possible, she decided. She just wasn't up to any arguments about Adrian Falkirk. Not today of all days. Why, why, why had her father picked this day to surprise her?

"Adrian's been in Murre Bay for a couple of weeks," she said flatly as she served the coffee.

Her father made no move to pick up his cup. His gaze had fixed itself on her face when she sat down opposite him. With difficulty, she met his eyes. "He's been ill," she explained. "Overwork, stress. He needed a vacation."

"Why the hell did he come here? Did he know you were here?"

She nodded. It had never been easy to lie to her father. What unkind fate, she wondered, had sent Adrian to the grocery store at the same moment in time as her father. "Did you speak to him?" she asked.

"What the hell would I have to say to him? He didn't even see me."

That was some consolation. She'd had a vivid image of her father haranguing Adrian in public.

The desperation that had been with her all morning suddenly swept over her again. What must Adrian be thinking? His face had looked so...bleak. How on earth could she explain to him what she couldn't explain to herself?

Her father's eyes had narrowed suddenly. "He was ill, you said. Does that mean he's your patient?"

Stick to the facts, only the facts. "He was. I've referred him to a doctor in Baxter."

"Hmph." He picked up his cup and sipped coffee in silence for a while. He was evidently running out of steam. Quick to anger, he always cooled off just as quickly. "He hasn't been bothering you, then?"

Define bothering, some small voice in the back of her mind suggested. Getting up, she put the pizzas in the oven, set the timer to six minutes and brought down a couple of plates from an upper cabinet. "Not at all," she said.

That was a lie all right, but Adrian certainly hadn't bothered her in the way her father had meant. "He's only here for a month," she added. "I doubt I'll see much of him at all."

His glance sharpened on her face. "You sound upset," he said, then sighed noisily as she shook her head. "Whatever happened to that nice man you told me you were seeing, the restaurant guy?" he asked unexpectedly. "You still seeing him? He sounded much more suitable than any of the Falkirks, salt-of-the-earth type."

This was a switch. He'd expressed the thought that Brian sounded like a wimp whenever she'd mentioned him before.·

"Nothing happened to him. He's still around." She should check on Brian, see how things were going at

Surf and Turf. No dammit, she was still upset with him for reporting Michael. "He had a fire in his restaurant on Thursday," she added, hoping her father would follow along that side road for a while and forget about Adrian Falkirk.

But Harris had evidently lost interest in Brian Milburn. He just grunted. He was looking down at the table, one finger compulsively tracing the wet ring his cup had left on the Formica. Handing him a paper napkin, Dani watched him wipe his hand, mop up the stain, then crumple the napkin into a ball. "That was a very humiliating experience, having to go in and tell all those people the wedding was off," he muttered. "Seeing Falkirk, not being sure which Falkirk he was, brought it all back."

"The wedding is history, Dad," Dani said softly.

"Is it?" His gaze was suddenly unusually penetrating. "Then what the hell is Adrian doing in Murre Bay?"

"I told you."

"But you're not telling me everything, are you?"

Anger shot through her, edged with guilt. "Don't you think I'm a little old to be accountable to you for everything I do?" she said tightly.

Her father winced. Damn, now she'd hurt his feelings. But what about her feelings?

The oven timer buzzed. Seizing the reprieve, Dani took the pizzas out of the oven, slammed them onto a cutting board and slashed them in half with a kitchen knife. Slapping a plate in front of her father, she served two of the sections onto it, put the salad in front of him and plunked down the bottle of salad dressing he'd brought.

Regarding her shrewdly, he reached around to the kitchen drawer for cutlery. "Why are you so mad at me?" he asked.

"I'm not mad at you," she said through her teeth. Which was the truth. So who was she mad at? At Adrian, for rushing off without giving her a chance to explain. As if there *was* any way to explain. She was mad at Brian for not letting her call Chet before he talked to the fire chief, mad at Michael for being Michael, mad at the whole damn world. Most of all she was mad at Dani Kelsey for ruining whatever had been growing between herself and Adrian Falkirk.

Shaking her head, she took a deep calming breath. "I'm sorry, Dad, I'm just irritable, I guess. I didn't sleep too well last night."

He picked up a piece of pizza and took a bite out of it, still watching her face. "Why not?"

Damn. He wasn't going to let it go, obviously.

She cut herself a small slice of pizza—mainly for something to do—she certainly didn't have any appetite. "Problems with a patient," she said for want of a better excuse.

"You're really not upset because Adrian Falkirk's here?"

"Why should I be?"

"Because he should have better sense than to hang around here, reminding you of the past, making you unhappy. You looked like you were going to burst out crying when I told you I'd seen him."

"I'm not unhappy," she said fiercely. "And I wasn't crying. I told you, I'm just tired." She took another breath. "Besides," she added quietly. "It was Jon who dumped me. Adrian is not Jon.'' The sentence struck her with ironic force. *Adrian is not Jon.* If only she could convince herself of that.

CHAPTER NINE

"WHAT'S WRONG, Kelsey?" Steff peered around the hood of her yellow slicker at Dani's face. "You seem awfully subdued."

It was early on Monday morning and they were walking on the beach, more slowly than usual, in consideration of Steff's recent surgery.

Dani smiled tightly. "I've got to get to the clinic by nine, Steff. There isn't enough time to tell you what's wrong."

"That bad, huh?"

"That bad."

"Would it have anything to do with Adrian Falkirk?"

Dani laughed shortly. "You've become a mind reader?"

Steff grinned. "Falkirk came by to fix my dinner last night. When I asked him where you were, he growled, 'How should I know?'"

Dani winced, but said nothing.

After a minute or two of unaccustomed silence, Steff said in her most gravelly voice, "You're right, it's none of my business."

"It's not that," Dani protested. "It's just..."

"You don't want to talk about it."

"Right."

"Okay. Let's talk about the weather. Look at that bank of clouds coming this way. Going to get even wetter, looks like."

Dani nodded, then there was another silence. "Adrian was pretty angry, huh?" Dani asked at last.

Steff thought for a minute. "Wouldn't say angry. More like . . . upset. He apologized right away, told me he'd had a bad day. Said Michael had hung around with him all day, driving him crazy with questions about some wildlife refuge he'd mentioned." She glanced at Dani sideways. "Said he was going to get Mike started on repairing his roof today. Guess he'll be home all day."

When Dani didn't respond, she sighed.

"I'm sorry, Steff," Dani said.

She'd intended going to see Adrian the previous evening, but her father hadn't left until ten o'clock and by then she'd been so wound up from having to pretend all day that everything was fine, she'd felt it was probably advisable to wait. She'd half expected to see Adrian on the beach this morning, but if he was expecting Michael to come to work he'd be waiting at home for him. Later, she thought. She had a tremendously busy day ahead of her at the clinic. After that, she'd have to grab her courage in both hands and go to Adrian's house. At the least she owed him an apology, even if she couldn't come up with a reasonable explanation.

"MR. FALKIRK isn't home," Mike informed her. The teenager was sitting on one of the Adirondack chairs on Adrian's deck, putting the finishing touches on a sketch of a pheasant. "He went into Baxter half an hour ago. Said he needed some diversion, whatever that is."

Well, she'd suggested he go to Baxter if Murre Bay didn't provide enough entertainment for him. "I'll catch him tomorrow," she told Michael, turning away.

He wasn't home the next evening, either. Nor was Michael, but judging by the number of new shakes on the roof the two of them had put in a productive day.

On Wednesday evening she snapped at poor old Stasny Stanislaus when they were working together at the free clinic in Baxter. All the old man had asked was if she was coming down with flu herself, like almost everyone else in the area. "You look peaked," he said defensively when she snarled that she was perfectly all right. She apologized at once, of course, but his lined face looked hurt and she realized she had to settle this thing with Adrian one way or another.

The trouble was that she didn't get home until too late to go calling on anyone. Tomorrow without fail, she decided.

She was halfway to Adrian's house at the end of her next workday when she saw his BMW turning the corner ahead. Flashing her lights at him—it had been a cloudy day and twilight had descended early—she pulled to the side of the road, rolling down her window as he made a U-turn and drew up alongside.

"I was on my way to your place," he said without inflection.

"I was coming to see you."

He looked at her, then gave a half smile that had no joy in it. "Maybe we should go back to my house, then. Not enough room in your trailer for me to pace."

That didn't sound good at all. But at least he was speaking to her, she reasoned as she followed him into his driveway. She hadn't been sure he would.

Inside the house, he turned on the living room lights then lit the fire that had already been laid in the fireplace. He hadn't shaved in a while, she noticed suddenly. Maybe not since she last saw him. Usually he was immaculate. The darkly shadowed jawline was somehow disturbing. Had her terrible mistake affected him that badly? Or was he just getting lazy about personal habits? The relaxed atmosphere of Murre Bay affected some people that way. Trouble was, the dark stubble made his appearance even sexier. She could feel that same languorous feeling taking over, making her want to touch him, go to him.

That was a joke. Stiff as he looked, he certainly wasn't about to welcome any advances from her. It was obvious that she had offended him irreparably.

Taking her coat, he hung it in the hall closet, then came back into the room and looked at her. "Wine?"

She nodded, more for a glass to hang on to than for the alcohol itself. "May I see the kittens?" she asked, following him into the kitchen area.

Boots was sitting proudly in a cushion-lined, obviously new wicker pet basket, surrounded by her babies. The kittens were fuzzier now and their eyes were open, shining like buttons against their black fur. "This is the only one that hasn't inherited its mother's white socks," Adrian said, picking up one of the kittens. The all-black kitten looked tiny in his large hand, but when Dani took it from him it felt fairly substantial. She stroked it lightly and placed it gently back beside its mother, who proceeded to wash it all over.

Watching Danielle, Adrian felt a twist of pain. If he could only turn the clock back to Sunday morning, do things differently. If he'd gone out to talk to Michael, let her wake up alone... What the hell good would that have done? Sooner or later he'd have found out her true feelings.

He noticed abruptly that there was some kind of yellow stain behind her left ear. Frowning, he bent down and touched it lightly. Makeup? He felt her tremble and realized what he was doing. Her hands had stilled on the edge of the basket. He wanted badly to let his fingers slide around to the side of her face, to touch her lips....

She stood up abruptly. "There's something behind your ear, something yellow," he said, his voice husky.

Straightening, she put her hand to the spot and smiled wryly. "We had a Halloween party for patients' kids this afternoon," she said. "I dressed up as a scarecrow. Yellow face, patched overalls and flannel shirt, synthetic straw up my sleeves and down my collar. Itchy stuff." She laughed. "Steff came to help, dressed as a witch."

"Something to see," he said, wishing again, wishing he could have helped her with the party, laughed with her, then brought her home and loved her. If only...

"It was fun." Her eyes were sad, wistful.

Reaching into a kitchen drawer, he took out a clean cloth, moistened it under the faucet and handed it to her. Looking embarrassed, she rubbed at the spot, then reached past him to rinse out the cloth.

He handed her a small towel to dry her hands. The air was thick between them. If he was to take one step forward...

"Is this mine?" she asked, indicating one of the glasses of wine he'd set on the island counter. When he nodded, she picked it up, taking a deep, shaky breath at the same time.

"My dad visited me on Sunday," she said as she preceded him into the living room and sat down in one of the armchairs that bracketed the fireplace. "He saw you in Phil's Market."

"That must have thrilled him no end." He sat down opposite her, stretching his long legs, another of those mirthless half smiles pulling at the corner of his mouth. "What did you tell him about my reasons for coming to Murre Bay?" he asked with obvious curiosity.

"The truth. That you were ill, and needed a peaceful place to recuperate."

An ironic gleam showed up in the back of his eyes. She braced herself for one of the sarcastic remarks the old Adrian would have made. But it didn't come. He just sat there, looking at her, waiting. His eyes were shuttered now, giving nothing of his thoughts away. Obviously he wasn't going to make any of this easy for her.

"About Sunday morning..." She gripped the stem of the wineglass. "I have no idea how I came to call you Jon. I wasn't really awake, I guess. I thought..."

"You thought I *was* Jon." His voice was harsh.

She swallowed. "I guess I must have done, but..."

"All along?"

She frowned, not sure what he meant.

"You were pretending all along that I was Jon?"

"Pretending? Good grief, no, I wasn't pretending." She had to be totally honest with him, obviously. "I can't deny that I've been confused ever since you came to Murre Bay," she admitted. "I seemed to have these feelings for you that were...unjustified, considering we had never been ... close, but I certainly wasn't pretending."

She was speaking the truth. Off and on she'd been confused by the strong resemblance Adrian bore to his brother, but when he'd made love to her, she had been fully aware that it was Adrian she was with.

Then why had she called him Jon? A moment of mental aberration? Was that all it had been?

The old derisive expression was back in his eyes as he watched her face. What was he deducing, she wondered and wished he could explain her to herself. Even now, sitting here, feeling such dreadful embarrassment and confusion, she could also feel his magnetism working on her, drawing her to him, so that she wanted to get up and walk over to him and lean down and . . .

"Are you still in love with Jon?" He set down his glass and leaned forward, looking at her directly, his blue eyes vivid in the lamplight, accusing.

"I don't think so," she said with scrupulous honesty. "I've come to see that Jon wasn't quite the man I once thought him to be. Away from him, I began to see several flaws in his character. But since you came here, I've felt confused. . . ."

He stood up and started pacing as he'd threatened to do, one hand going to rake through his dark hair in precisely the way Jon had always done when he was disturbed or angry. When he spoke, there was bitterness in his voice. "All my life I've been confused with Jon. All my life I've struggled to be recognized as a separate person, first by my parents and sisters, then by friends and business associates. Not that I blame anyone. I only have to look in a mirror to see . . ."

He stopped pacing and looked at her directly. "When you look at me, you see Jon. That about sums it up, doesn't it?"

"Not always, not every time."

He laughed shortly. "Here's something for you to ponder, Danielle. When I came to tell you Jon wasn't going to show up at your wedding, I thought you looked like the Snow Queen in your bridal gown. Do you know the Hans Christian Andersen stories about the Snow Queen?''

She gazed up at him, hating the coldness in his eyes, the cynical tone of his voice. "Something about a woman made of ice who carried a little boy away on a sled?'' she said hesitantly.

He nodded. "In the first story a wicked hobgoblin made a magic mirror. When it was broken, millions of glass splinters fell to earth and entered people's eyes, distorting their vision."

He smiled wryly. "I remember my mother telling me once that when she was a little girl she always thought when a person was old she must *feel* old. But when she reached sixty she still felt the same inside as she did at twenty. It was a shock, she said, to look in the mirror and see this person with gray hair and crow's-feet. Because her own image of herself was still youthful. It's the same for me, you see. I look in the mirror and see someone who looks exactly like Jonathan. But inside I'm a whole other human being, with different wants and needs and ideas and ambitions and feelings."

His eyes were intensely blue. "Did you ever think about how you are on the inside, Danielle, what a unique individual you are? It's so obvious that you have a calling to be a doctor—you're a care-giver, a nurturer, a wonderfully compassionate woman, you worked hard to become a doctor, you put yourself through school, almost single-handedly. Now, I'm sure your father has many sterling qualities, but imagine how it would be if people decided you had to be just like him, simply because you're related. Then add the possibility of looking so much like him you couldn't be told apart. Would that make you less of a unique individual on the inside?''

She wanted to get up and go to him and put her arms around him and tell him . . . tell him what? After what had happened, what could she possibly say?

"Surely Jon must have been confused with you also," she said inadequately.

"Of course he was, but he never seemed to mind, especially where woman were concerned. Even Marta—" He broke off and turned away, striding over to the sliding glass doors and looking out at the dark lake glimmering under the outside lights.

"Marta?" she prompted.

"I'm sorry, I shouldn't have mentioned . . ."

She sat very still. "Jon had an affair with Marta? Your wife?"

"It was very brief. No more than a one-night stand. Marta confessed all to me one night, after she'd had a little too much to drink." He shrugged, but the expression on his face, reflected in the glass, was far from casual. "According to Marta she had no idea . . ."

Dani felt sick. "She thought he was you? He pretended to be you?"

He didn't answer. He was still looking out at the lake, Dani caught her breath at the anguish in his face. How it must have tortured him, wondering if Marta really had known it was Jon making love to her.

Jon had known the difference. Jon had made love to his brother's wife, knowingly and with possible malice aforethought. No, not with malice. Jon had probably thought the whole thing was great fun. Which didn't say much for his character. But then, Jon always had been rather a weak character. Much weaker than Adrian.

Dani frowned. Where had that thought come from? It seemed important, even profound, yet frightening at the same time. Why frightening? Before she could examine the thought more closely, Adrian swung around and came toward her, bending down to put his hands on the arms of her chair, his face only inches from hers. "What about you, Danielle?" he asked hotly. "When you were with Jon, did it work for you the other way around? Did you ever think when you saw Jon that he was me? When you were with Jon, did you ever wonder if he could be me?"

Something stirred in her mind again, a thought that wouldn't quite come into being, an idea that had never developed, a memory that had been suppressed. Why did she suddenly have the feeling she was standing at the edge of an abyss, about to take a fatal step that would send her plunging downward? Adrian's question was ridiculous. Obviously. He was suggesting she might *never* have been able to tell the difference between him and his brother. "You were always so rude to me," she pointed out. "And sarcastic. My dad asked me once how I could tell the difference between you and Jon and I told him you always had a smirk on your face. You had, Adrian. You were *horrible* to me."

He straightened, looking sad. "I've been hoping," he began, then shook his head. "Obviously I've been very stupid. And I've forgotten that I was going to apologize to you. That's why I was coming to see you. On Sunday..." For a second his voice faltered, then came back stronger. "On Sunday I reacted in a ridiculous manner. Rushing off like that. Hardly mature behavior. I was just so..."

Again he didn't finish the sentence. What had he been about to say? Devastated? He had looked devastated.

She would never forget the look in his eyes. As though she'd slapped him.

He had gone to stand by the glass doors again, looking out as if he couldn't stand looking at her. And watching him, gazing at his reflection in the glass, his midnight-dark hair, his tall, lithe body clad in blue jeans and a loose off-white sweater that neither clung to nor concealed the muscles in his upper body, her mind filled with images of the night that had preceded that awful morning. His body moving against hers. His hands touching her. His mouth...

She felt empty, bereft, as if she had lost something, some part of herself that she couldn't imagine being without.

Was she still suffering from her breakup with Jon?

No. The answer came coolly but clearly into her mind.

She *had* stopped loving Jon.

When?

Once again, some other thought was trying to come through. Something to do with snowflakes shining on dark hair, a white silk scarf. The image couldn't quite seem to materialize. Instead, she found herself adding up the incidents that had impressed her since Adrian had arrived in Murre Bay. His compassion for Steff. The way he'd sat with her all day at the hospital. The expression on his face when he looked at the drawings of birds Michael had made. The way he'd gone running into the smoke-filled restaurant after little Timothy—without hesitation. The bemused expression on his face as he looked down at Boots and her babies, his hands holding the tiny kitten. Each time she had tried, and failed, to imagine Jon doing the same things. And she had felt... tenderness. Tenderness was not an emotion she'd ever associated with Jon. He had inspired passion in her, need occasionally, and love, yes, love certainly, but never tenderness.

Adrian isn't Jon, she'd said to her father. Was it possible that her mind had recognized the truth before her heart had?

What *was* the truth?

"Discussion is pointless, isn't it?" Adrian said abruptly. After another moment, he swung around and gazed at her across the room. "I had this crazy idea all along, you see, that you..." He shook his head. "I was wrong, obviously."

If only she could tell him with all honesty that there was no longer any confusion in her mind, no doubt...

Too late, the voice in her mind stated sadly.

Too late for what? she asked in return.

Too late to tell him her vision was no longer distorted. But was it? How could she be sure? If she couldn't be sure, how could she expect him to believe it? She couldn't. Not now. Not after Sunday.

He moved away from the glass doors and picked up his wineglass, draining it. "God, what I wouldn't give for a cigarette," he said bleakly.

"You've stopped smoking altogether?"

He glanced at her with another of those half smiles, with a touch of humor this time. "I had to. I told Mike I'd given it up. Now I'm stuck with setting a good example."

"How's it going with Mike?" she asked awkwardly.

"Fine. He's teaching me about birds. He really has a feel for the natural world. He's already checked every box and can in my garage to make sure I don't possess any substances that would affect the ecological balance of the area." He gestured toward the windows. "He's also put together several bird feeders. Daytime, my yard's full of red-winged blackbirds, sparrows, towhees, finches—and ducks snapping up the overflow."

"And Steff? Did you see her today?"

He shook his head. "She had a visitor." He hesitated as if he were going to say something more, then evidently thought better of it.

Was their discussion over? Dani wondered. Nothing was settled. Perhaps nothing ever could be settled. A sudden vista of emptiness seemed to stretch before her. "We could try being friends for a while," she suggested.

He laughed harshly. "I told you once before that wasn't possible, Danielle." Sitting down again, he looked at her, pain showing clearly in his blue eyes. "Right this minute I want to take you in my arms, in my bed, and make love to you. There's no confusion in *my* mind, you see. There never..." Again he broke off. "Dammit, Danielle, I've gone over all of this in my mind since Sunday, again and again. At first I was mad as hell, but that was just an automatic reflex, I guess. Then I thought that I wanted you so much I could take you on any terms you wanted to offer. But then the thought of you lying in my arms and thinking of Jon was so...repugnant to me, I knew I couldn't face it. So it seems to me that the only thing to do is stay away from you until you make up your mind, one way or the other. I'm damned if I can think of any alternative."

Too late, her mind echoed again.

She stood up abruptly. "I think I should go."

He stood up also. And looked at her. Desire spiraled inside her, but she fought it down. "I do wish," she started, then stopped. "I want you to know..." Again she broke off, looking at him helplessly.

"There isn't really anything more to say, is there?" His voice was sad.

She shook her head. "I'm sorry, Adrian. I just..." She couldn't bear it any longer, looking at him, wanting to touch him. Her eyes prickled with tears she couldn't possibly shed in front of him. "Could you give me my coat, please?"

In silence he brought it for her, held it while she shrugged into it, careful not to touch her. "I guess you'll be leaving Murre Bay pretty soon anyway," she said as he opened the front door for her.

He hesitated. "I'm not sure."

She couldn't bear it if he stayed on. Not the way he was now. He'd said a month originally and he'd been here more than three weeks. Alarmed, she glanced at him. "You're thinking of staying longer?"

The rueful grin that was almost his trademark, and Jon's, curled one corner of his mouth. "I seem to have become entangled. Life has a way of setting up strings that wind around you and keep you from making changes. Was a time, I didn't think I'd ever leave San Francisco. My wife wanted to live there and my work was there and my parents. But one by one the strings were severed. My parents decided the Bay area wasn't the great place to live that it once was, so they moved to Seattle. My wife—well you already know that story. And then my work lost its charm. Now I've acquired a whole new set of strings. The kittens need to grow a little before I move them. Mike is responding well, counting on me to introduce him to my friends at the wildlife refuge. Which I don't feel I can do until I know him better, and until he is totally clear of suspicion in regard to the fire at Surf and Turf. Then there's Steff, who seems...lonely sometimes. I've got a plan there, by the way, that might or might not work, and a project that..."

He broke off, to Dani's regret. As he talked his voice and expression had warmed considerably as if he were talking to a friend. Now, as though he'd suddenly remembered the way things were between them, he looked bleak again. "Well, anyway, I've decided to hang around a while longer, until I see how things go," he said ambiguously.

"You're actually thinking of moving away from the Bay area?"

"Let's just say I've entertained the possibility."

He couldn't possibly mean to stay in Murre Bay forever, of course. What was there to hold him here? He'd already admitted to boredom on occasion.

"Danielle," he said, and there was something tentative in his voice that made her think he was going to make one more try to straighten things out between them. But then he sighed and pulled the door wider, obviously wanting her to go through it. "Take care of yourself," he said softly as she passed him.

She nodded, on the brink of tears. "You too."

He watched her walk to her car, every fiber of his being telling him to call her back, take her in his arms, forget about Sunday morning.

But he couldn't forget. Her voice, caressing the sound of his brother's name, was imprinted on his memory.

Was he doing the wrong thing, sending her away? What else could he do? He had to take a chance, risk everything on the gamble that Dani would eventually come to see him as himself—and be able to prove it to him.

CHAPTER TEN

MIKE SET HIS long legs, braced the fence post and looked at Adrian enviously. "Sure wish I could grow a beard," he said. "Mine comes out all patchy."

"Give it a year or two," Adrian suggested, then added, "Hang on," as he pounded nails into the cross rail. Growing a beard was probably a ridiculous thing to do, he thought. Every day he decided to shave it off, every day he let it grow some more. Pretty soon, he'd need to have it professionally trimmed. It was coming off tonight, he decided, as he lifted the next section of rail into place.

Mike shifted restlessly. "Sure starts getting dark early now."

"That's what happens when you put the clocks back an hour." Adrian glanced up at the sky. Mike was right—the light was fading fast. Nevertheless, he positioned the hammer again. "Got another hour or so yet," he said, then pounded some more.

"Slave driver," Mike muttered.

Adrian grinned at him. "Why don't you just say you're bushed, instead of hinting around?"

Mike bridled. "I can work long as you can."

It worked every time. Relenting, Adrian laid the hammer on the fence rail and straightened his shoulders. "Bushed myself," he admitted. How many nails had he pounded since that fateful Sunday, he wondered, his glance going from the fence to the new boards in the deck to the huge patches of orange brown shakes that stood out against the weathered gray of the rest of the steep roof. Ten days and he just kept on pounding. Six days since he'd even seen her. Where would she be now? He glanced at his watch. She'd still be working. It was Wednesday, so she'd be going on to Baxter later for the free clinic.

He sighed, raking his hand through his hair. Was he going to spend the rest of his life checking his watch to see what Dani was doing? Would she ever stop appearing in his mind, short blond hair gleaming, smoky blue eyes opaque with tenderness, wide mouth curving in a smile. She had inhabited his mind for almost three years now, ever since that Christmas Eve when he'd first met her.

Slamming the door shut on that particular memory, he reached for the hammer again, then realized he'd lost his helper. Mike was standing at the edge of the bank, smoking a cigarette. Was that ever going to get easier, either? Would he ever be able to watch someone smoking without wanting a cigarette himself? Tobacco and Danielle. How was he supposed to get over two addictions at the same time?

It was ironic, he thought; he was probably in better physical shape than he'd been for years. In better spiritual shape, too. Murre Bay had brought him freedom from stress just as it was supposed to. But emotionally he was a mess.

"Hey!" Mike yelled suddenly, looking off to the west.

Throwing down his cigarette the teenager plunged down the bank into the shallow water at the edge of the lake, then started splashing at a furious rate through the tall reeds that bordered the bank, clumsy in the heavy combat boots he wore, arms flailing to beat down the rushes.

Dropping the hammer, Adrian leaped down the steps to the dock. "Where the hell are you going?" he yelled after the boy, feeling furious as he saw the flattened reeds. This time of the year there were no ducklings or goslings sheltering in the bulrushes but Mike was still upsetting the ecological balance that he supposedly prized so highly. So much for all his fine talk about his love of birds and animals and all parts of the natural world.

Mike was still traveling west, still flailing and stomping, and now Adrian could see, through the reeds and rushes, that something was moving ahead of him—a blur of gray feathers. Mike was carrying his zeal for getting close to birds too damn far.

Suddenly Mike pounced, and stretched his length in the water. A loud and raucous *grak, grak,* rent the evening air, sending a chill down Adrian's spine. A second later Mike was up and turning, hanging on with both arms to a large ungainly-looking bird, one hand clamped around its spearlike bill. A great blue heron, Adrian saw as Mike stumbled closer. Probably the same heron that had adopted Adrian's area of the lakeside as its territory. Every evening it could be seen stalking majestically through the reeds, its long bill darting to catch its food. Mornings, it often sat huddled on a branch of the huge Sitka spruce that marked the edge of the property, looking like a vulture as it surveyed its domain, its long neck and bill tucked into its breast. When it flew, rising up through mist over the water, its neck bent in an S-curve, large wings beating slowly and powerfully, it reminded Adrian of pictures he'd seen of a prehistoric pterodactyl. He'd become fond of the bird, had felt privileged that the heron no longer flew away whenever he appeared.

And now, for some ungodly reason, Michael had chased it down and captured it. "What the hell . . ." he began again as Mike reached the dock, breaking off when he saw the distress on the teenager's face.

"He's hurt, Mr. Falkirk," Mike gasped as he staggered up the steps to the front yard.

Following him, Adrian could see for himself that one of the big wings was trailing awkwardly and there were jagged areas in the outer part that were stained a brownish color. Blood. "Looks as if it's been shot," he exclaimed.

Mike grunted. "That's what I thought." He swore harshly, though his eyes were moist with sympathy as he looked at the damage. "Damn hunters. I heard some shooting off in the distance a couple of days ago. Some damn hunter getting bored, I'll bet, shooting at anything that came over. It's okay, big bird," he added in the gentlest voice Adrian had ever heard him use. "We're going to fix you up just fine."

The bird seemed frozen into immobility. It wasn't struggling in Mike's arms at all. Its eyes looked glazed. Adrian felt singularly helpless, not an emotion he was used to. He had no idea what to do.

"Could you call your friends, get some advice?" Mike suggested.

It was a good thing someone's brain was functioning, Adrian decided. "You think you can hang on to big bird a while longer?" The boy was soaked through, not shivering yet though—probably his blood was pumping fast enough to keep him warm for a while.

"Long as I hold on to his bill I'm okay," Mike said. "One thing I know about herons, they go for anything shiny. Eyes, for example."

Alarmed, Adrian turned and sprinted for the house. A few minutes later he was talking to his friend Jorge Rodriguez, trying to be as specific as possible about the nature of the bird's injuries. "Make sure you don't get anywhere near that bill," Jorge interrupted.

"Mike's holding on to it."

"Okay then, here's what you do." Adrian grabbed a pen and paper from the shelf under the telephone and started writing.

A few minutes later, he and Mike placed the bird carefully in the downstairs shower stall, closing the glass door quickly the instant Mike let go.

The heron made a few indistinct sounds but didn't start beating itself against the glass, as Adrian had feared. Through the frosted door he could see the long ungainly shape standing as still as a statue, but it seemed to him he could sense the almost palpable presence of the bird's fear. Or was that his own? "Keep an eye on him," he instructed Mike unnecessarily. Michael was already sitting on the closed toilet, obviously intending to guard the heron with his life if need be. "You did good," Adrian told him and he grinned tiredly.

A minute later Adrian handed a pair of his own blue jeans and a sweater in to Mike, along with some jockey shorts. The clothes would be loose on the boy's lanky frame but it was necessary to get him warm and dry.

In his car, Adrian sat for a few seconds before turning on the ignition, catching his breath. Then he took off for town, heading for Dani's clinic. Sure, he could go to the drugstore for the medical tape he needed, but the clinic was closer and he just might get to see Dani.

Pathetic, Falkirk, he jeered at himself.

"Terrific beard," Theresa greeted him. "You look like a gangster, all dark and mysterious." She batted her eyelashes. "What are you going to steal from me?"

"Only bandages." Adrian launched into the story of the great blue heron. Theresa, who had grown up in Murre Bay, grasped the problem immediately and grabbed three rolls of fairly wide tape out of a supply cupboard. As Adrian stuffed them into his parka pockets, Danielle came out of an examining room, accompanied by a huge bear of a man with a bandage on his hand. In the second before she saw him, he let his eyes fill with the sight of her, so clean and professional in her starched white coat, bow-tied blouse and dark skirt.

"I don't know what to say, Doc," the man said. "I sure am sorry, honest."

"What happened?" Theresa asked.

The man looked shamefaced. "I fainted. It wasn't bad enough I cut my hand trying to get a knife through a loaf of my wife's bread, but when Doc here started to sew it up, I passed out on her."

Danielle laughed. "It happens to loggers more times than you'd think, Joe," she assured him. "Nothing to do with courage. Just shock to the system. Be glad Laurie and I caught you before you hit the floor."

Her eyes were dancing, but when she caught sight of Adrian, her smile disappeared at once. She looked tired, he thought. Her pupils were dilated, giving her eyes the appearance of velvet. Quickly he explained his mission, appreciating the quick sympathy that showed on her face. "Is there anything I can do?" she asked.

For a split second he considered accepting her offer of help, just so he could look at her for a while longer, then he reminded himself that it had been his decision to stop seeing her. "Mike and I have everything under control," he said, adding, "I hope," under his breath. "We're going to take the heron to my friends' wildlife refuge tomorrow, but he's going to spend the night in my shower."

She nodded, then a small frown puckered the skin above her nose as she studied his face. She was looking at his beard, Adrian realized. Its presence puzzled her; obviously she hadn't seen through to its purpose. Just as obviously, she didn't think much of it.

"Good luck," she called after him as he turned away toward the door. He managed to stop himself from turning back to see if she was smiling or still frowning. *Pathetic,* he scolded himself again.

He hadn't imagined for a moment that it would be an easy task to treat the heron's wing, although Jorge had made it sound eminently simple. "Just tape it to the bird's body," he'd said.

But first they had to get the heron out of the shower, which was far more difficult than getting it in. Mike talked to it steadily, which certainly seemed to help keep the bird halfway calm. Finally, the job was done and the bird replaced. The cleanup took quite a while longer.

Exhausted, sweating, Adrian and Mike leaned against the bathroom wall, then glanced at one another and laughed. "I don't think he wanted his wing taped," Mike said, then his face sobered. "You think your friends can fix him up?"

"If anyone can." He looked at the teenager's troubled face, feeling a rush of fondness for the boy. Just as he'd thought, his clothing was definitely on the large side for Mike; the blue jeans trailed over his bare feet, the shoulder seams of the sweater hung so low he'd had to roll the sleeves half a dozen times. The oversize clothing made him look very young, and very vulnerable. "Your stock is way up tonight, Michael Caswell," Adrian said quietly.

Mike's hazel eyes gleamed. "You thought I'd lost my gourd, didn't you?"

"At first, yes. Until I realized what you were up to." Pushing himself away from the wall, he held out his right hand and they shook hands solemnly. Then Adrian suggested some food might restore their strength.

"Should we be feeding the heron?" Mike asked as he preceded Adrian into the kitchen.

"Not while he's under stress, according to Jorge. If he stays calm, we can give him some herring chopped up in some water. In the morning, I'll have to drive him to the refuge. There's probably one closer, but I know Jorge and Consuelo. I trust them. And their refuge has the official recognition of the State Game Department." Besides which, he thought, it would be a good way to introduce Mike to Jorge and Consuelo, see what the chemistry was like. No way was he going to mention that thought to Mike, though. "I had an appointment in Baxter tomorrow afternoon," he muttered instead. "But I can postpone that until Friday."

He frowned, looking down at Boots and the kittens. "Maybe Steff could take care of the cats," he added, glancing at Mike. Mike's thin face was one big question mark. Adrian grinned. "Of course you can go with me. Why don't you plan on spending the night here, and we'll get an early start in the morning."

"All right!" Mike exclaimed.

Adrian pulled a couple of cans of soup out of a kitchen cabinet. He was far too tired to bother with anything fancier tonight. He had planned to eat out at one of the restaurants in town, but he was too tired for that as well.

A thought struck him. "I suppose we'll have a horrendous cleanup job in the shower in the morning?" he said.

Mike grinned. "Count on it. We also have to figure out how to transport him."

"Jorge suggested a traveling container for a large dog. You know anyone might have one?"

Mike's brow furrowed. He had started setting up two places at the island counter without being asked. He was coming right along. "I'll get one if I have to call everyone in Murre Bay," he said. "Where do we get the herring?"

"Phil's, I guess. I'll run in to town after we eat."

"I could go," Mike offered at once.

Adrian looked at him. Most likely he wasn't thinking he'd ride the clunky old bike he used to get to Adrian's house every day. Which left only one alternative. "Okay," Adrian said evenly. "I'd appreciate that. You should stop in at home, too, and pick up some clean clothes, let your Mom and Chet know you might be gone a couple of days." He took a deep breath. "I guess you'd better take my car."

Mike's face shone as if a light had switched on inside it. It was a great moment for both of them.

MIKE WAS as enthralled with the wildlife refuge as Adrian had expected him to be. From the moment the road emerged from between the surrounding woods and he saw the sunlit meadow with its pens and outbuildings, the large rustic house with its neat borders of flowers, its lawn sloping down to a wind-rippled brook, his thin face glowed with excitement.

First he had to watch intently while Jorge treated the heron, retaped the wing and turned the heron loose in a netted pen at the side of a flight cage that was half the size of a football field. Then he went off with Consuelo on a complete tour of the facilities, admiring the efficiently equipped hospital, stopping to sketch the current patients—a pair of young screech owls that looked like stuffed toys, a slightly scruffy-looking bald eagle and a red-tailed hawk that had dived too fast after its prey and hit a fence.

After lunch, he helped Jorge feed the deer and Roosevelt elk that were now permanent residents, along with the raccoons and possums Jorge and Consuelo had raised from infancy, and a weasel that had come off the loser in a tussle with a barbed wire fence.

"People bring in animals almost every day," Consuelo explained to Mike, her plump pretty face soft with compassion as she changed the dressing on the flank of a yearling doe the teenager was soothing. "Sometimes someone'll take in a baby wild animal and find they can't control it when it grows up. Then in the spring we have more orphaned babies to feed than we have hands. The rest of the time there are traffic accidents or poison or pollution or young animals mauled by dogs."

She shook her head, her dark curls bouncing. "Always something," she added sadly, then brightened. "That's how we got started with the refuge," she explained. "Jorge and I were both teaching at the high school, hoping to develop a nursery garden out here, and a farmer brought in a basketful of baby raccoons he'd found huddled together under a hedge. A kid with a .22 rifle he'd got for Christmas had shot their mother. We managed to raise them and next thing we knew we were up to our ears in birds and animals and didn't have time to teach anymore."

"What's with you and the boy?" Jorge asked Adrian later. They were leaning on a fence watching Mike place scoops of peanut butter on a tree branch for the red Douglas squirrels to eat. He looked like the all-American boy today, Adrian thought. When he'd returned from the grocery store the previous evening Adrian had hardly recognized him. He was wearing faded but clean blue jeans, sneakers, and a gray cable knit sweater he said he'd borrowed from Chet. He'd also prevailed upon his mother to cut his straggly long hair. Obviously Mrs. Caswell was not an expert, but the improvement in Mike's appearance was astonishing. What had touched Adrian was the fact that he'd made the effort. This trip had obviously seemed important to him and he'd wanted to make a good impression.

"He's doing a few jobs for me," Adrian said vaguely, wanting to test the waters.

"Seems like a good kid. Has that mystical feeling for wild creatures you don't see often. Talks to 'em and they seem to understand him. Connie's the same way, soon as she speaks to an animal or a bird, it calms right down."

Adrian laughed. "Mike spent the night on a quilt on my bathroom floor, watching over his big bird. When I got up this morning, he was singing softly to it."

Jorge was silent for a while, then he said, "We get a lot of volunteer help, you know. People come out for a day or an evening. But it's hard getting anyone to stick around all the time. We could use someone like Mike."

"I thought you might be able to," Adrian admitted.

"Put up job, huh?"

"Thought I'd see how you took to him."

"Consuelo likes him. Anyone can communicate with birds is going to have numero uno place in her heart." He laughed fondly, his craggy face crinkling. "Takes kids to her heart in any case. Always wanted some of our own, but God didn't see fit. Kid looking for a job?"

Adrian nodded. "I'd like to hold off saying anything to him," he said slowly. "He's been hanging out with the wrong companions. May or may not have been involved in some trouble."

"You think he was?"

"No. But that's just my gut instinct."

"I'd trust your instincts over a lot of people's." Jorge grinned, aiming a punch at Adrian's shoulder. "Man, it's good to see you. We appreciate your donations, but nothing beats having you here in the flesh."

Jorge was right, he'd stayed away from the refuge too long. Ever since their college days, when he'd been majoring in business and management, and Jorge in biological sciences, he'd appreciated Jorge's easy and undemanding friendship, his ability to voice affection without embarrassment. "Maybe *I* should sign on as a helper," he suggested.

Jorge laughed. "Not you, old buddy. You may need a certain amount of rural environment, but this far out you'd go nuts with boredom. You're not the type."

"Mike calls me a big, rich, important dude."

"Nothing wrong with that. If the world didn't have big, rich, important dudes, it would fall apart."

Adrian looked at him. "You really believe that?"

Jorge nodded. "Who else is going to support a crazy no-profit place like this?"

IT WAS FRIDAY morning before they got away from the wildlife refuge. Consuelo insisted they couldn't make that long drive both ways in the same day. "It's been too long since we saw you, anyway," she said to Adrian. "Least you can do is bunk with us overnight."

Mike's eyes had pleaded eloquently. What could Adrian do but give in gracefully?

"We'll have to leave very early," Adrian warned Consuelo, thinking of his appointment in Baxter.

"That's no problem," she insisted with a laugh. "We're up with the birds around here."

Everyone groaned.

In the morning, she served up a hearty breakfast of *huevos rancheros* and *chorizo*. She hugged both Mike and Adrian before they left, and made them promise to come back to visit Mike's big bird soon. "I love you even if you do look like a pirate," she teased Adrian, rubbing her knuckles over his beard. With all the arrangements he'd had to make for the heron's transportation, he hadn't managed to shave it off as he'd intended.

Mike was subdued during the return drive. Adrian wasn't sure if he was just thoughtful or upset.

"Nice people," Mike finally said, after a long silence.

"The best," Adrian agreed.

"That Consuelo sure can cook."

"Yes."

"You didn't ask him, did you? Jorge, I mean. About me." His voice was tight.

He *had* been upset then. "I told you we'd have to see how it went," Adrian reminded him.

"You're still not sure I can be trusted."

"I'm still not sure I know you," Adrian amended.

Mike relapsed into silence again, and had little to say for the rest of the drive. When Adrian dropped him off at home, he turned around after getting out of the car and leaned in the open door, looking directly at Adrian. "I can be trusted, Mr. Falkirk," he said solemnly.

Adrian nodded, but didn't comment. Driving to his appointment in Baxter a little later he replayed Mike's words in his mind, hoping that the boy had spoken truly. Jorge and Consuelo were special people, he couldn't take a chance on Mike unless he was convinced the boy would never cause them pain.

He ran a hand over his newly smooth face. The beard had apparently not achieved the hoped-for result as far as Dani was concerned, so it had seemed unnecessary to hang on to it. Besides which, Consuelo's pirate or Theresa's gangster were not images he particularly wanted to present at this coming meeting. The meeting was important. It might very well change his life. At the very least, it promised a whole new direction.

"YOU SUPPOSE you might consider having dinner with me tonight?" Brian said humbly into the telephone. Clinic hours had just ended and Dani was in her office, clearing up paperwork.

"The restaurant's open?" she asked in surprise.

"Not yet, no. It's coming along though. I thought we could go to the Seaview Hotel. They have that great seafood buffet on Fridays."

"Hang on a minute," Dani said to give herself time, then leaned her elbows on her desk, considering. She had talked to Brian briefly a couple of times since the fire, but had felt their once comfortable friendship had been strained since Brian had reported Mike to the fire chief, after she'd expressly asked him not to. She must be mellowing, she guessed—she could understand now that he'd been distraught that night, angry about the vandalism and ready to strike out at anyone who might seem remotely responsible.

Abruptly, she realized she had picked up the little green bottle Adrian had given her and was holding it tightly. The note was still inside it. *Be kind to Adrian Falkirk.* Sitting upright, she pulled open a drawer, put the bottle in it and slammed it shut.

"Why not," she said to Brian, which was hardly gracious, but at least affirmative. Brian had caught her at a weak moment, she admitted to herself as she hung up the phone. During the week work was her anodyne, but as the weekend approached she felt . . . lonely.

She hadn't even seen Steff for a while. Whenever she called, she got Steff's gravelly voice on her answering machine saying, "I'm out and about. Catch you later." Steff always had kept busy, of course, but she'd usually been home in the evenings.

Dani sighed. Seeing Adrian for that brief moment on Wednesday had emphasized the emptiness of the social part of her life. She had to make an effort to get out more. This date with Brian would at least be a start.

On her way out of the clinic, she stopped to glance at Theresa's chalkboard. It read, We are never so happy nor so unhappy as we imagine.

"Tell me about it," she said out loud.

That evening, she took a shower in her own house for the first time in weeks. She'd moved her personal stuff out of the trailer the previous evening and Chet had arranged for her Hide-A-Bed sofa to be brought out of storage today. He'd stuck it in the middle of the now completed living room where it looked like an elegant cream-colored island in a sea of plywood. She would cut the evening short, she decided. She was looking forward to sleeping in her own house again.

Brian was his usual friendly self. He did make a gloomy comment about Adrian Falkirk still being in town, but when she shrugged and changed the subject, he perked up considerably and talked optimistically about the way the work was going at Surf and Turf.

"I still think you should have employed Chet for the job," she said as she sampled the jumbo prawns. His refusal to even consider Chet still rankled.

"Maybe so," he said mildly.

"Mike's not an arsonist."

"You're probably right."

Dani grinned at him. "You're determined not to get into an argument tonight, aren't you?"

He smiled back. "I've missed you, Dani."

"I've missed you, too." It was true in a way. She'd missed his undemanding companionship. She'd got used to telling him about her day's work, at least as much as she could without violating patients' privacy. Everybody needed somebody to talk to at the end of the day.

Maybe she should get a dog. Or a cat. Abruptly, she was visited with an image of Adrian's hands gently holding one of Boots's kittens.

It was hardly fair to Brian to look upon a dog or a cat as a substitute for his company, she scolded herself as her mind skittered away from thoughts of Adrian. Feeling guilty, she smiled at Brian, perhaps more affectionately than she should have done.

"How about coming to the dance with me next weekend?" he asked, using a more aggressive tone than usual.

Dani frowned. "I thought the Seaview dance wasn't until December."

"I don't meant that one, I mean the one at the Sandbox."

Dani stared at him for a moment, then murmured, "Gosh, yes, I remember now. Theresa said we received a flyer about a dance. I was busy at the time, didn't pay much attention. I didn't realize it was at the Sandbox."

Brian nodded. "Seems old Josh has put in a dance floor. He's got a live group coming from Tacoma. The grand opening is a week tomorrow. Semiformal yet, suits, ties, cocktail dresses, the works."

Typical of a high-powered Falkirk, she thought. Adrian suggests a dance floor, next thing you know, there it is. Actually Chet had told her about the dance floor—he'd put together a crew to work on it, along with a whole new decor which he couldn't talk about. It was supposed to be a surprise.

And as it looked as if Adrian had gone ahead and invested in the Sandbox as he'd intended, she thought in the next moment, he would no doubt be at the dance.

Dammit, why should she sit home just so she'd avoid seeing Adrian? She'd left Seattle to avoid Jon, she couldn't keep tailoring her life around Falkirks. "I'd love to go with you," she said, again more emphatically than she'd intended.

Brian's face lit up and he reached across the table to take her hand in his. She let him take it, but looked at him directly. "I'll be happy to go to the dance with you, Brian," she said gently. "But just as your friend, not your date. I don't want you getting all possessive the way you did at the fire. We don't have that kind of relationship."

He nodded eagerly. "I know, Dani, really I do. I just thought it would be more fun if we could go together."

That sounded very sensible, but at the same time his hand was pressing hers far too intimately, and she had the idea he was hoping the romantic ambience associated with dancing might cause her to change her mind.

What romantic ambience? she asked herself, remembering what Adrian had told her about the Sandbox.

She was going to have to remember Brian was too easily encouraged, she thought later as she got ready for bed. Pulling her robe over her nightgown, she went into the living room, pulled out the Hide-A-Bed mattress and made it up with sheets and a quilt and pillow.

She felt restless, she decided. Going upstairs, she looked around her new master bedroom, which was almost finished now, then wandered into the new bathroom. Turning on the light, she checked out the phenomenon she'd noticed earlier. Where the mirrors on two walls came together, she could see endless reflections of herself, stretching out into infinity. It seemed to her that if she looked at all those reflections long enough, she could begin to comprehend how Adrian felt about being confused with his twin brother.

Suppose one of those reflections was not a reflection after all. Suppose it was another person, not herself, even though it looked exactly like herself. How would she feel about that?

Confused.

Sighing, she turned out the light, went back downstairs and crawled into the Hide-A-Bed sofa. This was her first night back in her own house and she was going to close off her thoughts and go to sleep.

SHE AWOKE less than an hour later. It was midnight, she saw when she glanced at the digital alarm clock she'd placed on the floor next to the Hide-A-Bed. What on earth was she doing awake? It was profoundly dark. No moon.

Something had awakened her.

Listening, huddled under her quilt, she heard the surf beating on the beach, advancing and retreating, the wind moaning through the lock on the French doors that opened onto her new deck, and off in the distance, the mournful sound of a foghorn. And something else, something unfamiliar. A faint crackling sound.

Apart from the Hide-A-Bed sofa, the living room was empty. Probably the baseboard heaters had come on. The lack of furniture and carpeting created echoes.

Her nose twitched. What was that smell?

Sighing, she turned over, pulling the quilt with her. If she let herself imagine she smelled something, she'd come wide awake trying to figure out what it might be. It was probably just the new paint.

It wasn't paint.

Sitting up in bed, Dani inhaled deeply, analyzing.

Smoke.

But she hadn't lit the fire since the remodeling began. And she hadn't cooked in the house, either.

Probably it was her imagination, stimulated by Brian talking about the fire in his restaurant.

She glanced at the bay windows. Was it also her imagination that it didn't seem quite so dark out there after all?

Sliding her legs out from under the covers, she sat for a moment on the edge of the bed, decided she needed to go to the bathroom, and pulled on the robe she'd slung on top of the quilt earlier. Padding barefoot down the hall, muttering to herself about stupid people who couldn't sleep once they imagined something was wrong, even though they *knew* nothing could be wrong, she stopped dead. Beneath the door to the back bedroom she used as a home office, light was flickering where no light should be.

Flinging open the door, she gasped in horror. Around the closed slats of her new miniblinds radiated a light that was brighter than sunshine. Racing to the window, she yanked on the blind cord, so clumsy in her haste to get the shade up that she almost pulled the whole fitting from the frame.

For a full minute, she stood paralyzed, blinded by the orange glare. Behind the house, no more than twelve feet from where she was standing, the trailer she'd occupied until this morning was completely ablaze, flames leaping high as the wind from the ocean whipped around the house and sent them flaring. One small change in wind direction and the house itself would be in danger.

Rushing back to the living room, shock making her heart pound, she switched on a light, looked around wildly for the telephone and found it on a shelf in the built-in china cabinet. Grabbing it to her, she hurriedly punched out 911.

CHAPTER ELEVEN

ADRIAN'S MEETING had lasted well into the previous evening, the men and women present almost vibrating with excitement, such was the power of the Falkirk name—and the money it represented. Afterward, the mall developer and the owner of a discount clothing store, called for some unknown reason The Pink Flamingo, had insisted on taking Adrian out for a late dinner—which had made him even later—and had attempted to ply him with whiskey. After two drinks, Adrian had decided to spend the night at a motel in Baxter, rather than drive, for the third time in one day, the dark and winding road that linked Baxter to the coast.

At seven on Saturday morning, he pulled in to Murre Bay, feeling bleary-eyed and irritable. He must have become used to peaceful nights—highway traffic through Baxter had woken him up several times and each time he had lain awake for a while, feeling the unaccustomed alcohol racing around in his bloodstream. A hot shower and a good breakfast would perk him up, he decided as he pulled his tie loose. Maybe he could even get in a little clam digging this afternoon before returning to Baxter for the next round of talks. Judging by the brightness just becoming visible through the light cloud cover, it seemed possible that the sun might make an appearance sometime today.

He'd take time off tomorrow, he promised himself. He had to watch getting too bound up in work again, even if prospects did look great. He wished he could talk to Dani about his new project, but right now he was afraid she might find it threatening rather than exciting.

Without really meaning to, he had turned onto Seaview Way, he realized. Which was out of his way. Had he taken to driving past Dani's house now, like a lovesick teenager, just to be in the vicinity of the woman he loved and could not seem to win?

A couple of minutes later, he slammed on the brakes, stopping the car so abruptly he would have gone through the windshield if his seat belt hadn't been fastened. Behind Dani's house was a mound of charred rubble surrounded by a blackened metal skeleton, the whole thing roped off with yards of yellow fire department tape. Obviously, the debris represented what was left of Dani's trailer.

Adrian's heart contracted with shock into a hard ball. For a long moment he could only sit paralyzed behind the wheel, regarding the scene with stunned astonishment, while his brain tried to comprehend what had happened. Then he shot out of his car, vaulted over the tape and raced to Danielle's back door, on which he pounded for a full minute before realizing the house must be empty. Running around to the ocean side, he peered in the bay windows, confirming that no one was present.

Refusing to conjecture, because it was totally unthinkable that anything could have happened to Dani, he debated rousing neighbors, demanding to know where she was. But there were no vehicles parked outside any of the nearest houses—possibly they were in their owners' garages, or possibly the houses were used for vacation or weekend purposes only. In any case, if anything bad had happened to Danielle, he didn't want to hear it from strangers.

Steff, he thought finally, forcing his numb brain to come up with some logical course of action. Steff would know.

Afterward, he had no memory of driving to Steff's house, though he did remember his tires squealing around corners, so it seemed possible he might have exceeded the speed limit. Even so, it seemed to take forever for him to reach his destination.

Lights were on in Steff's house, shining upward into her glass tower. Dani's car was not parked in her driveway.

His stomach tied in a knot of anxiety, Adrian got out of his car and approached Steff's entryway. Now that he was here, he was almost afraid to knock. Gripping the doorjamb, he sent up a silent prayer that consisted mostly of Dani's name repeated over and over. This seemed to calm him and he managed at last to ring the doorbell.

Dani answered the door.

She was fully dressed in jeans and a pink sweater, her shining blond hair neatly combed into place, curving back over her ears. Her face was pale, her eyes deeply shadowed.

All of this Adrian noted as he continued to cling to the doorjamb, seemingly unable to release the death grip of his hand. His heart was still skittering around in his chest like a wild thing. "You're all right," he finally managed to croak out through a throat that had closed up on him.

She nodded and at last he was able to let go of the doorframe. "Could you possibly hold me for a minute?" she asked in a very small voice.

He opened his arms and she walked into them, laying her face against his shoulder. He held her without speaking for the longest time, feeling tremors go through her body, and possibly through his.

Her hair smelled of some mildly spicy shampoo, clean and lemony. He could feel her heart beating in counterpoint to his own. He thought that if he could just stand there forever, half inside Steff's doorway, with Dani in his arms, he would be a happy man. If he had lost her...

Had he lost her? He had sent her away, given her an ultimatum—see me as myself or forget the whole thing. She was remembering that now, he felt sure. Even though she was in his arms, there was constraint between them. Jon was between them, creating a barrier, smiling mischievously, pleased to be center stage. What if that didn't change? What if she never could see beyond Jon to Adrian?

She had to. Once on a shining December evening she had seen him clearly for one bright moment in time. Surely she would again. If he could just hold out long enough.

He felt exhausted suddenly, like a rag doll that had lost its stuffing. "I thought...God knows what I thought," he murmured against her hair.

"You saw the trailer?"

"Yes." Loosening his grip fractionally, he leaned his head back and gazed at her face. His brain still wasn't functioning properly. Since the moment he'd looked out at that mass of blackened rubble, he had apparently become incapable of coherent thought. All he could do was hold her, stare at her, try to convince himself that she really was okay. "I was terrified," he said huskily.

A ghost of a smile twitched one corner of her mouth. "Me too." She touched his face lightly with one cool hand. For just a second, her thumb grazed the corner of his mouth, then her eyes darkened and he knew she was remembering how it had been—the two of them together. Their eyes met and held, then abruptly she dropped her hand and moved out of his arms. The Snow Queen had retreated behind the palace walls one more time. "I guess your electric razor wasn't broken after all," she said in a stilted way.

Adrian managed to produce a rueful smile. You didn't like my beard, did you?"

She shook her head. "It didn't match the Falkirk image."

"That was the idea."

He watched her face carefully as she puzzled over his comment, but all she said was, "Did you *like* having a beard?"

"I hated it. It itched like the devil."

"Why did you grow it, then?"

Once more, he looked searchingly at her. "I grew it for you."

She opened her mouth to say something, closed it again, shook her head and again seemed about to speak when Steff's familiar gravelly voice interrupted. "Do you two suppose you could stop canoodling and come in and close that door?"

They both laughed, a little awkwardly, and turned away from each other. "Canoodling?" Adrian queried as he and Dani entered the kitchen.

Steff was standing at the sink, rinsing out a coffee decanter. She smirked at him. "Canoodling is an obscure term meaning to indulge in caresses and fondling," she informed him. "I certainly hope that's what you were doing. I try to live vicariously whenever I can."

"Steff," Dani protested.

Adrian made a face at the older woman, stopped to check on Boots and her kittens in their basket, then straightened to kiss Steff lightly on the cheek. "We were having a serious discussion about my formerly scruffy appearance."

She patted his face and grinned. "I liked the beard. Made you look dangerously sexy."

"I don't look sexy now?"

She gave him a penetrating once-over, her brown eyes glinting. "Yeah, you do, as a matter of fact. Never saw you in a suit before. Always was a sucker for a man in a suit. Especially a designer suit," she added, rubbing the fabric of his lapel between thumb and forefinger. "Have you been playing captain of industry?"

"Something like that."

She raised her eyebrows. "You had your meeting in Baxter?"

He nodded.

Steff glanced at Dani and he shook his head slightly. "Gotcha," she said. "I'll catch up later. You want some coffee? We're on about our fourth pot."

Adrian nodded and sat down at the kitchen table. Dani sat opposite him. "I've a thousand questions and I can't even frame the first one," he said.

"You could start with 'What the hell happened?'" Steff suggested over her shoulder.

Adrian laughed shortly. "Okay. Consider it asked."

Dani's hands were clasped so tightly on the table that her knuckles showed white. He wanted to cover them with his own, but was too aware of Steff's amused gaze and Dani's own wariness.

"I smelled smoke," Dani said flatly. "It was around midnight. I'd gone to bed fairly early. Then I woke up. The trailer was blazing like mad. I called the fire department but the trucks were already on the way—someone on the next street had seen the flames. The firemen had it out in no time. But I couldn't face staying alone in the house, and Kurt Webber didn't think it was a good idea, either."

"Arson?" Adrian asked.

She shuddered, her hands gripping each other even more tightly. Then she nodded.

Adrian swore.

"I called Steff," Dani went on as Steff poured coffee for all three of them. She hesitated, glanced at Steff, then back at Adrian. "Actually," she said slowly, "I called you first, but..."

She had thought of him first. In danger, frightened, she had thought of him. For the first time since that fateful Sunday he felt encouraged. "I was in Baxter," he explained. "I had a meeting, then a late dinner."

She frowned. "I thought you were probably still at your friends' place."

He shook his head. "We came back yesterday morning. I dropped Mike off at home, changed my clothes and went to Baxter. It was late when I got through, so I spent the night in a motel."

"You dropped Mike..." She broke off, shaking her head. "Anyway, when you didn't answer, I called Steff and she came and got me. I wasn't sure I was in any condition to even try to back my car out of the garage." She shrugged and attempted a smile that didn't quite come off. "I was a little shaky."

He put his hands over hers. "I'm sorry I wasn't there for you."

Her eyes looked huge in her pale face, their color somehow faded in the bright light of Steff's kitchen.

The image of that blackened rubble flashed into Adrian's mind and he gripped the cup Steff had put in front of him, feeling suddenly savage. If Dani had been harmed, he would have wanted to kill whoever was responsible. Even though she was sitting here in front of him, obviously unhurt, fury was racing through him, making him want to hit out at whomever had put her in danger.

Who, that was the question.

Steff sat down and stirred milk into her coffee cup. There was an odd expression on her lined face. "You dropped Mike off at home?" she asked.

Frowning, he nodded, then stiffened as his brain produced a possible reason for her question. "You're surely not thinking Mike was involved?"

"Kurt Webber said the MO was almost the same as at Surf and Turf," Steff said quietly. "Gasoline. Quite a lot of it. Apparently the arsonist or arsonists broke into the trailer, poured a gallon or so over the upholstery and set it alight."

"So they knew Danielle wasn't in there."

"It would seem so."

He let out a long breath, then shook his head. "Michael wouldn't have . . ."

"I didn't want to believe Mike had anything to do with the fire, either," Dani interrupted, her voice ragged. "But Kurt was going to barrel on over to the Caswells. So I called Chet. It must have been around two in the morning by then. Chet said as far as he knew Mike was still with you, he hadn't come home."

A familiar, tight band had wrapped itself around Adrian's temples—a sure sign of stress. He couldn't believe, didn't want to believe . . . "Not Mike," he said flatly.

"Face facts, Falkirk," Steff said. "It's entirely possible Mike was in cahoots with those two hoods for both fires."

Adrian shook his head. "There's no way I can reconcile arson with the boy who was almost in tears over an injured great blue heron. If you'd heard his voice when he spoke to that bird . . . So gentle."

"You're sure you're not just remembering your own teen years—you said you were misunderstood but you weren't guilty of anything. Maybe you're projecting that innocence onto Mike."

Again Adrian shook his head.

"Where is he, then?" Steff asked.

Tightening his grip on Dani's hands, Adrian asked her, "Did anyone see anything, or anybody?"

"Apparently not. Kurt's going to send someone to question more of the neighbors this morning. But those who came out when the fire trucks arrived—and there was quite a crowd—hadn't noticed anyone in the area before the fire started. It was dark of course, no moonlight, no streetlights. And the two houses behind me aren't occupied at this time of the year. The neighbors on either side are in, but their bedrooms are at the front of their houses to take advantage of the view. Anyone could have fooled around out back. Not much traffic on my part of Seaview Way at that time of night."

Adrian drank some of his coffee. It was hot and strong, revitalizing. "I think I'd better go look for Mike," he said grimly. He glanced at Steff. "Could you hang on to Boots and family for a while longer?"

"My pleasure," Steff said. "I've put a requisition in on the all-black kitten, by the way. I'm convinced she likes my kitchen better than yours."

Adrian smiled at her, feeling his tension lighten a little.

"The fire may not have anything to do with Michael's friends," Dani said slowly. "We don't even know for sure that they set fire to Surf and Turf—it's all conjecture...."

"You saw them hanging around outside the restaurant," Steff reminded her, her voice harsh. "You told Milburn, Milburn told the chief. And according to Chet, Mike had guessed that you'd reported the incident. If Michael mentioned that to his friends, they might have wanted revenge."

Dani sighed wearily. "That still doesn't mean Mike was involved."

"I'll find Mike," Adrian said. "But first I'd better call Chet, see if we can figure out what happened between the time I dropped Mike off and he disappeared."

Mike *had* gone home on Friday morning, Chet told him on the phone a couple of minutes later. His mother had been afraid to admit as much. Chet had wormed the truth out of her this morning. By the time Adrian had dropped Mike off, around eleven a.m., Chet had already gone to check on progress at the Sandbox, then he'd gone on to Doctor Kelsey's house. "The kids were in school, of course," he added. "Only Mom saw Mike. When I came home Mike wasn't there and Mom had gone to work at the hotel. I just took it for granted you'd both stayed over at the wildlife refuge another day."

He hesitated, and when he resumed speaking his voice sounded grim. "I don't know what to tell you, Mr. Falkirk. According to Mom, just before she went to work, around noon, Mike had a phone call. He didn't tell her who from. After school, the kids go to a neighbor's house until either Mom or I get home. They didn't see Mike, either. I've no idea where he spent the night."

Adrian swore again. Still sitting at the kitchen table, Steff and Dani looked at him with alarm. "Mike had a phone call soon after I brought him home," he told them, putting his hand over the telephone mouthpiece." His mother left for work right after that. Nobody's seen him since.

"I'm going to look for him," he told Chet. "Did he take his bike?"

"I didn't think to check," Chet said, then a minute later reported, "It's gone. So is his sleeping bag."

DANI INSISTED on going with Adrian to look for Mike, first calling Theresa at home to tell her to reschedule her morning appointments. "I wouldn't have been much use to my patients, anyway," she said as she settled herself in the BMW next to Adrian. "By now, knowing Murre Bay, they'll all have heard about the fire, so they won't be surprised when Theresa calls. None of them had urgent problems. Theresa's going to call Stasny and ask him to stand by at the clinic in case of any emergencies."

"You sure you're up to this?" Adrian asked. She'd regained a little color, but she looked . . . fragile.

She nodded. "I need to do *something*," she said. "I just don't want to believe Mike had anything to do with that fire."

"Me neither." Adrian remembered even as he spoke that Mike had seemed very subdued on their return trip from the refuge, and perhaps angry with Adrian for not arranging for him to go to work for Jorge. No, he thought at once, he wasn't going to suspect Mike just because he seemed a likely suspect. That kind of attitude caused more problems than it cured.

After stopping at Adrian's house so he could change his clothes, Dani hovering in the entryway as though she feared coming in any farther, they headed for the derelict car where they'd last found Michael hiding out. The police hadn't got around to towing it away yet, but it was empty. If there had been any footprints around it, they had washed away in the previous night's extrahigh tide. There was nothing inside it, no sleeping bag, no paper bag full of provisions, no sketchbook.

They checked the local parks, the pond where Dani said Mike had liked to go to watch birds, the schoolyard, the bus shelters, the marina, the beach closer to downtown. No Mike. Finally they drove to Dani's house. Dani paled again when she walked past the charred skeleton of her trailer. Adrian put his arm around her shoulders. She looked at him, but as far as he could tell, the only element in her expression was gratitude for being there. Her shoulders felt stiff, he thought.

Chet and one of his men were putting up wallpaper in Dani's new bedroom suite. Chet's face tightened when Adrian told him they hadn't come across Mike yet. "You have any ideas?" Adrian asked him. "Places he likes to go, places he might hide out in, friends' houses?"

Chet shook his head. "I called all his friends before coming over here. Nobody's seen him." He frowned, wiping his hands on an old rag. "He could have gone to Baxter, I suppose. He's hitched there on numerous occasions. Or he might have had a ride with someone I haven't thought of."

They were all silent for a minute, probably thinking, as Adrian was, that if Mike had been given a ride, it might have been with his two Tacoma friends, Ox and Scooter. And if he *was* with them, then he might have helped them fire Dani's trailer.

"I'd better go looking for him myself." Chet flexed his fingers. "One thing for sure, I'm going to throttle him when he turns up."

"*We'll* find him," Dani said hastily.

Adrian put a hand on Chet's shoulder. "No sense speculating. Mike might have gone anywhere, with anyone, or he might be somewhere perfectly innocent, alone."

A sudden thought occurred to him. Some time ago—the night of the Surf and Turf fire—Mike had said he'd been way down by the harbor, on the beach. "Let's go," he said to Dani, turning back to Chet as they headed for the stairs. "Don't worry, okay?" he added, more positively than he felt. "We won't give up until we find him."

Chet nodded, looking miserable.

DANI SAW THE WISPY column of smoke as Adrian slid the BMW into a parking slot. It hung above an area of the harbor beach where driftwood had been piled high by storms. It was strictly illegal, of course, to light a fire in amongst driftwood, but many people ignored that fact.

She pointed and Adrian nodded, looking grim. For a minute, they stood in the parking lot, gazing at the smoke. Probably Adrian felt as torn as she did. She wanted to find Mike, of course, but now that it seemed possible they had found him, she was afraid to find out why he'd disappeared.

She glanced at Adrian, standing silent and tense beside her. "How's your great blue heron?" she suddenly remembered to ask.

"He was doing okay when we left the refuge. Not happy, though. Jorge thinks he'll come out of it okay, but we won't know for a while if he'll be able to fly again. If he can, we'll bring him back here. If he can't, Jorge will keep him."

She nodded, appreciating the concerned tone in his voice. Now that he'd shaved off his beard, he was immaculate again, she thought, though the slight curl to his thick black hair saved him from appearing too neat. She could still feel the smoothness of his cheek against her fingers.

He also looked very sexy in jeans and a sweater and a leather jacket—a far cry from the elegantly suited Adrian Falkirk who had shown up at Steff's house earlier. That Adrian had reawakened a partial memory that kept hovering around the edges of her mind, haunting her. So far she hadn't managed to resurrect all of it. "Why on earth would you grow a beard for me?" she asked abruptly.

A wry smile glimmered in his blue eyes. "I'd hoped it would make me look different to you. Less like Jon."

Every once in a while he said something that left her absolutely speechless. It had never occurred to her that he would try to alter his appearance—for her. "Adrian," she began, but he put his hand on her shoulder and shook his head. "I know. It was a bad idea. I'm still

Jon's twin brother, beard or no beard." He took a breath and let it out on a sigh. "Shall we go?"

Mike had spiked a wiener on a peeled twig and was holding it over the fire when they scrambled over the driftwood and arrived at his campsite slightly out of breath. He'd had his hair cut, Dani noticed at once.

"Hey," he said. His eyes shifted away from their combined gazes almost immediately, but not before Dani saw a glimmer of relief in his expression as he looked at her. He knew about the fire, she thought with a sinking sensation in her middle. The question was, how had he known?

"You want a hot dog?" His voice sounded cheerful but had a pronounced tremor to it. "Got a packet of buns here." He nodded at the backpack attached to the back of the old bicycle lying next to him. "Fix you up in no time."

Dani couldn't think of anything she wanted less at this time of the morning, but Adrian accepted for both of them. Sitting on a log across from Mike, he took the wiener the teenager offered him and helped himself to a bun. After digging in his jacket pocket Mike handed over several tiny packets of ketchup and mustard of the kind given out in fast-food restaurants, then started cooking another wiener.

Without comment, Adrian dressed the bun and passed it to Dani. About to refuse, Dani met his steady gaze. Immediately, she sat down and took the hot dog from him. She could read his mind, it seemed. The code of the wild. Share food around a campfire and you build friendship . . . and trust. Okay, she could go along with that. She took a bite of the hot dog. To her surprise, it tasted delicious.

"You've been here all night?" she asked Mike as Adrian put together the next hot dog for himself.

Mike nodded.

He wasn't going to offer any gratuitous information, that was obvious. "Cold last night," she commented.

"Brought my down sleeping bag," he muttered.

Now what? She looked at Adrian for guidance, but he was finishing off his hot dog with every appearance of enjoyment.

There was a silence. Then Mike lit a cigarette. His hand was shaking, Dani noted. He was hunched down into his sheepskin-lined denim jacket, gazing into the small fire as if he saw visions there.

"You got a spare?" Adrian asked.

Mike's head came up in surprise. "Man, I thought you quit."

What happened to all that stuff about setting a good example? Dani wondered.

Adrian grinned at the boy. "Sometimes I have a weak moment."

Again Dani was able to guess at the workings of his mind. If he admitted to weakness perhaps the boy would admit to his. Very clever. But would it work?

The two of them smoked companionably for a minute, then Adrian stubbed out his cigarette and gazed around at the scenery. It was a lovely clear morning, cold but bright. "Mount Rainier's out," he commented.

"You should have seen it with the sun coming up." Mike had suddenly waxed enthusiastic. "Top of it looked like a strawberry ice-cream sundae. Beautiful."

Another silence. Then Mike said, "I guess you came looking for me."

Adrian nodded. "We got a little worried when Chet said you hadn't come home all night." He laughed. "I stayed out all night myself. In Baxter. Warmer than this though—I stayed in a motel."

"You make it in time for your meeting?" Mike asked.

"Just."

Dani wondered briefly about this meeting. It had been mentioned before. Steff had gone all mysterious when Adrian brought it up. They were two of a kind, Adrian and Steff—they both loved making mysteries. It was none of her business what Adrian did with his time, of course, but she was definitely curious. "Did you go to see Dr. Platt?"

Adrian nodded. "Several days ago."

So much for the devious approach.

"My trailer burned down last night," she said to Mike, keeping her voice as casual as Adrian had kept his.

He hunched down again. "I know."

Above his head, Dani and Adrian exchanged a swift glance. "Who told you?" Adrian asked.

Mike's head came up and he stared at Adrian. "Hey, man," he said with an obvious note of relief in his voice. "I was sure you'd think I did it."

"No way."

"Not on your life," Dani agreed as the boy swung his head to look questioningly at her.

Mike's smile was dazzling. "Wow," he exclaimed. "The minute I saw you, I thought for sure you were coming to drag me off so the cops could lock me up and throw away the key."

Adrian's smile showed what a ridiculous idea that had been. He was a terrific man, Dani thought. He was obviously working hard to win this boy's trust, just as obviously determined not to make any accusations, or reveal that he might have suspected Mike at all.

"I rode my bike into town real early," Mike said. "Went by Doc's place and saw the mess. I figured out what had happened."

"So then you came back here?" There was just a bare note of curiosity in Adrian's voice, but it was enough to cause sudden color to flush Mike's cheekbones.

Of course, Dani realized. If Mike was completely innocent, why would he come back here?

"I heard you had a phone call," Adrian said after another drawn out silence.

Mike nodded, looking miserable again. "Guess I'd better tell you what happened, huh?"

"It might be a good idea."

Mike took a deep breath, reached in his pocket and pulled out the pack of cigarettes again. He offered one to Adrian, but Adrian shook his head, smiling. "My moment of weakness is over." His steady gaze met and held Mike's.

Mike nodded as though he understood Adrian's underlying message, then lit up. It took three matches to get the cigarette going. "Ox called me from Tacoma," he muttered after a long drag. "Said he and Scooter were coming out to the coast and I should meet them at the little park on Scoter Lake, around nine o'clock."

"Last night?"

"You got it."

"Okay." Obviously Adrian had decided to let Mike tell this in his own way.

"I thought about going to meet them. Like I told you, they've been good to me, stopped guys hassling me and stuff. Promised me if anybody did anything wrong to me, they'd get hurt. It was a big power thing. Felt good, you know? But then I thought about Jorge and Consuelo and how nice they were to me, and I remembered what you said about being judged by the dudes you're hanging out with."

Dani was fairly sure Adrian had put the message a little differently, but it was obvious he'd made some headway with the teenager. It was also obvious he wasn't going to remind Mike that he had trusted him, that the chief had let him go only because Adrian accepted responsibility for him. Reminders like that would put pressure on Mike. It was much better to give him a chance to reach a decision to come clean by himself. Once again, she tried to imagine Jon doing all Adrian had done for Mike, and couldn't.

"I take it you didn't go to meet them," Adrian said.

Mike sighed. "Tell you the truth, Mr. Falkirk, part of it was being scared of what they might be planning to do."

"Did they mention any plans?"

"Nope. But Ox had this, like . . . excited sound in his voice, so I guessed they had something in mind." He turned to look at Dani, hunching into his collar again. "If I'd known what it was, I'd have told you, Doc," he said firmly. "Cross my heart and hope to die."

"I know you would, Michael," she said softly.

Mike had turned back to Adrian. "I called you to see what I should do, but you weren't home."

Adrian winced. "See if I spend a night in Baxter ever again." He looked at Mike with that steady gaze that always affected Dani so strongly. "You could have told Chet." It was the closest he had come to criticism.

Mike flushed. "The old Chet, maybe. Not the way he is now."

"Chet's had a lot on his mind. I think maybe things are picking up for him. You might find him more like his old self pretty soon."

"Yeah?" There was a lot of doubt in Mike's voice. He shook his head. "Anyway, I decided to split for a while. Then this morning, when I saw Doc's trailer, I was scared again, afraid someone would say I'd done it. People make up their minds to something like that, no way in the world I could prove I didn't do it."

"Are you saying Ox and Scooter set fire to the trailer?" Adrian said.

Mike looked at him earnestly. "I've no way of saying they did or they didn't."

"But you think they did? You said they seemed to be planning something. Did they set the fire at Surf and Turf?"

Mike shrugged. "I don't know that, either, Mr. Falkirk. I swear. They were mad about being thrown out, but they never said anything to me about torching the place. And all Ox said to me last night was it was a good thing the cops didn't know where they lived."

"Did you take that as a threat?" Adrian asked.

Mike looked miserable. "They're my friends, Mr. Falkirk."

"Do you know where they live?" Dani asked very softly.

He glanced at her, fear showing stark in his hazel eyes. He didn't answer. Dani glanced at Adrian and he nodded slightly. Yes, Mike knew.

"When I saw that trailer, I thought maybe you had been in it," Mike said. "When you came across that driftwood just now I was real relieved, you know."

He hunched further down into his jacket. He was obviously torn. On the one hand, he felt loyalty to the two men he thought of as his friends. On the other was his new-found loyalty to Adrian and perhaps some respect for Dani. Mixed with all that was fear. The back of his neck, exposed by his recent haircut, was paler than the rest of his skin. It made him look extremely vulnerable.

Adrian looked at him steadily. "What do you think you should do now?"

Another silence. Dani wanted to touch the boy's shoulder, let him know she understood his dilemma, but she was afraid to make any motion that might upset the delicate balance of a moment that had the potential of changing Michael Caswell's life forever.

Abruptly, Mike stood up and climbed over the driftwood, then walked toward the water, head down, hands in jacket pockets. Dani glanced at Adrian and he shook his head. In silence they watched the teenager. He stood still for some time, gazing in the direction of Mount Rainier's distant peak. Then he turned his attention to the small birds skittering at his feet. Finally he came back and sat down again. "Sanderlings," he said to Adrian.

Adrian raised his eyebrows. "*Calidris alba,*" he said, then glanced at Dani as Mike grinned. "Mike and I have a competition going," he explained. "Who can memorize the most Latin bird names. He's way ahead of me, of course."

He directed a look of patient enquiry at Mike and the boy nodded. "I guess I have to go to the police," he said.

Dani saw Adrian let out a long breath. "You do know your friends' address?"

Mike nodded again and Adrian reached over and clasped his shoulder. "Seems to me you just became a man," he said softly.

Mike beamed. "Will you come with me to the police station?"

To Dani's surprise, Adrian shook his head. "I think you should ask Chet to go with you."

Mike thought that over for a minute, the expression on his face starting with a frown that cleared eventually to produce a pleased grin. Standing up, he kicked sand over his fire. "Okay," he said.

Behind him Dani and Adrian exchanged a relieved smile.

DANI AND ADRIAN stood in one of Dani's bay windows, looking out at the ocean. After shaking Adrian's hand with obvious relief and gratitude, Chet had gone off to the police station with Mike, putting his arm around his brother's shoulders as they left the house.

While she and Adrian had been talking to Mike, Dani's shower stall had arrived and above their heads several workmen were struggling to get it in place. So much banging, sliding, and general clattering was going on that Dani wondered, shuddering, if the shower stall and men were about to come crashing down through her ceiling.

The sun was high, the ocean dappled with dancing light, the edges of the waves frothing white. It was well past noon and the tide was out. Several hundred clam diggers were assaulting the sand with shovels and the silver metal cylinders called clam guns. Already the beach looked like a lunar landscape, pitted with mini-craters.

"Do you think the police will hold Mike?" she asked.

"Unfortunately, no."

Astonished, she stared at Adrian's stern profile. "You want him to be arrested?"

He sighed, turning to look at her. For someone who had just persuaded a rebellious teenager to act like a responsible adult, he didn't look at all happy. Bleak might be a better description of the expression in his eyes. "He might be safer in jail."

A cold chill jolted along Dani's spine. "You think he'll be in danger?"

"Those so-called friends of his are possibly gang members. Gangs don't usually take kindly to informers."

Dani shivered.

"I talked to Chet about it," Adrian said, rubbing the back of his neck. Dani remembered him taking Chet aside while Michael was in her downstairs bathroom, freshening up to present a good appearance to the police. "I wasn't sure if Chet would realize the dangers. But he was way ahead of me. We agreed that if the police don't hold Mike, one of us will be with him at all times until those two are arrested."

"You're a good man, Adrian Falkirk," Dani said softly.

He smiled at her and lightly touched her face. She thought for a moment he was going to take her in his arms, perhaps even kiss her, but then his expression hardened again and his hand dropped to his side. "Has it occurred to you that you could be in danger yourself?"

"I don't see why I would be," she protested, even though her blood was running cold again. "I do think it's probable the burning of my trailer was an act of revenge, but now they've had their revenge, why would they bother with me?"

"Because once Mike gives their address to the police, they'll wonder who talked him into doing that. And might possibly come up with your name. Besides which," he added as she began to protest again, "gang members don't always worry about logic." He shook his head. "You can't stay here, that's for sure."

"Adrian!" Her voice was almost a wail. "I just moved back in after weeks of rattling around in that damn trailer."

He held her gaze. "Grow up, Danielle," he said harshly. "You're in danger here."

About to yell at him for treating her like a child, she realized she was acting like one. "You're right, of course," she muttered. "If there's any possibility of danger, I'd be stupid to stay here alone. I'll ask Steff if I can sleep at her place for a while."

He frowned. "I'm not sure that's any better."

"Sure it is. My answering service will forward my calls without anyone being any the wiser. I certainly won't tell anyone I'm staying there. I can put my car in Steff's garage."

"Anyone could follow you there."

"So I'll take a circuitous route, make sure I'm not being tailed." She shook her head. "Good grief, I can't believe we're talking all this cloak-and-dagger stuff, not in Murre Bay."

"You could stay with me."

Startled, she met his gaze. His eyes were a curiously electric blue in the strong light reflected off the ocean. "Oh, well, I hardly think..."

He shook his head. "You're quite right. You're too well known here—the town doctor—it wouldn't be good for your reputation."

It wasn't her reputation she was worried about. How could she possibly stay under the same roof as Adrian when her entire nervous system became battle-ready when she merely looked at him. Nothing had changed. Yes, she still wanted to make love with him, but that didn't mean her body wasn't still responding to old memories. *Make up your mind, one way or the other,* Adrian had said. But how could she ever be sure?

Adrian had not shifted his gaze while these thoughts scurried through her mind. And judging by the sad expression in his eyes, those same thoughts had transmitted themselves through the small space between them as clearly as if she had spoken them aloud. After all, if sexual impulses could arc between a man and a woman, why not thoughts?

"I guess I will sleep at Steff's, then," she said awkwardly.

He nodded, still not taking his gaze from her face. He seemed to be mulling something over. For a moment she thought she might be reading his mind again. Was he going to suggest she might spend the rest of the day with him? What would her answer be?

She'd say yes, she thought, almost with despair.

"I have to go into Baxter," he said abruptly and turned away. Glancing out at the clam diggers once more, he sighed in an almost wistful way, then shook his head. "I'll check with Chet tomorrow," he said briskly, heading toward the door. "I'll probably be late getting home tonight." Stopping abruptly, he looked back at her and again she thought he might intend arranging to see her later, but instead he said, "Make sure Steff locks her doors," which was solicitous of him, but hardly romantic.

Grow up, Dani Kelsey, she scolded herself.

CHAPTER TWELVE

THE CHANGE IN the Sandbox was incredible. After checking their coats in the small foyer, Dani and Brian stopped just inside the doorway to the main room, staring around in amazement. Dance music was playing, the place was crowded and the majority of the customers were young couples, though Murre Bay's older population was fairly well represented. But what was truly astonishing was the look of the place, which Chet's crew, in a very short period of time, had transformed into a replica of a traditional English pub.

The wall that had separated two fairly large rooms had been cut back to form an archway; wainscoting and blackened beams had been added and the upper walls painted white. Even the low ceiling, formerly slightly claustrophobic, now seemed perfect for the decor. The long, well-scrubbed bar was the same, but the front of it had been panelled with rustic-looking wood. A huge mirror hung behind it, visually enlarging the space.

Each of the small round tables clustered near the bar had a candle lantern on it and enough cushioned chairs to seat four. Beyond the archway several pairs of dancers gyrated on a good-size dance floor, their music provided by a three-piece band on a raised platform.

"This is fantastic," Dani exclaimed as a waitress showed them to a table near the archway.

"Looks as if Josh aims to give me some competition," Brian said.

Dani sighed. Did he always have to find something negative to say? "He's hardly likely to draw the dining and drinking crowd," she pointed out tartly.

On each table was a drink list—a variety of fresh juices, just as Adrian had suggested, several espresso-type drinks, a virgin Bloody Mary, and the virgin strawberry daiquiri Adrian had decried.

Adrian. Why must her brain constantly toss up the man's name? she wondered, choosing to ignore the fact that she had been darting glances around the place ever since she got here, looking for that familiar, dark-haired, muscular figure. Well, it was odd that he wasn't here, considering the interest he had shown in the place.

And of course, at that precise moment, she caught sight of Adrian at one of the tables around the dance floor. He was wearing one of his beautifully tailored dark suits, his black hair tousled slightly over his forehead. Belatedly, she realized he was sitting with a beaming Steff, who was all dressed up in an apricot silk two-piece that made her look as elegant as her escort.

"Look at Steff," Dani exclaimed. "Isn't she beautiful?"

Brian swung his head, then scowled as he caught sight of Adrian. "You look very nice, too," he said loyally, turning back to Dani.

Very nice. Dani was wearing a sinfully expensive chemise in a shade of smoky blue chosen to match her eyes. It had a plunging neckline trimmed with bugle bead embroidery and it fitted her as if it had been made for her. She'd bought it on her last trip to Seattle before joining her father for *The Rocky Horror Picture Show.* Looking in the full-length mirror on the back of her bedroom door she had decided, rather smugly, that she looked definitely sexy.

Very nice. She sighed. Brian never had caught on to the knack of paying compliments.

Steff was waving. Now she was wending her way between tables toward them, followed, naturally, by Adrian. The compliment Brian hadn't quite managed showed clearly in Adrian's blue eyes as he looked at Dani. Either someone had turned up the Sandbox's thermostat or her traitorous body was betraying her again. Images coursed through her mind—images of flames dancing in a fireplace, casting shadows on two bodies that clung and parted and came together again.

"Isn't this exciting?" Steff exclaimed as she reached them. Her gaunt but beautiful face glowed. "You look marvelous, Kelsey. Doesn't she, Falkirk?"

Adrian smiled. "Fabulous," he said, which was a whole lot better than "very nice." Bending over the table, he touched the fabric of her sleeve. "Crepe de chine?" he asked, and when she nodded, looked her over fairly thoroughly, making heat rise to her cheeks. "Did you buy it at Falkirk's?"

"Nordstrom's Gallery," she said just as solemnly, unable to keep from laughing when he winced.

"What do you think of the Sandbox now?" Steff asked. "Look how many people are here. Oh, it's going to be a big success, I'm sure of it. I was so afraid the storm would hit early and nobody would come. There's one on the way from the southeast, and you know what that means. The wind will go whipping around the harbor and hit us like a ton of bricks." She looked around happily, sniffing. "Not a whiff of smoke in the whole place. Not that I'm militant about smoking," she added

apologetically to Adrian, "but it does seem whole-
some, doesn't it?"

Before Adrian could answer, she went on again, telling Brian, who had stood up, to sit down. "We aren't
staying, though Falkirk and I would love to join you
later, wouldn't we Falkirk? But we really have to talk to
Andersen."

With that she darted off toward the bar, Adrian once
more following after giving Dani a rueful smile that ef-
fectively whipped her nervous system into a frenzy.

"Why don't we dance?" she suggested to Brian,
feeling an abrupt need to move.

They joined the crowd on the dance floor, to various
greetings. Murre Bay's residents were a gregarious lot
and most of them knew Dani and Brian. The band was
good and the music lively—a medley of hits from the
fifties through the eighties, with a little country and
western thrown in for good measure. Pretty soon everyone was swapping partners—except for Adrian and
Steff who showed up for a couple of slow dances then
disappeared again. When the band finally took a break,
after a particularly wild number, both Dani and Brian
were perspiring. The waitress brought them fresh juice,
which tasted wonderful. Somebody opened a window
for a few minutes and the fresh sea air wafted in.

"I guess Josh is going to make a speech," Brian
commented.

Dani looked up to see big Josh Andersen standing in
front of the bar, holding a microphone and smiling
broadly. "Are we having fun yet?" he asked, and the
crowd roared "Yes."

His smile grew even wider. "We're going to do this
every Saturday from now on. We want you to let us
know if you have any suggestions for us in the way of

entertainment, or alcohol-free drinks. We want this to be a place you come to during the week to relax, and on weekends to party.''

More applause.

Then Josh said, ''In case you're all wondering who I mean by 'we,' I'd like to introduce you to my partner. The person responsible for all this.'' He waved his hand vaguely around. ''Not a silent partner by any means,'' he added with a robust laugh.

Dani braced herself for Brian's remarks once he found out Adrian Falkirk was behind this transformation but to her total astonishment the name that Josh spoke into the microphone was ''Steff Carmody.''

''Thank you,'' Steff said when the applause died down. ''Like Andersen, I want to welcome you to the Sandbox. We have a few more improvements in mind and we hope you'll help us make it something Murre Bay can be proud of. To start us off, we want you to stop by the notebook on the bar before you leave tonight, and write down your suggestions for a new name to go with our new look. We also want to inform you that we'll be working on the back room next, turning it into a meeting room that can be rented for private parties or group meetings. Thank you for your support.''

She had never seen Steff look quite as happy as she looked this evening, Dani decided, as the band began playing again. Perhaps the glow that surrounded her like an aura was entirely due to the apparent success of her new enterprise, or perhaps it had something to do with the bear hug Josh Andersen had given her as she finished her little speech.

''No wonder you've been the invisible woman lately,'' Dani said accusingly when Steff came over to join them. ''She's been coming in all hours of the night,'' she told

Brian. "I leave for the clinic in the morning, she's still asleep. I come back to the house at night, she's gone. Fine roommate, wouldn't you say?" She was joking, of course, but all the same, it had been a long and lonely week.

Steff grinned. "Surprised hell out of you didn't I? I was watching your face."

"I was expecting . . ."

"Falkirk, yes, I know." She put her hand on Dani's arm. "Don't be mad at him for not telling you, Kelsey. I made him promise. Chet, too. I've been dying to confide in you, but I felt like a kid before Christmas and I *liked* the feeling. It's been one hell of a long time since I had a secret of my very own. Andersen and I have all kinds of plans. We're going to take a trip up to Vancouver, British Columbia, in a month or so. Evidently there's a store there that specializes in pub stuff—horse brasses, toby jugs, dart boards. Andersen did some research and found out there's a special kind of dart board made with some kind of bristles that you just have to have for authenticity. We're going to put in a piano, too, and on Friday nights we plan to have sing-alongs like they do in real English pubs. 'Knees up Mother Brown,' 'The Lambeth Walk,' something called the 'Hokie Cokie.'" Her smile was radiant. She seemed at least twenty years younger. "Oh, it's all such fun."

"Looks as if you made a new friend, too," Dani said dryly, glancing to where Josh was tossing peeled oranges into the enormous juicer.

Steff grinned again and poked Dani's shoulder. "Don't go getting ideas, Kelsey. Andersen and I are just very good friends, as the saying goes. I must say though," she added with a flirtatious grin at Brian, "it's nice to be around male persons once in a while. Perhaps you can come up with a name for us, Milburn?''

Brian smiled. "How about the Queen's Arms?'' he suggested, which was amazingly witty for him.

"Might be too suggestive.'' Sometimes Steff's smile was positively wicked. "Andersen's rooting for the Rooster and Fox—customers to guess which of us is which.'' With an abrupt movement, she suddenly leaned across the table and touched Brian's hand. "How about a dance, Milburn, this one sounds staid enough for an old lady.''

"I'd be delighted.'' Brian stood up at once, though he looked strangely annoyed by the invitation.

Dani saw why in the next moment when Adrian Falkirk slid into the seat next to her. Obviously Steff was running interference again. "Danielle,'' Adrian said softly, with that same sensual note he always gave to her name.

She gripped the stem of her juice glass. "I hear you didn't have anything to do with all this, after all,'' she said lamely.

"Just in the suggestion stage. Steff took it from there as I'd hoped she would.''

"You do seem to get involved in other people's lives, don't you?''

"A man ought to have a hobby, don't you think?'' His voice was light, but his eyes showed her comment had hurt.

"I'm sorry,'' she said at once. "I can't seem to refrain from making nasty remarks to you.''

"It's okay, Danielle. You still owe me a couple of shots from the old days.''

There was a pregnant silence, which she broke by asking how he was getting along with Michael Caswell.

She'd heard from Chet that Mike had told the police everything he knew about Ox and Scooter, the previous weekend. He had not been held, but had been told not to leave town, which sounded rather alarming.

"We're doing fine," Adrian said. "I'm running out of jobs for him to do, though. We spend a lot of time jogging and fishing. I'm not sure how good that is for Mike's character, but it's certainly beneficial to my health."

"You look well," she said awkwardly. The understatement of the year. He looked fantastic—wind-tanned, well rested, his blue eyes clear. Obviously he wasn't losing any sleep over her, whereas she...

"Soon as the police catch up with Mike's former buddies and the fire incidents are settled, I'm going to take Mike back to the wildlife refuge," Adrian went on. "He calls Consuelo almost every day, checking on big bird, who is doing remarkably well, by the way."

He frowned down into the juice glass the waitress had put in front of him. "God, I'd give anything for a beer," he exclaimed.

Dani laughed. "I was just thinking a minute ago I could go for a glass of wine. Bad, aren't we?"

"Totally decadent." His smiling glance held hers just long enough to set her blood racing, then he drank some of his juice, his face sobering again. "Jorge and Consuelo are anxious to have Mike, and Mike's not exactly patient about waiting, but until this whole thing gets settled, we can't do much about it. Tacoma police are watching out for Ox and Scooter, but so far they haven't turned up at the address Mike provided. Someone must have tipped them off."

"You're still sure Mike can be trusted?"

"All the way." He paused and half turned in his chair, inclining his head as if he were listening to something. "He just needs a little maturing," he added in a vague way.

Dani sighed. "I'll be glad myself when they catch those guys. I can't wait to move back into my house even if I still don't have any furniture in it."

As if he hadn't heard her, he stood up abruptly. For one awful moment she thought he was going to walk away from her, and was immediately furious with herself for feeling bereft, but he didn't go, he took hold of the back of her chair and leaned over her. "I think they're playing our song," he murmured.

She laughed nervously as she accompanied him to the dance floor. "I didn't know we had one."

"Didn't you?" He smiled directly into her eyes, laugh lines crinkling, his own eyes glinting with some message she couldn't quite interpret. "I'm disappointed. I requested it especially for you."

His right arm slid around her, his left hand took hers. There was none of the usual uncertainty that often occurred with an unfamiliar dance partner; her feet seemed to have a life of their own, following automatically as he swung her expertly out to the middle of the floor.

His hand was firm against her spine, his shoulder solid against her cheek. The floor was even more crowded now and it was necessary to dance very close. Dani could hear a pulse beating in her ears that had nothing to do with the tempo of the music and everything to do with the tall, silent man steering her unerringly between the other couples. Their bodies moved well together, swaying and turning in perfect cadence. She was fully aware of the moment they danced past

Steff and Brian, aware of Brian's frown and Steff's just as predictable, approving smile. But some part of her brain was teasing her, trying to figure out what tune the band was playing.

And then Adrian began singing it softly in her ear. He had a pleasant voice, low and husky, precisely on key.

Winter Wonderland.

"A bit Christmassy, isn't it?" she murmured. "We haven't even had Thanksgiving yet."

Adrian leaned his head back, looking at her. The same message that had glinted in his eyes earlier was there again. And suddenly, seemingly out of nowhere, there came into her mind a vivid picture of him standing in a doorway, wearing an overcoat over a tuxedo, a white silk scarf. Snow crystals were shining in his dark hair.

She caught her breath and stumbled. Smoothly, Adrian changed step. He was smiling now. Lifting her right hand, he brushed his lips across her knuckles, then held her hand close to his chest. "The night we met," he murmured.

There was no way in the world she could look away from those vivid blue eyes. The expression in them was intense, almost hypnotic. "Yes," she whispered.

They continued to dance, looking at each other, their bodies moving automatically, but by no means jerkily. The music surrounded them, supporting Dani so that she floated on it. He was holding her even closer now, his fingers splayed across her back, pulling her in so that their lower bodies touched and moved together in a rhythm that was like lovemaking. Somehow without her noticing it, her left hand had moved from his shoulder to the back of his neck.

Adrian was no longer smiling. His eyes seemed heavy lidded, somber, his mouth stern. Such a beautiful mouth. She wanted to touch it.

And still the music played. The drummer was singing the words now, nudging Dani's mind to produce images of a Christmas tree, an ivory silk brocade dress, someone playing a piano, people singing. And always she came back to the picture of Adrian standing in a doorway with snow shining in his hair.

It was a shock to her whole system when the song ended. She felt disoriented, almost dizzy. Slowly, reluctantly, Adrian released her, his solemn blue gaze still holding hers. People started leaving the dance floor. Brian came over to her and took her arm, easing her away from Adrian. Gallantly, Adrian took Steff's arm and escorted her back to their table. All four of them sat down. Josh Andersen came over.

For the rest of the evening, Dani moved and talked like an automaton. Afterward, she couldn't remember a thing anybody had said. There was Steff's laughter and Josh Andersen's booming voice joining in. People came to the table, chatted, moved on. She must have answered them. She *was* conscious of an ominous silence from Brian, which proved he wasn't nearly as insensitive to atmosphere as she'd sometimes thought him. And always there was Adrian, catching her glance from time to time, a faint smile hovering around his mouth, that same message glinting in his eyes.

She danced with Brian, with Josh, with a couple of her patients. She danced with Adrian exactly four times. They didn't speak. They didn't need to.

And then the party ended and it was time to go home. Walking out of the door with Brian, standing there while he helped her into her coat, she couldn't imagine what she was doing there with him. Or what she was going to do with him now.

As it turned out, this last was no problem. Brian was angry. He let her know that in no uncertain terms as he drove her to Steff's house. Looking out at wind-tossed trees and bushes, she was able to block out most of what he was saying, but a few phrases seeped through. Making an exhibition of herself with Adrian Falkirk. Dancing as if they were glued together. People would wonder what the hell she was doing, climbing all over Adrian Falkirk when she had gone to the dance with *him*.

This last sentence came just as he drove into Steff's driveway. It needled her into speech. "I behaved with perfect decorum," she informed him. "All I did with Adrian was dance." And that was true, she assured herself. Unfortunately, it seemed Brian had been watching closely—he must have noticed the electricity that had sparked and crackled between her and Adrian, the glances exchanged, the glances held.

"It's none of my business, of course," Brian said stiffly. "You warned me not to get possessive about you. I'm just concerned that people will talk."

"I understand, Brian," she said softly as she got out of the car.

He didn't even wait to see her in safely. Which was understandable, she supposed. Buffeted by the wind, fumbling the key Steff had given her into the lock, she wondered why she didn't feel more let down. After all, in spite of the promise in Adrian's eyes, here she was, coming home alone again. But she didn't feel disappointed, she felt . . . patient. Sooner or later, she would see him again, and then . . .

He came in with Steff, of course. She must have known he would. That was why she'd just drifted into

Steff's living room and sunk down in an overstuffed chair, waiting, still wearing her wool coat.

He loomed over her in the lamplight. "Steff's making hot chocolate," he informed her.

She smiled up at him. "That's nice. It was a good party, wasn't it?"

He nodded. He wasn't taking his coat off, either, she noticed. About then, Steff came into the room. Dani saw her grin as she looked from one to the other. It was a very wicked-looking grin. "You know what?" she said. "I'm suddenly overcome with the wearies. Too much excitement for an elderly lady. Maybe I'll let you make your own chocolate." She inclined her head to one side. "Come to think of it, I don't think I even have any. You got any at your house, Falkirk?"

"Pounds of it," he said dryly, his left eyebrow raised in the cocky way that used to irritate hell out of Dani and now seemed the sexiest thing imaginable.

Steff yawned. "Best you and Kelsey go have your nightcap there then, don't you think?"

Smiling, Dani stood up and hugged her. "You're a wicked woman, Steff Carmody."

She returned the hug. "Aren't I just, though?"

Adrian had to be hugged, too, then Steff walked them to the door, closing it behind them and shooting home the bolt in an excessively loud manner. Evidently she wasn't expecting Dani back all night.

Dani laughed. "I love that woman."

"Me too," Adrian said.

They stood for a moment on the lighted porch looking at his car parked in the driveway. "Perhaps we should go to my house rather than yours," Dani said thoughtfully. "Mike just might show up at your place early in the morning."

For a second a shadow moved across his face. Probably he was remembering that disastrous Sunday morning. But almost immediately he grinned. "I thought you said you didn't have any furniture?"

"I have a bed."

He laughed and there was a husky note in his voice. "Why, Doctor Kelsey, I do believe you're planning to seduce me."

"You hadn't realized that?"

He put his arms around her and kissed her very lightly on the mouth. Evidently he felt her question didn't need an answer. Which, of course, it didn't.

CHAPTER THIRTEEN

THE WIND WAS getting stronger, gusting so fiercely that Adrian and Dani had to hang on to each other as they ran from the car to the house. Dani spared a glance for the empty blackened space where the trailer had stood, then determinedly put all thought of the fire out of her mind.

In the living room, as they caught their breath, Adrian cast a speculative glance at the cream-colored sofa that sat in the middle of the uncarpeted floor. "It's a Hide-A-Bed," Danielle said with a nervous laugh, then went off to hang their coats in the hall closet.

Adrian walked over to the stone fireplace, glancing with approval at the brass scuttle filled with alder wood and topped with kindling. At the side of the raised hearth was a folded newspaper.

By the time Dani returned, he had the fire laid and was looking around for matches. "On the mantel," she said huskily. He could almost feel her nervousness vibrating the air.

When the flames flared up, he slid closed the glass screen and turned to look at her. Drawn into her own stillness, she was sitting on the very edge of the sofa, looking wary but infinitely beautiful in her elegant blue chemise, her hands clasped in her lap like a little girl's. She had turned on the hall light, which barely penetrated the shadows in the large room. Her eyes looked enormous.

"Did you really want hot chocolate?" she asked with just a hint of a mischievous smile. "I'm not sure I have any. Would coffee do?"

What he wanted was to take her in his arms and kiss her breathless, but on the way over here he had decided they must first determine a few things. He wanted no accidental repeat of their last confrontation. "How about a glass of wine?" he suggested gravely.

She looked at him uncertainly for a moment, then got up and left the room. God, she moved gracefully. He wanted her desperately.

When she gave him his glass, he sat down on the edge of the hearth and after a moment's pause she returned to the sofa, sitting on the edge again, tugging her dress down so it covered her knees.

He raised his glass in a silent toast, then set it down beside him. "I think perhaps we should first set the scene," he said.

A puzzled expression moved across her face, then cleared. "The night we met."

He nodded. "Almost three years ago. Christmas Eve."

She took a deep breath, then glanced at the windows. "It's starting to rain," she muttered. Wind was whistling through the keyhole on the French doors. The chimney cap rattled as it rotated. The sound of the surf beat against the walls.

"Danielle," he said encouragingly, knowing she was nervous, purposely delaying.

"Okay." She smiled faintly, took a sip of her wine, then met his gaze. "Roxanne invited me to your father's house for the annual Christmas Eve party. She and I were decorating the tree by the staircase. It was an enormous tree and there were boxes and boxes of ornaments. I'd never seen so many ornaments.''

She paused and he took up the story. ''I let myself into the house with my key. I'd come straight from the airport, alone. Marta had stopped off to visit a friend. When I came into the foyer, you were passing an ornament up to Roxanne. A crystal star. It shone in the light from the chandelier. You were wearing a cream-colored dress. Brocade, I think. Trimmed with silver. Christmas music was playing on the radio. Aretha Franklin singing *Winter Wonderland.*''

He took a breath, his gaze still holding hers steadily. ''Roxanne said something to you and you laughed. Then you felt the draft from the doorway and turned around just as I closed the door. You still had the remnants of laughter on your face. I thought I had never seen anything as beautiful as your face.''

''You looked so big,'' she murmured. ''It seemed to me you filled the doorway. You were wearing a tuxedo, a dark overcoat, a white silk scarf with fringed ends. There were snowflakes shining in your hair.''

''I fell in love with you at that precise moment,'' he said evenly.

Her heart beat painfully against her ribs, her blood clamoring through her veins. She stood up, then wasn't sure where she thought she was going. She could hardly dash right out of her own house into the night, into the storm. Fight or flight instinct, some clinical part of her brain informed her.

She sat down again. ''You were rude to me later,'' she said. ''When Jon came.''

''I didn't know what I was saying. If you'll remember, by that time, my wife had arrived also. I had to cover up what I was feeling. As it was, Jon suspected. He kept looking from me to you, remember?''

She shook her head.

He reached for his wineglass, took another sip. "We're getting ahead of ourselves. Before Jon came, before Marta came, we talked. Do you remember what we talked about?''

"Childhood memories," she said after a short pause. "I'd forgotten about that. I told you about going fishing with my dad, and you said you'd never gone fishing with your father, he was always too busy.'' Her face lit up, making Adrian want to get to his feet and pick her up in his arms and carry her off to... where? According to what she'd said earlier, this was it, this bare room with its lonely settee.

"We talked about school," she said. "You told me you were a math whiz and I said I was, too, and you challenged me to prove it and we spent half an hour making up ridiculous arithmetic problems for each other. If Jane spent four hours on the train and Robert six and the engineer drove at sixty-five miles an hour...''

She was laughing now, as she had laughed then, the merry sound tugging at his heart.

She frowned. "I can't remember what came next.''

"My sister Jacqueline played the piano.''

"So she did. Christmas carols. She played beautifully. I remember thinking it wasn't fair for one family to have so much talent.''

"We sang," he murmured. "You knew all the words to 'The Twelve Days of Christmas.' ''

"And you did an impression of Elvis Presley singing 'Blue Christmas.' ''

They both laughed, and just as quickly sobered.

"And then Marta arrived," Adrian said slowly.

Her eyes accused him. "You hadn't told me you were married."

"There wasn't an opportunity. What could I say, Hi, I'm Adrian Falkirk, I'm married. The subject just didn't come up. I was too busy having a good time." He hesitated, then went on. "I don't think I knew I'd already fallen in love with you. I just knew I was strongly attracted. It wasn't until later that I realized . . ."

"Why were you so rude to me?"

"I saw you look at Marta and then at me and it came to me that I'd been married for twelve years and expected to be married until death did us part. By then Jon had got into the act and was competing for your attention. I don't think I've ever envied my brother so much as I did at that moment when I realized he was free to court you and I wasn't."

He stood up, opened up the fire screen and poked the fire, then put another log on it. Walking over to her, he took her glass from her and set it down on the floor. Then he sat down beside her, taking both her hands between his. "I knew I had to kill whatever it was that had sparked between us. The quickest way to kill it was to say something unkind. I don't even remember what it was, do you?"

Her lips tightened. "I've never forgotten that part. You said in this awful, drawling voice, 'She's a little skinnier than your usual wench, isn't she, brother?' "

He winced, then put his hand to her cheek and stroked her mouth with his thumb. "I'm sorry, sweetheart. It must have hurt."

She nodded, moisture shining in her eyes at the memory.

He kissed her lightly, then attempted a grin. "It was true, though," he said, hoping she'd see the remark as a way of lightening the atmosphere.

She did. She laughed. "You're just as mean as you ever were."

He became serious again. "Don't you see, Danielle, I had to be rude. And then, you became engaged to Jon within the month. So I had to continue to be rude every time I saw you. I had to think of you as an adversary, an enemy, which you were, to my peace of mind. And body. I had to make you angry, because I couldn't bear it if you smiled at me."

"Oh, Adrian." She put her hand to his forehead, gently stroking his hair back from his brow. "I had no idea. Even after you came here, I didn't realize that all that time ago..."

"It didn't stop, Danielle," he said urgently. "I kept thinking my feelings would turn brown around the edges and fade away but they never did. My love for you feels as fresh today as it did in the beginning. Why do you think I came to Murre Bay?" The light that she'd always thought of as slightly derisive was there in his blue eyes again, but it didn't look derisive to her now. Nor did the lift of his eyebrow look arrogant. He looked...loving.

"You said you were curious."

"I was. Desperately curious to find out if there was still something between us, something we could build on."

His gaze wouldn't let hers go. She could feel his intensity in the air between them. He was waiting now, waiting for something only she could provide. What was it? What did he want from her? "I don't know what you want me to say," she whispered.

"I want you to admit you felt it, too. I want you to admit you fell in love with me that night, just as I did with you."

Shocked, she stared at him. "Where did you get that radical idea? It just isn't so, Adrian. I remember now that I thought you were very attractive, very handsome. I'd forgotten that. I'd even forgotten that I met you before I met Jon. I'd forgotten the whole evening." Her face clouded, then she smiled faintly. "When I was a very little girl, I heard someone talking about a shadow box. I had no idea what it was, but the sound of it intrigued me. Finally I decided it must be a box to put your shadow in. You know, a matchbox is for matches, a chocolate box is for chocolates. I imagined reaching down and rolling up my shadow, folding it up real small and putting it into its box. Later, of course, I found out a shadow box was a deep wooden frame meant to hold small ornaments and keepsakes, but I always preferred my definition. Sometimes I've thought that we all have shadow boxes in our brains. Places where we put memories for safekeeping and then forget all about them."

"We remember what we want to remember," Adrian said.

"I suppose that's true, but..."

"Why would you *not* want to remember that night? Unless you didn't want to remember that it was me you loved, not Jon?"

"We only spent a couple of hours together before Jon came," she protested.

"Time doesn't make any difference," he said firmly. "When I saw you, I *recognized* you, as if I'd been waiting all my life for you. And you felt the same. You looked at me when I came in that door, and I saw it happen, Danielle. While we were together, I felt it intensify—*between* us. There was nothing one-sided about it." He touched her cheek lightly again. "I also saw you deny it to yourself when Marta arrived. Just as I had to deny it to myself. But it was there. Between us. Both of us. That's why you became engaged to Jon. You've never confused me with Jon, it was Jon you confused with me."

"No." She was standing again, without any clear memory of getting to her feet.

He looked up at her. "Tell me when you fell in love with him then?"

"When I first met him. Almost right away." She shook her head violently and went to stand by the French doors, looking out, though she couldn't see a thing. Rain was pounding the windows, driving against the roof, pouring noisily down the drainpipes. "I know what you're saying, Adrian, you're saying I fell in love with you and projected it onto Jon as soon as he turned up, because you were... unavailable." She had tried to make her voice firm, but it had a definite tremor to it. She turned and looked at him. "That would mean my eight months with Jon were a lie."

"Weren't they?"

She came back to sit beside him and he couldn't bear the anguish in her face. "Does it really matter what happened back then? Don't you see, I can't admit what I don't know. And I really don't know, Adrian." Her gaze was steady, still anguished, but direct and truthful. "I stopped loving Jon, Adrian. I don't know exactly when, but I do know that I love you, only you. Surely that's all that matters?"

For a moment more, he gazed at her. He'd wanted a reassurance which it seemed she couldn't give him.

There was disappointment in that, but it was over-whelmed by the joy of knowing she loved him, of knowing that at least she'd remembered their meeting.

"Oh, the hell with it," he said, and took her in his arms.

THEY PULLED OUT the bed and made it up together, then Adrian put another log on the fire. They didn't bother closing the blinds—in this storm, who would be walking the beach or dunes, what ships would be risk-ing the high seas?

With great care, Adrian helped Dani remove her lovely dress, panty hose and lacy underwear, then she returned the favor, assisting him out of his own cloth-ing. Restraining the passion that wanted him to throw their clothing on the bare floor and pull her down on the bed, he gathered up their garments and hung them in the hall closet. Naked, he came back to find her lying on top of the quilt, her ivory body gently illuminated in the firelight.

"Everybody should always make love by firelight," he murmured as he lay down beside her and pulled her into his arms.

She laughed softly. "In Murre Bay, you could do it most of the year."

He touched the gleaming cap of her hair, making himself go slowly. He wanted to savor her, relish her. With gentle fingers, he traced the line of her hair as it curved behind her ear, following it around to the charmingly boyish peak it made at the nape of her neck. Her arms were around him, her hands moving deli-cately on his body with a feather-light touch that was beginning to drive him mad. But still he held back, tracing her face now, the soft bird's wing eyebrows, her eyelids, touching the spiky edges of her mascaraed lashes, the classic line of her cheekbones, the hollows beneath them, the soft curving line of her mouth.

Finally, unable to restrain himself any longer, he touched his mouth to hers, brushing it gently with his own, letting his lips tease hers into motion.

For a long time they kissed, silently, hungrily, but not yet passionately, letting the magic build between them as it had before, getting comfortable with each other, getting to know each other.

Dani thought that she would never get tired of his mouth. It was such a firm mouth, a strong mouth, yet it had an interesting tremor to it when she touched it lightly with her tongue. Could anything be more tantalizing than a strong man who was not afraid to tremble? She could feel his solid male pressure against her lower body, but his hands moved slowly over her, obviously unwilling to hurry. She stretched luxuriously as he finally touched her breasts, giving him access to her body, putting space between them so she could touch him too, releasing his mouth, for the moment only, so that he could bend his head to her breasts.

She touched his hair as his tongue teased her nipples and made them hard, tangling her fingers in it, feeling it curl around her fingers. Then as his mouth and hands moved lower, she pressed her hands against his head, holding it against her, lifting her body to his seeking mouth.

She could hear the wind whooshing under the eaves, the rain driving against the windows, the wood crackling in the fireplace as the flames sent shadows leaping across the ceiling. The sound of the surf was almost violent now, beating against the shore in time to the beating of her heart as Adrian lifted her and touched

her and set pressure building in her. She clung to him,
her eyes closing tightly, feeling the pressure, feeling his
touch, waiting, waiting for the release that was bound
to come at any moment.

And then he stopped.

He loomed over her, leaning on his elbows, smiling
down at her, his eyes shining brilliantly in his shadowed face. He didn't speak, but she understood, exactly as if he had spoken, that she wasn't to be allowed
a release just yet. There were miles to go, kisses to be
exchanged, the shapes of bodies to be learned. Then,
and only then, would her passions be allowed to ex-
plode, and then, only in conjunction with his.

"The games people play," she murmured, and saw
him smile his satisfaction at her understanding. He
looked too satisfied, she decided, almost smug.

Looping her right foot around his leg, clasping her
hands behind his back, she lifted suddenly and rolled
with him so that he was on his back. Then she said,
"Stay," and proceeded on a lengthy exploration of her
own, kissing her way across his face, then down to the
hollow of his throat, brushing her lips lightly over the
mat of dark hair on his chest, blowing lightly to tease
him, feeling him stiffen. But, obediently, he didn't move
and she continued on over the clean-tasting, clean-
smelling flesh of his lean muscular body, feeling his
muscles tense though he continued to hold himself still.

Neither of them spoke, but the sound of their
breathing gave away their rising passion. And at last, as
though he could contain himself no longer, Adrian
groaned and reached for her and pulled her to him and
then under him and rising, entered her slowly, deliberately, his gaze holding hers. The firelight, less bright

now, flickered mystery into his eyes and shone on his black hair so that it seemed to glisten.

The memory of the night she'd met Adrian was passing once again through her mind, like a strip of film held against the light, passing slowly, frame by frame, so that it seemed to overlay Adrian's shadowed features, uniting past and present. Why had she suppressed the knowledge that the man in the dark overcoat with snowflakes gleaming in his hair and the naked man above her, loving her so thoroughly, so wonderfully, were one?

CHAPTER FOURTEEN

SOMEONE WAS KISSING HER, teasing her out of the dark cocoon of sleep into the light of morning. She could see the light beyond her closed eyelids—a gray light that was alive with sound and fury. The storm was still raging.

She came awake slowly. She always came awake slowly—not a good trait in a doctor, but there it was. She could feel breath against her mouth now, blowing lightly.

She opened her eyes. He was leaning over her, supporting himself on one hand, gazing lovingly at her. She smiled at him. "Adrian," she sighed.

In the instant before he kissed her again, she glimpsed relief in his face. A chill twisted around her heart. Was he always going to doubt? Would she always have to reassure him, in word or deed?

Always? What always?

Adrian would be leaving Murre Bay. He didn't seem sure where he would be going, but go he would, sooner or later. The chill deepened, clutching at her stomach, then thawed as his lips continued to brush lightly against her own.

Carpe diem. The phrase came to her out of old school textbooks. *Carpe diem.* Seize the day.

Winding her arms around his neck, she kissed him back. "The fire's gone out," she murmured, feeling another chill—the chill of the air in the room this time.

"I've been busy," he said against her mouth.

She laughed softly. "It was quite a night."

"Some kind of world record. Also some kind of storm. It sounded like the *1812 Overture*—all that was missing were the bells." He lifted his head and gazed down at her. "I love you, Danielle."

"I love you."

For a second she thought he was going to say something more, but instead he shook his head and rolled away from her to sit upright on the edge of the Hide-A-Bed sofa. "I'm starved," he informed her. "Do you have any food in that flashy new kitchen?"

"Lots of it. I stocked up yesterday."

He looked a question at her.

"I'm going to move back in today," she told him. "I let Steff know last night at the dance. I can't go on hiding out, Adrian. It's been a week now and those so-called friends of Mike's haven't shown up. Seems to me if they know what's good for them they never will."

His face registered doubt, then he smiled. "We'll talk about it later. Do you have any eggs?"

"A few."

"Cheese?"

"What do you have in mind?"

"I make a mean omelette."

She shook her head. "Too much cholesterol."

He groaned. "What then?"

"Oatmeal?"

He made a face.

"I have grapefruit." She relented. "I could make pancakes—I have a healthy recipe using whole wheat flour."

"You're on, Doctor. Shower first, then food." He glanced at the windows. Rain was blowing hard against the glass. "Looks as if we're homebound for the day." He gave her a wicked grin. "Isn't that too bad?"

"We could light another fire. There's wood in a rack in the garage."

"We'll leave the bed down. More room to sprawl. Or play."

Happiness was a palpable thing, she thought as he padded barefoot to the bathroom. She could feel it glowing out of her, lighting her up from inside, touching the bare room with magic, turning it into a safe haven against the storm.

She sat up and swung her legs to the floor, wincing as they met the cold boards. One more week, Chet had told her the previous day. One more week and her house would be a home again.

The question was, would Adrian still be here?

THE STORM CONTINUED. Two and a half hours later, after breakfast by the fire, Dani stood in one of her bay windows, looking out at the ocean through her binoculars. Behind her the fire crackled and sparked and she was cosily warm in a fleecy white sweatshirt and her French-cut jeans. Adrian stood beside her, finishing his final cup of coffee, looking cosy himself in an extra-large Washington Huskies sweatshirt she'd loaned him and the suit pants he'd worn the night before.

"The sea sure is rough," he murmured.

Dani nodded. Because of the sudden driving bursts of rain, visibility was poor, but she could see enough to tell that the ocean was an angry gray green, the waves piling in as high as a house.

Handing the binoculars to Adrian she went to her back door to see if her Sunday newspaper had arrived. It had, neatly bundled in a sturdy plastic bag. Scanning the headlines as she returned to the living room, it was a moment before she realized Adrian had exclaimed.

He'd twisted sideways in the bay window, training the binoculars to the south.

"You looking at the jetty?" she asked. "Spectacular isn't it? How high do you suppose that spray goes?"

"I thought..." he broke off. "I thought I saw someone, on the rocks."

She went to the window and took the binoculars from him. "I hope you're wrong," she exclaimed. "We're always having problems with people climbing on the jetty to watch the storms. Silly idiots don't realize how dangerous..." She broke off, having finally got the jetty in focus. "You did see someone," she said quickly to Adrian. "Of all the stupid...look at those waves...it must be right on high tide."

A second later, she was heading for the hall to find jackets. Throwing one her father had left behind to Adrian, along with a knitted hat, she wrapped herself up warmly, grabbed the telephone and punched in 911, which she seemed to be doing a lot lately.

"Start your car up," she called to Adrian. "Soon as I get the police we'll drive to the jetty. We can probably beat them there, there's not a moment to lose."

Adrian hit the accelerator while she was still closing her door. Speeding up Seaview Way, she filled him in on the last disaster on the rock jetty. Five people, standing out there watching a storm, had been swept off the rocks into the water and pulled along by the undercurrent with such force some of them had lost their clothing and had almost lost their lives.

"You can see the problem at low tide," she explained. "There are sand bar formations farther out, which cause pockets or channels, some wide, some narrow. There's a hellacious rip goes through there when the tide's in, running like a freight train. There are warning signs, but there are always people who think the signs aren't meant for them."

They hit the beach running, without breaking stride as they passed a pickup parked at the entrance to the beach. When they reached the rocks, they scrambled straight up them to the top of the jetty. Squinting through the wind-driven rain and spray as she stumbled along, Dani thought at first the person she'd glimpsed through the rain had already been swept over into the sea, but then she saw movement ahead. "Two people," she yelled over her shoulder. "No, three."

Adrian was making fairly good time behind her, though he was sliding from time to time, which was hardly surprising, considering he was wearing the dress shoes he'd worn the previous night. Slipping herself, drenched by spray, she kept going, shouting warnings now, wondering why the hell the three people were still working their way onward. They appeared to be hanging on to each other, pulling each other along. No, the two on the outside were pulling the middle one. What the hell were they up to?

She saw the huge comber the instant before it reached the rocks ahead of her. Awed, she paused automatically, Adrian coming up short behind her. "My God," he exclaimed and put his arms tightly around her.

The wave rose up like a wall on the south side of the jetty, curled over and hit the rocks with the force of a cannon, knocking the three figures off their feet and down the other side. No, not all three, Dani realized, one of them was lying flat, clinging to the rocks with desperate fingers. Leaping over the rocks toward him, she grabbed him under the armpits, yelling at him to get up, even as she realized it was Michael Caswell. "I've got you," she shouted. "Come on, we have to get out of here. Now."

As they reached the top of the jetty, she saw that Adrian had clambered down the rocks on the north side. With her heart in her mouth, she watched him reach the bottom, yank off his jacket and kick off his shoes, before plunging forward into the boiling waves. Ahead, another huge swell was rolling in. "No," she protested, meaning it as a shout, but producing only a whimper, her heart leaping as she heard the unmistakable sound of sirens.

Mike was shuddering, his face bleached white, his clothing soaking wet. Half dragging, half pushing, she got him started along the jetty, then let go of him and yelled at him to keep going, intending to go back and help Adrian rescue the other two. "I can't," Mike moaned, falling to his knees. Would he be safe here? She couldn't be sure. Grabbing his arm, she pulled it over her shoulders and yanked him a few more yards.

"Oh God, Doc," he moaned. "I've never been so glad to see anyone in my life. Oh God, they were going to scare me good, they said." His hands clutched at her, almost knocking her off balance. "They were going to make me pay for snitching on them. Thank you, Doc, thank you. I'll never do anything bad again in my life,

I swear it. I'll do anything you say, anything Mr. Falkirk says.''

He was near hysteria, she recognized. Still supporting him, she turned, squinting through the still spewing water, pushing her wet hair away from her forehead with her free hand. Somewhere along the way she'd lost her hat. She couldn't see Adrian anywhere. All she could see was angry water, heaving and roiling, thundering against the rocks. Mike was still babbling, promising to go to church like his Mom wanted him to, he was going to get a job, a good job, give all his money to his mother and the kids.

Easing him down to a sitting position, she told him to stay put, he was safe now, and started down the rocks to the beach, her eyes still straining, scanning the waves. *Was that a dark head? There where the foam was boiling. Yes. One head or two?* She couldn't tell. In the shallows someone was dragging himself toward the beach, on his knees. He fell flat as a wave hit him from behind, then slid backwards as the wave retreated. Not Adrian. Her heart plummeted.

Not stopping to remove any clothing, she sloshed into the water after the man, lifting him so that his head was out of the water, trying to pull his dead weight forward.

A heartbeat later, three dark figures in wetsuits raced past her a few yards along the shore. They ran into the waves, shouting, just as a fourth figure showed up beside her. Barney Grey, one of the local police officers on the surf rescue team, had grabbed the man from the other side and was heaving with her. They pulled him high onto the beach. "I'll take care of him," Dani gasped out to Barney. "Mike's on the jetty. Mike Caswell."

As Barney dashed away, Dani saw that the man they'd rescued had pulled himself to his knees and started vomiting. He was one of the men she'd last seen loitering with Mike outside Surf and Turf, she realized. It looked as if he was going to be okay, and she spared a moment to look over her shoulder.

Two members of the surf rescue team were just reaching shore, a man supported between them. Mike's other friend. Not Adrian. Adrian was still nowhere in sight. Biting down hard on her lower lip, feeling as if her heart had solidified into a rock-hard lump of ice inside her, Dani got to her feet.

And there, stumbling a little, came Adrian, escorted by an officer who was keeping a wary hand near his elbow. Thanksgiving welled up inside her, making her weak.

A paramedic came up beside Dani and put a blanket over her shoulders, then knelt down to put another over the man. He had stopped throwing up, but was still on his knees, his head wagging from side to side. "I'll see to this guy," the paramedic said.

Dani hadn't even realized she was shivering. Knotting the blanket around her neck she ran to the other man as the officers laid him down on a litter. "Can't find a pulse," one of the men said.

Dani and the officer immediately began CPR, Dani slipping her hand under the victim's neck and giving him mouth-to-mouth resuscitation, the officer compressing his chest and counting out the rhythm.

A few seconds and Dani felt the rush of returning air. A moment later the man began vomiting and Dani quickly turned him onto his side. When he was done, she cleared his mouth and checked that he was breathing on his own. He had relapsed into unconsciousness and was obviously in shock. His skin was pale, almost blue, his pulse rapid, his pupils, when she raised his eyelids, dilated. Swiftly, Dani placed a rolled up blanket under his legs to raise them, then checked him over. She could find no injuries. As the officer swaddled him in blankets, she stood up, looking around for Adrian.

He was squatting nearby, a blanket around his shoulders, one arm around Mike. Wet black hair straggled over his forehead. His feet were bare, his wet trousers and shirt plastered against his body. He looked . . . wonderful.

"You did real good, man," Barney Grey was saying to him as Dani approached. "If you'd tried to swim to shore 'stead of taking that guy in a parallel line for a ways, you'd never have made it through that rip."

"Are you okay?" Dani asked. Her legs felt like rubber and her heart was ricocheting around in her chest, constricting her breathing. Reaction was setting in.

Adrian nodded, his blue eyes sending her a message that was perfectly clear. He was not only okay, he was tremendously relieved that she was okay.

She knelt down beside Michael, who was also swathed in blankets. He'd regained a little of his color, but his hazel eyes appeared dazed, the pupils enlarged. "He looks a little shocky," Dani said to Barney. "We'll take him along in the ambulance." She turned back to Adrian.

"I'll be fine," he said. "You don't have room for everybody. All I need are dry clothes and hot chicken soup."

She touched his cheek, using the pretext of testing his skin temperature, trying to communicate that she didn't want to leave him, but she had to go with the ambu-

lance. He nodded, leaning his cheek into the palm of
her hand to let her know he returned the feeling. In spite
of her wet clothing, welcome warmth flooded her body.
"I'll see Mr. Falkirk gets home okay," Barney said,
grinning broadly from Dani to Adrian, obviously aware
of what was going on between them.

The officers were already carrying the litters toward
the beach exit. Helping Mike to his feet, Dani and
Adrian assisted him off the beach and up into the ambulance. As Dani was about to follow him in, Adrian
took her hand and held it tightly for a second, lifting it
to his lips, before letting it go with obvious reluctance.
In the moment before Grey closed the doors, she exchanged a glance with Adrian and as the doors slammed
shut, she allowed herself, for the first time, to realize
how close she had come to losing him forever. A violent shudder ripped through her. "You okay, Doc?"
Michael asked her, bending his head to look up into her
face.

"I'm fine," she said, and meant it. Adrian was alive.
She was alive. Life was good.

IT WAS FOUR O'CLOCK in the afternoon before she got
home again, catching a ride from Baxter with one of the
police officers who had followed the ambulance to the
hospital. One of the nurses had loaned her a pair of
sweats and someone else had routed out some sneakers
that were only a little too large. Dumping her soggy
clothing in the laundry room, she went immediately to
the telephone in the living room and punched out
Adrian's number. She'd had to dial information from
Baxter to get it when she'd tried to call him from the
hospital earlier. Strange to realize she hadn't ever called

him before. Then a busy signal had sounded in her ear. His phone was ringing now, though.

A moment later, his voice answered. "Hi," she said softly.

There was a pause, then he said, "Is everybody okay?" in a voice that didn't sound right.

She frowned, then decided he'd probably been sitting there worrying. Possibly he'd been trying to reach the hospital earlier. "Mike's fine," she assured him. "We're keeping him overnight at the hospital just to be sure. Chet's with him, and his mother, the police called them right away. The other two are going to be okay, too. The one you brought in was totally exhausted. Another minute or two and I don't know if he'd have made it. Both of them suffered from hypothermia and had taken in substantial amounts of saltwater, but they are stable now."

"Good," Adrian said. "And you? Are you still at the hospital?"

Why was his voice so stiff? Some reaction of his own? "I'm home and I'm in great shape." She paused. "Is anything wrong, Adrian?"

"No, it's just..." His voice trailed off. "I'm relieved you're all right."

"Are you coming over—I'm going to get the fire going again, make a pot of coffee."

"I—hang on a minute will you?"

He still sounded stiff. Something was wrong. He hadn't gone away from the phone, he was still holding on to it—she could hear the soft sound of his breathing.

Dani gazed out through the French doors while she waited for him to speak again. The storm had blown itself out while she was in the hospital, but the sea was still fairly rough. The wind had dropped, however, and a few people were straggling along the beach, one of them throwing a stick for his dog—an Irish setter that still retained some of the awkwardness of puppyhood. Weekenders, Dani decided. They'd probably stayed holed up in their cabins or motels during the storm and wanted to get at least a few minutes of salt air before driving back to the cities they'd come from. Probably none of them even knew of the near tragedy that had occurred.

The tide was well out now, the waves around the end of the jetty occasionally sending up fountains of spray that were comparatively gentle. In the sky the sun was valiantly breaking through the cloud layer, sending down biblical rays of light to touch the water.

"Hello," Adrian said at last. "Listen, I'm not... I think—I'll come over later, okay? An hour or two?"

She felt... flattened, she decided as she hung up the phone. What on earth had happened to the man who had looked at her so lovingly four hours earlier, the man who hadn't wanted to let go of her hand?

Perhaps he was ill. Alarm shot through her. His body had taken quite a battering in that angry sea. He'd looked okay, had seemed okay—but perhaps she should have insisted on him checking into the hospital to make sure. Surely he'd have had the sense to get out of his wet clothing right away. If he had delayed—he wouldn't have gone searching for her father's jacket or his own shoes, would he? Surely not.

Grabbing an old jacket from her hall closet, she kicked off the borrowed sneakers, rammed her feet into some flats of her own and headed to the garage, filled with anxiety. Only illness could explain that flat note in Adrian's voice. She had to make sure he was okay.

THERE WAS A WHITE Ferrari parked in Adrian's driveway, next to his own BMW. Washington plates. She didn't know anyone who owned a Ferrari. But, she thought, with a catch of her breath in her throat, she did know someone who preferred white cars.

Her heart beating erratically against her ribs, her mind in turmoil, she walked slowly toward the house, suddenly not at all sure she had done the right thing by coming here.

Adrian opened the door before she reached it, and stood looking solemnly at her. He was wearing trim jeans and sneakers and the loden green sweatshirt he'd worn once before—the first time she'd gone to his house. He looked fit and vigorous, but strained around the eyes.

"I was afraid you were sick," she said as she reached him.

He took her hand and held it tightly, shaking his head. "I'm fine."

"You sounded sick," she said.

He smiled faintly, but didn't comment. "We were a pretty good team today."

"We were. You were very brave, Adrian. I was terrified."

"No more than I."

She glanced over her shoulder at the white car. "Is that who I think it is?"

He nodded, watching her face.

"You didn't want me to see him?"

He gave her a wry smile. "I have some fears of my own, I guess."

He stepped back, releasing her hand. She took a deep breath and moved past him. Jonathan Falkirk was sitting in one of the chairs that bracketed the fireplace, also wearing jeans and a sweatshirt, a blue one, drinking a beer. Her mind flashed an image of herself in her elaborate wedding gown, standing beside her father, looking at herself in the mirror while Harris asked her if she was sure Jon Falkirk was the right man for her. Dear God, it was then, at that precise moment, that she had realized . . .

Before the thought had quite crystallized, Jon saw her, set down the bottle and got to his feet in one lithe movement, smiling his old familiar dazzling smile, taking her hand between both of his. "Dani, this is a surprise! Adrian said you'd called but couldn't get away just yet."

Dani glanced at Adrian, smiling wryly at the sheepish expression on his face. "I didn't want to come, looking such a mess," she said, letting Adrian off the hook. She indicated her oversize sweatsuit. "The nurse who loaned me these was a size 16, I think. And I didn't have time to wash my hair."

"I didn't think the outfit was your usual style," Jon commented. "You look great all the same," he added enthusiastically. "Beautiful."

She'd forgotten how enthusiastic Jon always was, full of a restless energy that seemed to radiate from him. He was as handsome as ever, as handsome as Adrian, still a mirror image, his eyes as blue as Adrian's, hair as thick and black, body as strong and muscular. And he was still holding her hand. Gently, she extricated it.

"I'm the one who's surprised," she said. "I understood none of the Falkirks knew where Adrian was."

Jon laughed. "I've known for some time. I was down in San Francisco two weeks ago. I charmed Charlotte, Adrian's secretary, into telling me where he was hiding. Didn't tell the folks, though, not until Adrian missed the monthly get-together yesterday. Then Dad got worried and was all set to call the police out on a search of the Oregon coast. So then I had to give him away." He laughed. "Dad kept calling here last night and there wasn't any answer." He glanced from Dani to Adrian, obvious curiosity brimming in his blue eyes.

Somehow Dani prevented herself from turning to see how Adrian was handling all this. At the moment, she didn't dare meet his eyes.

"Dad decided he'd either had a car wreck or a nervous breakdown," Jon went on merrily. "Why else would a Falkirk miss a business meeting? Only way I could keep him from tearing out here, when Adrian still didn't answer his phone this morning, was to promise to come out myself and find out what was up. I called Dad an hour or so ago to let him know the long-lost son had been found."

Dani nodded. That explained the busy signal. There was a short silence while Jon glanced again from Dani's face to his brother's. Then Adrian said, "Would you like some coffee, Danielle?"

The stiffness was back in his voice. Jon must have been listening when she called him a little while ago. She nodded, still afraid to look at him. A moment later, he put a cup in her hand and she sat down in the chair opposite the one Jon had vacated. "I expect Adrian told you about our adventure this morning," she said when he sat down.

He grinned. "I'd just driven in when he arrived with a police escort, looking like something the cat dragged in. I'm not sure he said as much as he might have about his own part in the rescue. He gave most of the credit to the police rescue team."

"The man would have died if Adrian hadn't acted so promptly...and courageously," Dani said, amazed that her voice could sound so even. Not so amazing though, she thought as she sipped the scalding coffee. Like the storm that had raged earlier, her own personal turmoil had disappeared. She felt completely calm, totally in control.

"Adrian tells me the two of you have become friends," Jon said, laughing again. "I guess miracles do happen. Never thought I'd see the day."

Friends.

What did she expect, that Adrian would have confided they were lovers? She'd have been furious if he had. All the same, there had been a note in Jon's voice, a slight emphasis, that made her think he had probably guessed. Feeling stupidly awkward, she drank some more of her coffee.

"Roxanne said to say hello if I saw you," Jon went on. "She's missed you. Everyone has. We had no idea you were still in Washington."

"I've missed Roxanne, too," she said truthfully. It hadn't seemed possible to maintain her friendship with Jon's sister under the circumstances. It had seemed wisest to stay away from all Falkirks.

Until one of the Falkirks tracked her down.

Adrian still wasn't saying anything. Why not? He hadn't even sat down, had gone to stand by the island counter that separated the living room from the kitchen area. She could feel him looming there, watching her, watching Jon, tension emanating from him like a live thing. Feeling awkward again, she got up and took her coffee cup to the kitchen sink, then bent to say hello to Boots and her kittens.

One of the kittens, the one Steff wanted, was out of the basket, lapping milk from a saucer. The other three were asleep, cuddled up against Boots's side. All four kittens were healthy-looking balls of black fluff now. She picked up the adventurous one and stroked it, laughing softly when it nibbled on her finger, its baby teeth sharp as needles. Gently, she placed it back in the basket, took a deep breath and returned to the living room.

Jon was on his feet now, finishing the last of his beer. Handing the bottle to Adrian, he smiled at Dani. "Guess I'd better run along. It's a long drive and I have an early meeting tomorrow. It was good seeing you, Dani. Don't be such a stranger, okay?"

Typical Jon. Acting as if they were just old friends who hadn't seen one another in a while. Nothing on his face to show he remembered that the last time they had seen each other was two days before their proposed wedding.

"Say hello to Roxanne for me," she managed to say just as casually.

He nodded, then abruptly leaned over to kiss her lightly on the cheek. "Take care of yourself, okay?" he said warmly. A second later he was shaking his brother's hand. "You want me to talk to the old man about your Baxter project?" he asked as he headed for the door. "Pave the way, so to speak."

"I'd rather tell him about it myself," Adrian said, following him out.

Sinking into her chair, Dani waited for Adrian to come back, hearing the two of them talking in the small entryway, their voices almost indistinguishable from each other. She heard Jon's car start up, the front door close, Adrian's footsteps on the polished floor.

He was standing over her, looking down at her. She smiled up at him. For a second, he stared down at her solemnly, studying her face, then he dropped to his knees in front of her and took her hand. Lovingly, she watched the solemn expression fade from his face, to be replaced by one of distinct relief. "It's all right, isn't it?" he said slowly.

She touched his face with her free hand, realizing exactly how tense he had been by the residual harshness present in his voice. "It's very definitely all right."

"You didn't feel . . ."

"I felt nothing," she assured him. "I guess the piece of distorting glass you talked about must have washed out of my eye in the rain."

His eyes brimmed with light, then his mouth brushed against hers gently, so gently it was more like a sigh than a kiss. His arms went around her and he kissed her again and this time there was nothing gentle about it. It was a lover's kiss, demanding and urgent and hungry.

"Adrian," she said softly. "There's something I need to tell you."

"Later," he murmured against her mouth. He thought that this time he would never let her go. He had died a thousand deaths watching her with Jon, searching her face for clues to what she might be feeling, finding none. He had been so afraid, not exactly that she would discover she still loved Jon, but that the unexpected encounter would make her even more confused. But now her lips, her eyes, the pressure of her body were all telling him he had nothing to worry about. And just to make him doubly sure, she murmured, "I love you, Adrian Falkirk."

Releasing her mouth, he looked an urgent question at her and she nodded, laughing. "I should probably take

a shower first," she said lightly. "I didn't have a chance
at the hospital and I called you the minute I got home."

"No shower," he said. "There isn't time."

"We have all night," she pointed out, tangling her
fingers in his hair.

"If your beeper doesn't beep, or Steff doesn't come
by, or Mike decide to call, or Chet." He was already
pulling her up, easing her toward the hall, intending to
get her up the stairs before any of these possibilities
came to pass.

Laughing, she allowed herself to be hustled upward.

"Mike is definitely okay?" he asked as he followed
her into his bedroom.

"More than okay, a reformed character," she told
him, sitting down on the wobbly edge of the water bed.
"He had some kind of epiphany up there on the jetty.
He kept telling me he was going to do everything right
from now on, including going to church."

Adrian sat down and put his arm around her shoulders, holding her close to his side. "He was in shock
when I tried to talk to him. Those two were going to kill
him?"

"He doesn't know. He thinks they just wanted to
scare him. They'd guessed of course, that he'd told the
police where they lived. Evidently someone had warned
them the police were checking the neighborhood. They
lay low for a while, then drove out here this morning.
Ox called Mike and told him if he didn't meet them at
the jetty they were going to lie in wait for his brother,
Chet, and take it out on him. Mary Caswell and Chet
and the kids were at the Methodist church when Ox
called." Her eyes met his. "Today was the anniversary
of Tom Caswell's death. Mike didn't want to go to the
church, and there was a bit of a scene. Chet finally de-

cided it was safe to leave Mike for a short time. Mike asked where Ox was and he said he was calling from Phil's Market, which of course is pretty close to the church. So Mike felt he had no choice but to meet him and Scooter.''

Adrian shuddered, wishing he'd kept Mike under surveillance the whole time. It hadn't occurred to him Chet would leave him alone. "Did the police ask Ox and Scooter about the fires?''

"They did indeed. Informed them they were 'persons of interest' to the police in Tacoma and got confessions from both of them, to the fires here and some warehouse vandalism in Tacoma. They also got confirmations that Mike hadn't known about either fire. Ox insisted, by the way, that they had followed me home and saw me go into the house. Then they hung around long enough to know I wasn't going to come out before they set fire to the trailer. Anyway, Mike's definitely in the clear.''

Adrian took her in his arms and kissed her softly. "Sounds as if there's a happy ending all around.''

She shook her head. "I don't want our story to have a happy ending.''

Not at all sure what she meant, he stared at her and she smiled, looking so beautiful his heart seemed to turn over. "I don't want it ever to end,'' she said, then she pulled at his shoulders abruptly, catching him off balance, hauling him down with her onto the water bed, the two of them bouncing like mad for at least two minutes before the thing stopped rocking.

But somehow in the middle of all the jouncing, she managed to scramble out of her oversize sweats and he was able to pull off his own clothing, not without danger of being bounced overboard.

It felt so good to laugh, so damn good.

But it felt just as good to stop laughing, to draw her naked body into his arms and hold the length of her against him. Touching her, kissing her lovely firm breasts, her flat abdomen, he was suddenly haunted by the memory of angry water rolling around him, threatening to drag him down.

He pushed the images out of his mind. He was safe, he was warm and dry and he was with his own love, the woman he had wanted for almost three years. When this much happiness was granted a man, no other thoughts should be allowed to intrude. Lifting himself over her, he smiled down at her. Her face was flushed from his kisses, her blond hair tousled over her forehead, her smoky blue eyes clear and untroubled. The palace gates were open wide in welcome. "You taste extremely salty," he told her.

"I knew I should have taken a shower."

He shook his head. "I like it. Maybe I'm developing a fetish. I may have to dredge you with salt whenever we make love. Be sure to put a case of salt on the household shopping list every month."

The laughter that had glowed in her eyes gave way to a suddenly sober expression. "Household?" she queried.

"Later," he said. And then he entered her, slowly and lovingly, watching her face, moved by the awe that showed there as her response took hold, feeling awe himself at the magnitude of his own emotions.

Moving with her in a rhythm that seemed to come naturally, he marveled that two bodies could fit together so well, as though they had been made to accommodate one another. Her pupils were dilating with passion as they moved, her face tightening as pressure built inside her. Slowing his motion, he tried to hold on to his own pressure until she was completely ready, but it just wasn't possible and he had finally to let it go, revelling in the raw power of it. Not a half second behind him, she cried out his name, *his* name, and arched against him, her arms wound tightly around him.

"I love you, Danielle," he murmured as her body went limp beneath him and her eyes closed. Across her face, light moved, as her lips parted in a radiant smile. Looking up at him, her eyes were clear, the whites pristine, the smoky irises brimming blue. There were no shadows anywhere.

"WHAT BAXTER PROJECT?" Dani asked abruptly.

They had come down to the kitchen half an hour ago to rummage through the refrigerator and cupboards in search of food, having simultaneously reached the conclusion, after showering and shampooing together, that they were ravenously hungry. "That's what swimming does for you," Adrian had joked, making Dani groan.

At her question, he stood very still for a moment, a loaf of French bread clutched in his right hand. Setting the bread down on the island counter, he reached in the drawer for a serrated knife and began cutting meticulously even slices of a size that would fit in the toaster.

At the other end of the narrow kitchen, Dani was leaning over the stove, stirring a mixture of lima beans, split peas, barley, onions, potato, celery, various spices and water—a concoction that would make a truly delicious and nutritious soup, she'd assured him.

"Ah yes," he muttered, feeling extremely nervous. "The Baxter project."

He took a deep breath, thinking that now was the time for a cigarette. Every once in a while, he allowed himself to think that the craving was over, but whenever a crisis loomed, he instinctively longed for the soothing comfort of tobacco. *Deceptively* soothing comfort, he reminded himself. "I've been going into Baxter quite a lot lately," he told her.

"So I've heard. Mysterious meetings were mentioned." As she stirred the soup, she gazed into the steamy pot as if she were hoping for a revelation of the future. Her voice had been light, but there was tension in the grip of her fingers on the wooden spoon. Sensitive as always, she had obviously guessed the Baxter project was important, not only to him, but to her.

Plunge right in, he instructed himself. But still he delayed, pulling out the bottle of Fume blanc he'd stuck in the refrigerator to chill, carefully removing the cork and pouring a small amount into two glasses. Putting one next to her on the kitchen counter, he took a sip of his own, following it up with a deep breath. "There's a store in the mall— The Pink Flamingo."

Her nose wrinkled. "Not exactly top drawer stuff."

"But a terrific building."

"I suppose."

Plunge, he told himself again. "I'm buying it out. I'm going to gut the interior, remodel it along Falkirk lines, open up a branch of Falkirk's there. Not as large as my store in San Francisco of course, but still full service. The mall developers are ecstatic. Falkirk's will pull in more business for the entire mall."

He paused. She was still stirring the soup, a small frown on her face. "I thought I'd ask Chet to do the remodel."

She swung around, delight showing in her smile. "That's wonderful, Adrian. It will really get Chet's business off the ground. God, he'll be so thrilled—he's really getting into construction now, you know, he told me about some people who'd been watching him do my place and how proud it made him when they complimented him.''

Adrian nodded. ''He told me, too.'' Great, he thought, the only pleasure she'd registered was for Chet. What about his idea, his project?

She was frowning again. ''I suppose it'll be a while before you open?''

''Several months. There's a lot to be done, even before we start ordering merchandise, hiring people.''

''You'll hire local people?''

''Of course.''

She laughed suddenly. ''Steff will be thrilled. So will a lot of other women in Murre Bay. We do have some great shops here, but nobody in the area is serving your end of the market—the upscale department store with lots of energy and sizzle. People have to drive all the way to Olympia or Tacoma or even Seattle.''

''So I'd heard. That's what gave me the idea in the first place. That and finding out The Pink Flamingo was looking for a buyer.''

''Will you be personally involved in the remodeling?'' she asked carefully, gazing down into the soup pot again.

Ah, at last it was beginning to dawn on her that there might be more here than met the eye. ''I certainly will,'' he said, then added in the most casual voice he could come up with, ''And in the managing.''

She reached out to turn the heat down under the soup, and finally turned around to face him fully. ''What are you saying, Adrian?'' Her voice was definitely shaky.

He grinned. "I'm saying I'm going to start up a branch of Falkirk's in Baxter and I'm going to manage it myself. I showed Jon my feasibility study and I'm going to put it before the whole family at a specially called meeting next week. I don't foresee any arguments. We're in an expansion mode, three new stores opening in the Pacific northwest. The opportunity's here and I didn't want to stand by and do nothing. Jon was doubtful at first, but when I suggested he might take over Falkirk's San Francisco he became quite enthusiastic. He's always wanted that store, and evidently Claude is restless in Seattle." He watched her face, but no emotion registered. "Claude wants to start up a fashion magazine of her own. She'd much prefer to do it in California, according to Jon."

"You're going to manage the Baxter store yourself?" she echoed in a dazed voice, as though that was all she'd heard.

"I certainly am. I've got some compelling reasons for sticking around, you see. But besides that, I'm excited about the fact that it will be a much smaller store. I can get in there and do things myself instead of just attending meetings all the time. And still have time for fishing and loafing."

"You're going to live in Baxter?"

"No way," he said, and as the light that had begun to glow in her eyes faded, he added hastily. "I'm going to live in Murre Bay. Steff's made a believer out of me. This is my territory, my natural habitat." He paused for effect. "I like it here."

The glow was back. He could feel the warmth of her smile at six paces. Six paces too many. Covering ground rapidly, he pulled her into his arms. "I know this doctor," he said slowly, gazing directly into her shining eyes. "She has this house that's getting to look pretty good. A show house, you might even say. Quite a large house. Plenty of room for two. Terrific view of the ocean. I'm hoping she might share some of that space with me. I'd be happy to share the mortgage payments, of course."

She raised her beautiful bird's wing eyebrows. "You're saying you want to live with me?"

"And be your love. But not without benefit of clergy."

She put her hands on his shoulders and shook him, a ferocious scowl on her face. "Adrian Falkirk, if you don't do this properly, I'm going to..."

She had to swallow the rest of the sentence as his mouth captured hers and held it, kissing the scowl away. When he released her, her eyes were shining again. He took her face between his hands and let all of his love for her show. "Danielle," he said, his voice lingering tenderly on her name. "Will you please marry me?"

She sighed. "I thought you'd never ask."

He grinned. "Well, you have to admit I had cause to pause. Since I've been here I've become involved with two fires, a shot-up heron and a near drowning, not to mention getting to know a boy who talks to birds. For a place that was billed as a peaceful retreat from the hustle and bustle of the city, Murre Bay has shown me quite a lot of action." He took a breath, then said, "Now, will you please answer my question?"

"You're sure you don't have any doubts? You do believe I see you clearly now?"

"I do," he said firmly, but she thought she detected a slight hesitation. There must never be any hesitation, she decided. All doubt must be banished. Immediately. She brushed her thumb lightly across his closed mouth, then placed her hands on his shoulders. "I have something to tell you, first. Something important."

A frown puckered his forehead. He was still holding on to her, but his hands had stiffened, betraying his sudden tension. "I never did like my wedding gown," she said slowly. "It was too elaborate, you see. All that embroidery and beading and flounces. Pam Hunter talked me into it. It was the style, she said. I realized on my wedding day, my proposed wedding day, that it wasn't *my* style, but somehow it didn't seem to matter."

She paused, still looking directly into his eyes, which showed complete bewilderment. "My dad asked me if I was sure I was doing the right thing, marrying Jon, and I felt this moment of panic. And I remembered..."

His eyes were clearing now. Pulling her in close to him, he looked directly into her face. "You remembered what?" he asked urgently.

"The same thing I remembered when I saw Jon this afternoon." She took a deep breath. "I remembered that when I first saw you standing in that doorway at your father's house, with snowflakes shining on your hair, I felt this extraordinary rushing sensation that seemed, just for an instant, to be pulling me toward you. I remembered the extraordinary closeness between us when we sang and when we made up those ridiculous arithmetic problems. On my wedding day, I wondered, for just a moment, before I buried the thought away in my shadow box, if it was only the wedding dress that was a mistake. But of course, at that late date, I wasn't about to admit to myself that I might have been wrong." She paused again, then added very softly, "Wrong all along."

He closed his eyes momentarily, and she felt a tremor go through him. Then he opened them again and they had never looked so blue. "You loved me from the beginning."

"From the minute I saw you." There wasn't even a shadow of doubt in her voice, or in her mind.

A grin spread slowly across his strong features. "Then I guess you're finally ready to answer my question."

She nodded. "I love you, Adrian Falkirk," she said firmly. "Of course I'll marry you."

CHAPTER FIFTEEN

DANI GRINNED through her veil at the mirrored reflection of herself and her father, standing together in the church's dressing room. Excitement was a drumbeat throbbing in her breast. "We look pretty good, don't you think, pops?"

He smiled and nodded. "I like your dress."

The dress was ivory-colored, a simple high-waisted Empire style, flattering to Dani's tall slender figure, relatively unadorned. Her veil was held in place with a brocade-covered headband. She'd bought the whole outfit at Falkirk's. Of course.

The church was in Murre Bay, a small church—overlooking Dani's beloved Pacific ocean. Everything at this wedding, she and Adrian had decided, should fit the tone of their life-style.

"I must confess I was a little worried," Harris said.

Tension curled around Dani's stomach. Surely he wasn't going to express doubts now.

As she frowned at him, he grinned and nodded at the snow falling thickly against the night-dark panes of the tall mullioned windows. "I was afraid the snow would keep people away." He shook his head. "I didn't think it ever snowed out here."

"It doesn't do it very often," Dani said softly. "But it had to snow today."

He frowned, obviously not understanding. Which was okay with Dani. She and Adrian understood.

"I don't need to ask if you're sure this time," Harris said, taking her hand and tucking it under his arm. "The answer shines out all over you. And out of Adrian." He laughed. "He got to the church ahead of you, guess he must be eager."

"He didn't want me to worry," Dani said softly.

Harris's handsome features twisted into a frown that was belied by the gleam in his eyes. "He still owes me a jacket, by the way."

"I'll make sure you get a gift certificate."

He groaned. "I suppose I have to shop at Falkirk's exclusively now."

She nudged him with her elbow. "There are worse fates. Look upon it as a contribution to your family's welfare."

"Are you sure people won't think I look ridiculous?" Steff's gravelly voice asked from behind them.

Dani swung around, laughing. "You look fabulous, and you know it."

"Well, certainly," Steff said. "I wasn't questioning *that*. It's the idea of a seventy-two-year-old lady being a maid of honor that seems a bit . . . unusual."

"Since when have you worried about being unusual?" Dani demanded.

Steff was wearing a dress of the same style as Dani's—of a pale blush that reflected youthful color into her gaunt but beautiful face. When she'd finally agreed to stand up with Dani, she'd proposed wearing bright scarlet. "A Christmas Eve wedding should be red and white," she'd insisted, but Dani had persuaded her she'd look even more beautiful in a paler shade. Which she did.

"It's time to go," Pam Hunter said from the doorway. "The church secretary just waved at me." She smiled at Dani as she opened the door wide. "Good luck," she said.

Dani smiled back at her gratefully. Her old friend Pam had been completely understanding about accepting the role of bridesmaid this time, especially after she'd met Steff for herself, even more so when she met Walt Johnson, the friend of Adrian's selected as her escort. He was waiting for her now, a tall young man with Scandinavian features, blond hair and a mischievous smile that gave him a roguish appearance.

"Okay, Pops, this is it," Dani murmured as Steff walked into the vestibule, Pam and Walt following.

Harris squeezed her hand between his arm and his body. "Be happy, honey," he whispered.

And then the majestic notes of Wagner's "Bridal Chorus" rang out and Dani walked down the aisle on her father's arm, smiling through her veil at the faces turned to greet her. Mike Caswell was there, she noted, standing with Jorge and Consuelo Rodriguez, looking wonderfully grown up in a neat blue suit, white shirt and navy tie. Chet was beyond him, grinning at her. Josh Andersen was there. So was Brian Milburn, not smiling, but at least not looking too gloomy. There were patients galore on her side of the church, all looking remarkably healthy today, which was very considerate of them.

On the other side were Adrian's friends from San Francisco and Seattle, a couple of new friends from Baxter, and standing there in the front pews, of course, Falkirk after Falkirk. They all seemed cheerful—evidently they'd recovered from the combined shock of

Adrian giving up his position in San Francisco and Dani Kelsey coming back into their lives.

They hadn't needed all those candles, Dani thought as she looked at Adrian. The confidence shining in his blue eyes could have lighted the entire church. He looked wonderfully virile in his black tuxedo—no cutaway coat and elaborate cravat this time. Everything he felt for her was showing in his smile, and it was obvious that what he felt was love.

Beyond him stood Jon, also smiling. But then Jon always smiled. As usual, he looked like a mirror image of his brother, but to Dani Kelsey there was no mistaking which Falkirk was which.

She handed her bouquet to Steff. Steff grinned at her and winked. Judging by the smug smile on her lined face, she was taking full credit for this happy outcome, as though she'd single-handedly arranged it herself.

As Dani's father lifted her veil and stepped around behind her to take his seat, she put her hand in Adrian's and smiled. His hand squeezed hers lightly, discreetly, then lifted it to his mouth and brushed it with his lips.

She gazed at him in a bemused way as the minister cleared his throat and prepared to begin the service. How odd, she thought, how wonderfully odd. As far as she knew he hadn't gone outside since his arrival, but looking at him now, with the candles flickering light across them both, she could swear there were snowflakes shining in his hair.

WATCH FOR

COWBOYS AND CABERNET
by Margot Dalton

Tyler McKinney is out to prove a Texas ranch is the perfect place for a vineyard. Vintner Ruth Holden thinks Tyler is too stubborn, too impatient...too Texas. And far too difficult to resist!

COWBOYS AND CABERNET
Book Two of

A town where you'll find hot Texas nights, smooth Texas charm and dangerously sexy cowboys.

A series of twelve books that feature the rugged individuals who live and love in the Lone Star State. And each one ends with the same invitation...

Y'ALL COME BACK...REAL SOON!

In March, don't miss Book One of Crystal Creek: DEEP IN THE HEART by Barbara Kaye. Then in April, look for Book Two: COWBOYS AND CABERNET by Margot Dalton!

HARLEQUIN®

my Valentine
1993

The most romantic day of the year is here! Escape into the exquisite world of love with MY VALENTINE 1993. What better way to celebrate Valentine's Day than with this very romantic, sensuous collection of four original short stories, written by some of Harlequin's most popular authors.

**ANNE STUART
JUDITH ARNOLD
ANNE McALLISTER
LINDA RANDALL WISDOM**

**THIS VALENTINE'S DAY, DISCOVER ROMANCE
WITH MY VALENTINE 1993**

Available in February wherever Harlequin Books are sold. VAL93

HARLEQUIN SUPERROMANCE®

HARLEQUIN SUPERROMANCE WANTS TO INTRODUCE YOU TO A DARING NEW CONCEPT IN ROMANCE...

WOMEN WHO DARE!
Bright, bold, beautiful...
Brave and caring, strong and passionate...
They're unique women who know their
own minds and will dare anything...
for love!

One title per month in 1993, written by popular Superromance authors, will highlight our special heroines as they face unusual, challenging and sometimes dangerous situations.

Travel through time next month with:
#537 WINGS OF TIME by Carol Duncan Perry
Available in February wherever Harlequin Superromance
novels are sold.
